# The
# PARISIAN
# NIGHTS

*The House of Pleasure*

# The
# PARISIAN NIGHTS

### of
## GUY DE MAUPASSANT

A New Redaction by
## MARIE  LORENZ

New York
AVALON PRESS, Inc.
1945

# CONTENTS

7

# first night

*A great banker makes a marriage of convenience—hides his mistress in the upper story of a friend's house— with consequences amusing to all concerned except the great banker.*

ROYAUMONT's enormous haunches quivered with laughter from just remembering the story he had promised his friends. Spreading himself back in his great arm-chair, which he completely filled, that *picker of bits of pinchbeck,* as they called him at the club, finally began:

"It is not to be denied that Bordenave is beholden to no one, and can go through any street he likes and publish those famous memoirs of sheriff's officers, which he wrote during the ten years when he did not dare go out, and in which he carefully described the characters and peculiarities of all those generous distributors of stamped paper with whom he had had dealings, their tricks and wiles, their weaknesses, their jokes, their ways of performing their duties, sometimes with brutal rudeness and at others with cunning good nature, now embarrassed and almost ashamed of themselves, and again ironically jovial, as well as the tricks of their clerks to get a few crumbs from their employer's cake. The book will soon be published and Machin, the Vaudeville writer, has promised him a preface, so that it will be a really amusing work. You are surprised, eh? Confess that you are absolutely surprised, and I will lay you any bet you like that you will not guess how our excellent friend, whose existence is an inexplicable problem, has been able to settle with his creditors, and suddenly produce the exact amount required."

"Do get to the facts, confound it," Captain Hardeur said, who was growing tired of all this verbiage.

"All right, I will get to them as quickly as possible," Royaumont replied, throwing the stump of his cigar into the fire. "I will clear my throat and begin. I suppose all of you know that two better friends than Bordenave and Quillanet do not exist; neither of them could do without the other, and they have ended by dressing alike, by having the same gestures, the same laugh, the same walk and the same inflections of voice, so that one would think that some close bond united them, and that they had been brought up together from childhood. There is, however, this great difference between them, that Bordenave is completely ruined and that all that he possesses are bundles of mortgages, laughable parchments which attest his ancient race, and chimerical hopes of inheriting money some day, though these expectations are already heavily hypothecated. Consequently, he is always on the lookout for some fresh expedients for raising money, though he is superbly indifferent about everything, while Sebastien Quillanet, of the banking house of Quillanet Brothers, must have an income of eight thousand francs a year, but is descended from an obscure laborer who managed to secure some of the national property, then he became an army contractor, speculated on defeat as well as victory, and does not know now what to do with his money. But the millionaire is timid, dull and always bored, the ruined spendthrift amuses him by his impertinent ways, and his libertine jokes; he prompts him when he is at a loss for an answer, extricates him out of his difficultes, serves as his guide in the great forests of Paris which is strewn with so many pit-falls, and helps him to avoid those vulgar adventures which socially ruins a man, no matter how well ballasted he may be. Then he points out to him what women would make suitable mistresses for him, who make a man noted, and have the effect of some rare and beautiful flower pinned into his buttonhole. He is the confidant of his intrigues, his guest when he gives small, special entertainments, his daily familiar table companion, and the buffoon whose sly humor one simulates, and whose worst witticisms one tolerates."

"Really, really," the captain interrupted him, "you have been going on for more than a quarter of an hour without saying anything."

So Royaumont shrugged his shoulders and continued:

"Oh! you can be very tiresome when you please, my dear fellow! . . . Last year, when he was at daggers drawn with his people, who were deafening him with their recriminations, were worrying him and threatening him with a lot of annoyance, Quillanet got married. A marriage of reason, and which apparently changed his habits and his tastes, more especially as the banker was at that time keeping a perfect little marvel of a woman, a Parisian jewel of unspeakable attractions and of bewitching delicacy, that adorable Suzette Marly who is just like a pocket Venus, and who in some prior stage of her existence must have been Phryne or Lesbia. Of course he did not get rid of her, but as he was bound to take some judicious precautions, which are necessary for a man who is deceiving his wife, he rented a furnished house with a courtyard in front, and a garden at the back, which one might think had been built to shelter some amorous folly. It was the nest that he had dreamt of, warm, snug, elegant, the walls covered with silk hangings of subdued tints, large pier-glasses, allegorical pictures, and filled with luxurious, low furniture that seemed to invite caresses and embraces. Bordenave occupied the ground floor, and the first floor served as a shrine for the banker and his mistress. Well, just a week ago, in order to hide the situation better, Bordenave asked Quillanet and some other friends to one of those luncheons which he understands so well how to order, such a delicious luncheon, that before it was quite over, every man had a woman on his knees already, and was asking himself whether a kiss from coaxing and naughty lips, was not a thousand times more intoxicating than the finest old brandy or the choicest vintage wines, and was looking at the bedroom door wishing to escape to it, although the Faculty altogether forbids that fashion of digesting a dainty repast, when the butler came in with an embarassed look, and whispered something to him.

"Tell the gentleman that he has made a mistake, and ask him to leave me in peace," Bordenave replied to him in an angry voice. The servant went out and returned immediately to say that the intruder was using threats, that he refused to leave the house, and even spoke of having recourse to the commissary of police. Bordenave frowned, threw his table napkin down, upset two glasses and staggered out with a red face, swearing and stammering out:

"This is rather too much, and the fellow shall find out what going out of the window means, if he will not leave by the door." But in the ante-room he found himself face to face with a very cool, polite, impassive gentleman, who said very quietly to him:

"You are Count Robert de Bordenave, I believe, Monsier?"

"Yes, Monsieur."

"And the lease you signed at the lawyer's, Monsieur Albin Calvert, in the *Rue du Faubourg-Poissonnière,* is in your name, I believe?"

"Certainly, Monsieur."

"Then I regret extremely to have to tell you that if you are not in a position to pay the various accounts which different people have intrusted to me for collection here, I shall be obliged to seize all the furniture, pictures, plate, clothes etc., which are here, in the presence of two witnesses who are waiting for me downstairs in the street."

"I suppose this is some joke, Monsieur?"

"It would be a very poor joke, Monsieur le Comte, and one which I should certainly not allow myself towards you!"

The situation was absolutely critical and ridiculous, the more so, that in the dining-room the women who were slightly *elevated,* were tapping the wine glasses with their spoons, and calling for him. What could he do except explain his misadventure to Quillanet, who became sobered immediately, and rather than see his shrine of love violated, his secret sin disclosed and his pictures, ornaments and furniture sold, gave a check in due form for the claim there and then, though with a very wry face. And in spite of this, some people will deny that men who are utterly cleared out, often have a stroke of luck.

# second night

*A woman who loved beautiful furs, and a man who loved the woman well enough to buy her the furs and take a beating from her, too, for his pains.*

LOVE IS STRONGER than death; it is also stronger than the worst thing which can befall us.

A young, and by no means bad-looking stockbroker, one of the barons of the Almanac of the *Ghetto*, used to go very frequently to the Universal Exhibition in Vienna in 1873, in order to divert his thoughts, and to console himself amidst the varied scenes, and the many objects of attraction there. One day he met a newly married couple in the Russian section, who had a very old coat of arms, but on the other hand, a very modest income.

This latter circumstance had frequently emboldened the stockbroker to make secret overtures to the delightful little lady; overtures which might have fascinated certain Viennese actresses, but which were sure to insult a respectable woman. The baroness, whose name

15

appeared in the *Almanach de Gotha,* therefore felt something very like hatred for the stockbroker, and for a long time her pretty little head had been full of various plans of revenge.

The stockbroker, who was really, and even passionately in love with her, got close to her in the Exhibition buildings, which he could do all the more easily, since the little woman's husband had taken to flight, foreseeing mischief, as soon as she went up to the show-case of a Russian fur dealer, before which she remained standing in rapture.

"Do look at that lovely fur," the baroness said, while her dark eyes expressed her pleasure; "I must have it."

But she looked at the white ticket on which the price was marked.

"Four thousand roubles," she said in despair; "that is about six thousand florins."

"Certainly," he replied, "but what of that? It is a sum not worth mentioning in the presence of such a charming lady."

"But my husband is not in a position . . . "

"Be less cruel than usual for once," the man from the *Ghetto* said to the young woman in a low voice, "and allow me to lay this sable skin at your feet."

"I presume that you are joking."

"Not I . . . "

"I think you must be joking, as I cannot think that you intend to insult me."

"But, Baroness, I love you. . . . "

"That is one reason more why you should not make me angry."

16

"But . . . "

"Oh! I am in such a rage," the energetic little woman said; "I could flog you like *Venus in Furs* did her slave."

"Let me be your slave," the Stock Exchange baron replied ardently, "and I will gladly put up with everything from you. Really, in this sable cloak, and with a whip in your hand, you would make a most lovely picture of the heroine of that story."

The baroness looked at the man for a moment with a peculiar smile.

"Then if I were to listen to you favorably, you would let me flog you?" she said after a pause.

"With pleasure."

"Very well," she replied quickly. "You will let me give you twenty-five cuts with a whip, and I will be yours after the twenty-fifth blow."

"Are you in earnest?"

"Fully."

The man from the *Ghetto* took her hand, and pressed it ardently to his lips.

"When may I come?"

"Tomorrow evening at eight o'clock."

"And I may bring the sable cloak and the whip with me?"

"No, I will see about that myself."

The next evening the enamored stockbroker came to the house of the charming little Baroness, and found her alone, lying on a couch, wrapped in a dark fur, while she held a dog whip in her small hand, which the man from the *Ghetto* kissed.

"You know our agreement," she began.

"Of course I do," the Stock Exchange baron replied. "I am to allow you to give me twenty-five cuts with the whip, and after the twenty-fifth you will listen to me."

"Yes, but I am going to tie your hands first of all." The amorous baron quietly allowed this new Delila to tie his hands behind him, and then at her bidding, he knelt down before her, and she raised her whip and hit him hard.

"Oh! That hurts me most confoundedly," he exclaimed.

"I mean it to hurt you," she said with a mocking laugh, and went on thrashing him without mercy. At last the poor fool groaned with pain, but he consoled himself with the thought that each blow brought him nearer to his happiness.

At the twenty-fourth cut, she threw the whip down.

"That only makes twenty-four," the beaten would-be, *Don Juan,* remarked.

"I will make you a present of the twenty-fifth," she said with a laugh.

"And now you are mine, altogether mine," he exclaimed ardently.

"What are you thinking of?"

"Have I not let you beat me?"

"Certainly; but I promised you to grant your wish after the twenty-fifth blow, and you have only received twenty-four," the cruel little bit of virtue cried, "and I have witnesses to prove it."

With these words, she drew back the curtains over the door, and her husband, followed by two other gentlemen came out of the next room, smiling. For a moment the stockbroker remained speechless on his knees before the beautiful woman. Of all the things which occurred to him to say, he could utter only one word, and that a really silly one. He made a futile gesture with his shoulders and said:

"*Crash!*"

# *third night*

> *To disillusion her idealistic admirer,*
> *the little actress granted him a whole*
> *night. Disillusion? It almost killed*
> *him. . . .*

AMONG MY MANY Viennese friends, there is
one who is an author, and who has always amused me
by his childish idealistic prattle.

Not by his idealism from an abstracted point of view,
because in that way I am something of an idealist myself; and because I am perfectly well aware of this, I
as a rule never laugh at people's idealism, but his sort
of idealism was really too funny.

He was a serious man of great abilities who only just
fell short of being learned, with a clear, critical intellect; a man without any illusions about society, the state,
literature, or anything else, and especially not about
women; but yet he was the craziest optimist as soon as
he got upon the subject of actresses, theatrical princesses and heroines; he was one of those men, who, like
Hacklander, cannot discover the Ideal of Virtue any-
where, except in a ballet girl.

My friend was always in love with some actress or other; only Platonically, of course, and from preference for some girl of rising talent, whose literary knight he constituted himself, until the time came when her admirers laid something much more substantial than laurel wreaths at her feet; then he withdrew and sought for fresh talent which would allow itself to be modestly patronized by him.

He was never without the photograph of his ideal in his breast pocket, and when he was in a good mood he used to show me one or other of them, whom I had never seen, with a knowing smile, and once, when we were sitting in a *café* in the *Prater*, he took out a portrait without saying a word, and laid it on the table.

It was the portrait of a beautiful woman, but what struck me in it first of all was not the almost classic cut of her features, but her white eyes.

"If she had not the black hair of a living woman, I should take her for a statue," I said.

"Certainly," my friend replied; "for a statue of Venus, perhaps for the Venus of Milo, herself."

"Who is she?"

"A young actress."

"That is a matter of course in your case; what I meant was, what is her name?"

My friend told me, and it was a name which is at present one of the best known on the German stage, with which a number of terrestrial adventures are connected, as every Viennese knows, with which those of Venus herself were only innocent toying, but which I then heard for the first time.

My idealist described her as a woman of the highest talent, which I believed, and as an angel of purity, which I did not believe; on that particular occasion, however, I at any rate did not believe the contrary.

A few days later, I was accidentally turning over the leaves of the portrait album of another intimate friend of mine, who was a thoroughly careless, somewhat dissolute Viennese, and I came across that strange female face with the dead eyes again.

"How did you come by the picture of this Venus?" I asked him.

"Well, she certainly is a Venus," he replied, "but one of that cheap kind who are to be met with in the *Graben*, which is their ideal grove. . . . "

"Impossible!"

"I give you my word of honor it is so."

I could say nothing more after that. So my intellectual friend's new ideal, that woman of the highest dramatic talent, that wonderful woman with the white eyes, was a street Venus!

But my friend was right in one respect. He had not deceived himself with regard to her wonderful dramatic gifts, and she very soon made a career for herself; far from being a mute character on a suburban stage, she rose in two years to be the leading actress at one of the principal theaters.

My friend interested himself on her behalf with the manager of it, who was not blinded by any prejudices. She acted in a rehearsal, and pleased him; whereupon he sent her to star in the provinces, and my friend accompanied her, and took care she was well puffed.

She went on the boards as Schiller's *Marie Stuart,* and achieved the most brilliant success, and before she had finished her starring tour, she obtained an engagement at a large theater in a Northern town, where her appearance was the signal for a triumphant success.

Her reputation, that is, her reputation as a most gifted actress, grew very high in less than a year, and the manager of the Court theater invited her to star at the Court theater.

She was received with some suspicion at first, but she soon overcame all prejudices and doubts; the applause grew more and more vehement at every act, and at the close of the performance, her future was decided. She obtained a splendid engagement, and soon afterwards became an actress at the Court theater.

A well-known author wrote a racy novel, of which she was the heroine; one of the leading bankers and financiers was at her feet; she was the most popular personage, and the lioness of the capital; she had splendid apartments, and all her surroundings were of the most luxurious character, and she had reached that height in her career at which my idealistic friend, who had constituted himself her literary knight, quietly took his leave of her, and went in search of fresh talent.

But the beautiful woman with the dead eyes and the dead heart seemed to be destined to be the scourge of the Idealists, quite against her will, for scarcely had one unfolded his wings and flown away from her, than another fell out of the nest into her net.

A very young student, who was neither handsome,

nor of good family, and certainly not rich or even well off, but who was enthusiastic, intellectual and impressionable, saw her as *Marie Stuart* in *The Maid of Orleans, The Lady with the Camelias,* and most of the plays of the best French play writers, for the manager was making experiments with her, and she was doing the same with her talents.

The poor student was enraptured with the celebrated actress, and at the same time conceived a passion for the woman, which bordered on madness.

He saved up penny by penny, he nearly starved himself, only in order that he might be able to pay for a seat in the gallery whenever she acted, and be able to devour her with his eyes. He always got a seat in the front row, for he was always outside three hours before the doors opened, so as to be one of the first to gain his Olympus, the seat of the theatrical enthusiasts; he grew pale, and his heart beat violently when she appeared; he laughed when she laughed, shed tears when she wept, applauded her, as if he had been paid to do it by the highest favors that a woman can bestow, and yet she did not know him, and was ignorant of his very existence.

The regular frequenters of the Court theater noticed him at last, and spoke about his infatuation for her, until at last she heard about him, but still did not know him, and although he could not send her any costly jewelry, and not even a bouquet, yet at last he succeeded in attracting her attention.

When she had been acting and the theater had been empty for a long time, and she left it, wrapped in valuable furs and got into the carriage of her banker, which was waiting for her at the stage door, he always stood there, often up to his ankles in snow, or in the pouring rain.

At first she did not notice him, but when her maid said something to her in a whisper on one occasion, she looked round in surprise, and he got a look from those large eyes, which were not dead then, but dark and bright; a look which recompensed him for all his sufferings and filled him with proud hopes, which constantly gained more power over the young Idealist, who was usually so modest.

At last there was a thorough, silent understanding between the theatrical princess and the dumb adorer. When she put her foot on the carriage step, she looked round at him, and every time he stood there, devouring her with his eyes; she saw it and got contentedly into her carriage, but she did not see how he ran after the carriage, and how he reached her house, panting for breath, when she did, nor how he lay down outside after the door had closed behind her.

One stormy summer night, when the wind was howling in the chimneys, and the rain was beating against the windows and on the pavement, the poor student was again lying on the stone steps outside her house, when the front door was opened very cautiously and quietly; for it was not the banker who was leaving the house, but a wealthy young officer whom the girl was letting out; he kissed the pretty little Cerebus as he put a gold coin into her hand, and then accidentally trod on the Idealist, who was lying outside.

They all three simultaneously uttered a cry; the girl blew out the candle, the officer instinctively half drew his sword, and the student ran away.

Ever since that night, the poor, crazy fellow went about with a dagger, which he concealed in his belt, and it was his constant companion to the theater, and the stage door, when the actress's carriage used to wait for her, and to her house, where he nightly kept his painful watch.

His first idea was to kill his fortunate rival, then himself, then the theatrical princess, but at last, he lay down again outside her door, or stood on the pavement and watched the shadows that flitted hither and thither on her window, turned by the magic spell of the lovely actress.

And then, the most incredible thing happened, something which he could never have hoped for, and which he scarcely believed when it did occur.

One evening, when she had been playing a very important part, she kept the carriage waiting much longer than usual; but at last she appeared, and got into it; she did not shut the door, however, but beckoned to the young Idealist to follow her.

He was almost delirious with joy, just as a moment before he had been almost mad from despair, and obeyed her immediately, and during the drive he lay at her feet and covered her hands with kisses. She allowed it quietly and even merrily, and when the carriage stopped at her door, she let him lift her out of the carriage, and went upstairs leaning on his arm.

There, the lady's maid showed him into a luxuriously

furnished drawing-room, while the actress changed her dress.

Presently she appeared in her dressing gown, sat down carelessly in an easy chair, and asked him to sit down beside her.

"You take a great interest in me?" she said.

"You are my ideal!" the student cried.

The theatrical princess smiled, and said:

"Well, I will at any rate be an honest ideal; I will not deceive you, and you shall not be able to say that I have misused your youthful enthusiasm. I will give myself to you. . . ."

"Oh! Heavens" the poor Idealist exclaimed, throwing himself at her feet.

"Wait a moment, wait a moment," she said with a smile. "I have not finished yet. I can only love a man who is in a position to provide me with all those luxuries which an actress, or, if you like, which I can not do without. As far as I know, you are poor, but I will belong to you only for tonight, however, and in return you must promise me not to rave about me, or to follow me, from tonight. Will you do this?"

The wretched Idealist was kneeling before her; he was having a terrible mental struggle.

"Will you promise me to do this?" she said again.

"Yes," he said, almost groaning.

The next morning a man, who had buried his Ideal, tottered downstairs. He was pale enough; almost as pale as a corpse; but in spite of this, he is still alive, and if he has any Ideal at all at present, it is certainly not a theatrical princess.

# *fourth night*

*Different women like different smells—*
*The Countess was young, witty, and a*
*beauty. With only one real weakness, the*
*love of anything which smelled of the*
*stable ...*

Three charmers belonging to that class of society which has nothing useful to do, and therefore does not know how to employ its time sensibly, were sitting languidly on a bench in the shade of some pine trees at Ischl, discussing their preference for all varieties of smells.

One of the ladies, Princess F——, a slim, handsome brunette, said there was nothing like the smell of Russian leather; she wore dull brown Russian leather boots, a Russian leather dress suspender, to keep her petticoats out of the dirt and dust, a Russian leather belt which spanned her wasp-like waist, carried a Russian leather purse, and even wore a brooch and barcelet of gilt Russian leather; people added that her bedroom was lined with Russian leather, and that her lover was obliged to wear high Russian leather boots and tight breeches, but that on the other hand, her husband was excused from wearing anything at all in Russian leather.

Countess H——, a very stout lady, who had formerly been very beautiful and of a very loving nature, but loving after the fashion of her time *à la* Parthenia and Griseldis, could not get over the vulgar taste of the young Princess. All she cared for was the smell of hay, and she it was who brought the scent *New Mown Hay* into fashion. Her dream was of a freshly mown field in the moonlight, and when she rolled slowly along, she looked like a moving haystack, and exhaled an odor of hay all about her.

The third lady's taste was even more peculiar than Countess H——'s, and more vulgar than the Princess's, for the small, delicate, light-haired Countess W—— lived only for — the smell of stables. Her friends could absolutely not understand this; the Princess raised her beautiful, full arm with its broad bracelet to her Grecian nose and inhaled the sweet smell of the Russian leather, while the sentimental hay-rick exclaimed over and over again:

"How dreadful What dost thou say to it, chaste moon?"

The delicate little Countess seemed very much embarrassed at the effect that her confession had had, and tried to justify her taste.

"Prince T—— told me that that smell had quite bewitched him once," she said; "it was in a Jewish town in Gallicia, where he was quartered once with his hussar regiment, and a number of poor, ragged circus riders, with half-starved horses came from Russia and put up a circus with a few poles and some rags of canvas, and the Prince went to see them, and found a woman among them, who was neither young nor beautiful, but bold and impudent; and the impudent woman wore a faded, bright red jacket, trimmed with old, shabby, imitation ermine, and that jacket stank of the stable, as the Prince expressed it, and she bewitched him with that odor, so that every time that the shameless wretch lay in his arms, and laughed impudently, and smelled abominably of the stable, he felt as if he were magnetized.

"How disgusting!" both the other ladies said, and involuntarily held their noses.

"What dost thou say to it, chaste moon?" the haystack said with a sigh, and the little light-haired Countess was abashed and held her tongue.

At the beginning of the winter season the three friends were together again in the gay, imperial city on the blue Danube. One morning the Princess accidentally met the enthusiast for the hay at the house of the little light-haired Countess, and the two ladies were obliged to go after her to her private riding-school, where she was taking her daily lesson. As soon as she saw them, she came up, and beckoned her riding-master to her to help her out of the saddle. He was a young man of extremely good and athletic build, which was set off by his tight breeches and his short velvet coat, and he ran up and took his lovely burden into his arms with visible pleasure, to help her off the quiet, perfectly broken horse.

When the ladies looked at the handsome, vigorous man, it was quite enough to explain their little friend's predilection for the smell of a stable, but when the latter saw their looks, she blushed up to the roots of her hair, and her only way out of the difficulty was to order the riding-master, in a very authoritative manner, to take the horse back to the stable. He merely bowed, with an indescribable smile, and obeyed her.

A few months afterwards, Viennese society was alarmed at the news that Countess W—— had been divorced from her husband. The event was all the more unexpected, as they had apparently always lived very happily together, and nobody was able to mention any man on whom she had bestowed even the most passing attention, beyond the requirements of politeness.

Long afterwards, however, a strange report became current. A chattering lady's maid declared that the handsome riding-master had once so far forgotten himself as to strike the Countess with his riding-whip; a groom had told the Count of the occurrence, and when he was going to call the insolent fellow to account for it, the Countess covered him with her own body, and thus gave occasion for the divorce.

Years had passed since then and the Countess H—— had grown stouter and more sentimental. Ischl and hayricks were not enough for her any longer; she spent the winter on lovely *Lago Maggoire,* where she walked among laurel bushes and cypress trees, and was rowed about on the lukewarm, moonlight nights.

One evening she was returning home in the company of an English lady who was also a great lover of nature, from *Isola Bella,* when they met a beautiful private boat in which a very unusual couple were sitting; a small, delicate, light-haired woman, wrapped in a white burnoose, and a handsome, athletic man, in tight white breeches, a short, black velvet coat trimmed with sable, a red fez on his head, and a riding whip in his hand.

Countess H—— involuntarily uttered a loud exclamation.

"What is the matter with you?" the English lady asked. "Do you know those people?"

"Certainly! She is a Viennese lady," Countess H—— whispered; "Countess W——."

"Oh! Indeed you are quite mistaken; it is a Count Savelli and his wife. They are a handsome couple, don't you think so?"

When the boat came nearer, she saw that in spite of that, it was little Countess W—— and that the handsome man was her former riding-master, whom she had married, and for whom she had bought a title from the Pope; and as the two boats passed each other, the short sable cloak, which was thrown carelessly over his shoulders, exhaled, like the old cat's skin jacket of that impudent female circus rider, a strong *stable perfume*.

# *fifth night*

*A whole house of 'kind girls' were at
his disposal, and they could not understand his failure to 'collect' from
them favors for which other men
paid so dearly and readily, until he
explained. . . .*

F̲RIDAYS, ABOUT ELEVEN o'clock in the morning, regularly, he came into the court-yard, put down
his soft hat at his feet, struck a few chords on his guitar
and sang a ballad in his full, rich voice. Soon at every
window in the four sides of that dull, barrack-like building, some girls appeared, one in an elegant dressing
gown, another in a little jacket, most of them with their
breasts and arms bare, all of them just out of bed, with
their hair hastily twisted up, their eyes blinking in the
sudden blaze of sunlight, their complexions dull and
their eyes still heavy from want of sleep.

They swayed backwards and forwards to his slow
melody, gave themselves up to the enjoyment of it, and
coppers, and even silver, poured into the handsome
singer's hat, and more than one of them would have

liked to have followed the penny which she threw to him, and to have gone with the singer who had the voice of a siren, and who seemed to say to all these amorous girls; "Come, come to my retreat, where you will find a palace of crystal and gold, and wreaths which are always fresh, and happiness and love which never die."

That was what they seemed to hear, those unhappy girls, when they heard him sing the songs of the old legends, which they had formerly believed. That was what they understood by the foolish words of the ballad. That and nothing else, for how could anyone doubt it, on seeing the fresh roses on their cheeks, and the tender flame which flickered like a mystic night-light in their eyes, which had, for the moment, become the eyes of innocent young girls again? But of young girls, who had grown up very quickly, alas! who were very precocious, and who very soon became the women that they were, poor vendors of love, always in search of love for which they were paid.

That was why, when he had finished his second ballad, and sometimes even sooner, concupiscent looks appeared in their eyes. The boatman of their dreams, the water-sprite of fairy tales, vanished in the mist of their childish recollections, and the singer re-assumed his real shape, that of musician and strolling player, whom they wished to pay, to be their lover. And the coppers and small silver were showered on him again, with engaging smiles, with the leers of a street-walker, even with: "p'st, p'st," which soon transformed the barrack-like court-yard into an enormous cage full of twittering birds, while some of them could not restrain themselves, but said aloud, rolling their eyes with desire: "How handsome the creature is! Good heavens, how handsome he is!"

He was really handsome, and nobody could deny it, and even too handsome, with a regular beauty which almost palled on people. He had large, almond-shaped, gentle eyes, a Grecian nose, a bow-shaped mouth, hidden by a heavy moustache, and long, black, curly hair; in short, a head fit to be put into a hair-dresser's window, or, better still, perhaps, onto the front page of the ballads which he was singing. But what made him still handsomer, was that his self-conceit had a look of sovereign indifference for he was not satisfied with not replying to the smiles, the ogles, and the *p'st's, p'st's,* by taking no notice of them; but when he had finished he shrugged his shoulders, he winked mischievously, and turned his lips contemptuously, which said very clearly: "The stove is not being heated for you, my little kittens!"

Often, one might have thought that he expressly wished to show his contempt, and that he tried to make himself thought unpoetical in the eyes of all those amorous girls, and to check their love, for he cleared his throat ostentatiously and offensively, more than was necessary, after singing, as if he would have liked to spit at them. But all that did not make him unpoetical in their eyes, and many of them, most of them, who were absolutely mad on him, went so far as to say that *he did it like a swell!*

The girl, who in her enthusiasm had been the first to utter that exclamation of intense passion, and who, after throwing him small silver, had thrown him a twenty-franc gold piece, at last made up her mind to have an explanation. Instead of a *p'st, p'st,* she spoke to him boldly one morning, in the presence of all the others, who religiously held their tongues.

"Come up here," she called out to him, and from habit she added: "I will be very nice, you handsome dark fellow."

At first they were dumbfounded at her audacity, and then all their cheeks flushed with jealousy, and the flame of mad desire shot from their eyes, from every window there came a perfect torrent of:

"Yes, come up, come up." "Don't go to her! Come to me."

And, meanwhile, there was a shower of half-pence, of francs, of gold coins, as well as of cigars and oranges, while lace pocket handkerchiefs, silk neckties, and scarfs fluttered in the air and fell round the singer, like a flight of many colored butterflies.

He picked up the spoil calmly, almost carelessly, stuffed the money into his pocket, made a bundle of the furbelows, which he tied up as if they had been soiled linen, and then raising himself up, and putting his felt hat on his head, he said:

"Thank you, ladies, but indeed I cannot."

They thought that he did not know how to satisfy so many demands at once, and one of them said: "Let him choose."

"Yes, yes, that is it!" they all exclaimed unanimously.

But he repeated: "I tell you, I cannot."

They thought he was excusing himself out of gallantry, and several of them exclaimed, almost with tears of emotion: "Women are all heart!" And the same voice that had spoken before, (it was one of the girls who wished to settle the matter amicably), said: "We must draw lots."

"Yes, yes, that is it," they all cried. And again there was a religious silence, more religious than before, for it was caused by anxiety, and the beatings of their hearts may have been heard.

The singer profited by it, to say slowly: "I cannot have that either; nor all of you at once, nor one after the other; nothing! I tell you that I cannot."

"Why? Why?" And now they were almost screaming, for they were angry and sorry at the same time. Their cheeks had gone from scarlet to livid, their eyes flashed fire, and some shook their fists menacingly.

"Silence!" the girl cried, who had spoken first. "Be quiet, you pack of huzzys! Let him explain himself, and tell us why!"

"Yes, yes, let us be quiet! Make him explain himself in God's name!"

Then, in the fierce silence that ensued, the singer said, opening his arms wide, with a gesture of despairing inability to do what they wanted:

"What do you want? It is very amusing, but I cannot do more. I have two girls of my own already, at home."

# *sixth night*

*He was so virtuous, he liked to feel that he was righteous even when he visited a house of pleasure. . . . But that sort of thing can be overdone, as you will see. . . .*

He DID NOT THINK of himself as a saint, nor had he any hypocritical pretensions to virtue, but, nevertheless, he thought as highly of himself as he did of anybody else, and perhaps, even a little more. And that, quite impartially, without any more self love than was necessary, and without his having to accuse himself of being self conceited. He did himself justice, that was all, for he had good moral principles, and he applied them, especially, if the truth must be told, not only to judging the conduct of others, but also, it must be allowed, in a measure for regulating his own conduct, as he would have been very vexed if he had been able to think of himself:

"On the whole, I am what people call a perfectly honorable man."

Luckily, he had never (never, really!), been obliged

to doubt that good opinion which he had of himself, which he liked to express thus, in his moments of rhetorical expansion:

"My whole life gives me the right to shake hands with myself."

Perhaps a psychologist would have found some flaws in this armor of integrity, which was sanctimoniously satisfied with itself. It was, for example, quite certain that our friend had no scruples in making a profit out of the vices or misfortunes of his neighbors, provided that he was not in his own opinion, the person who was solely, or chiefly responsible for them. But, on the whole, it was only one manner of looking at it, nothing more, and there were plenty of materials for casuistic arguments in it. This kind of discussion is particularly unpleasant to such simple natures as that of this worthy fellow, who would have replied to the psychologist.

"Why go on a wild goose chase? As for me, I am perfectly sincere."

You must not, however, believe that this perfect sincerity prevented him from having elevated views. He prided himself on having a weakness for imagination and the unforeseen, and if he would have been offended at being called a dishonorable man, he would, perhaps have been still more hurt if anybody had attributed middle-class tastes to him.

Accordingly, in love affairs, he expressed a most virtuous horror of adultery, for if he had committed it, it would not have been able to bear that testimony to himself, which was so sweet to his conscience:

"Ah, As for me, I can say I never wronged anybody."

While, on the other hand, he was not satisfied with pleasure which was paid for by the hour, and which debases *the noblest desires of the heart,* to the vulgar satisfaction of a physical requirement. What he required, so he used to say, while lifting his eyes up to heaven was:

"Something rather more ideal than that!"

That search after the ideal did not, indeed, cost him any great effort, as it was limited to not going to licensed houses of ill-fame, and to not accosting street-walkers with the simple words: "How much?"

It consisted chiefly in wishing to be gallant even with such women, and in trying to persuade himself that they liked him for his own sake, and in preferring those whose manner, dress and looks allowed room for suppositions and romantic illusions, such as:

"She might be taken for a little work-girl who has not yet lost her virtue."

"No, I rather think she is a widow, who has met with misfortunes."

"What if she be a fashionable lady in disguise!"

And other nonsense, which he knew to be such, even while imagining it, but whose imaginary flavor was very pleasant to him, all the same.

With such tastes, it was only natural that this pilgrim followed and pushed up against women in the large shops, and whenever there was a crowd, and that he especially looked out for those ladies of easy virtue, for nothing is more exciting than those half-closed shutters, behind which a face is indistinctly seen, and from which one hears a furtive: *"P'st! P'st!"*

He used to say to himself: "Who is she? Is she young and pretty? Is she some old woman, who is terribly skillful at her business, but who yet does not venture to show herself any longer? Or is she some new beginner, who has not acquired the boldness of an old hand? In any case, it is the unknown, perhaps, that is my ideal during the time it takes me to find my way upstairs;" and always as he went up, his heart beat, as it does at a first meeting with a beloved mistress.

But he had never felt such a delicious shiver as he did on the day on which he penetrated into that old house in the blind alley in Ménilmontant. He could not have said why, for he had often gone after so-called love in much stranger places; but now, without any reason, he had a presentiment that he was going to meet with an adventure, and that gave him a delightful sensation.

The woman who had made the sign to him, lived on the third floor, and all the way upstairs his excitement increased, until his heart was beating violently when he reached the landing. At the same time, he was going up, he smelt a peculiar odor, which grew stronger and stronger, and which he had tried in vain to analyze, though all he could arrive at was, that it smelt like a chemist's shop.

The door on the right, at the end of the passage, was opened as soon as he put his foot on the landing, and the woman said, in a low voice:

"Come in, my dear."

A whiff of a very strong smell met his nostrils through the open door, and suddenly he exclaimed:

41

"How stupid I was! I know what it is now; it is carbolic acid, is it not?"

"Yes," the woman replied. "Don't you like it, dear? It is very wholesome, you know."

The woman was not ugly, although not young; she had very good eyes, although they were sad and sunken in her head; evidently she had been crying, very much quite recently, and that imparted a special spice to the vague smile which she put on, so as to appear more amiable.

Seized by his romantic ideas once more, and under the influence of the presentiment which he had had just before, he thought—and the idea filled him with pleasure:

"She's a widow poverty has forced to sell herself."

The room was small, but very clean and tidy, and that confirmed him in his conjecture, as he was curious to verify its truth, he went into the three rooms which opened into one another. The bed-room, came first; next there came a kind of a drawing-room, and then a dining-room, which evidently served as a kitchen, for a Dutch tiled stove stood in the middle of it, on which a stew was simmering, but the smell of carbolic acid was even stronger in that room. He remarked on it, and added with a laugh:

"Do you put it with your soup?"

And as he said this, he laid hold of the handle of the door which led into the next room, for he wanted to see everything, even that nook, which was apparently a store cupboard, but the woman seized him by the arm, and pulled him violently back.

"No, no," she said, almost in a whisper, and in a hoarse and suppliant voice, "no, dear, not there, not there, you must not go in there."

"Why?" he said, for his wish to go in had only become stronger.

"Because if you go in there, you will have no inclination to remain with me, and I so want you to stay. If you only knew!"

"Well, what?" And with a violent movement, he opened the glazed door, when the smell of carbolic acid seemed almost to strike him in the face, but what he saw, made him recoil still more, for on a small iron bedstead, lay the dead body of a woman fantastically illuminated by a single wax candle, and in horror he turned to make his escape.

"Stop, my dear," the woman sobbed; and clinging to him, she told him amidst a flood of tears, that her friend had died two days previously, and that there was no money to bury her. "Because," she said, "you can understand that I want it to be a respectable funeral, we were so very fond of each other! Stop here, my dear, do stop. I only want ten francs more. Don't go away."

They had gone back into the bed-room, and she was pushing him towards the bed:

"No," he said, "let me go. I will give you the ten francs, but I will not stay here; I cannot."

He took his purse out of his pocket, extracted a ten-franc piece, put it on the table, and then went to the door; but when he had reached it, a thought suddenly struck him, as if somebody were reasoning with him, without his knowledge.

43

"Why lose these ten francs? Why not profit by this woman's good intentions. She certainly did her business bravely, and if I had not known about the matter, I should certainly not have gone away for some time. . . . Well then?"

But other obscurer suggestions whispered to him:

"She was her friend! . . . They were so fond of each other! Was it friendship or love? Oh! love apparently. Well, it would surely be avenging morality, if this woman were forced to be faithless to that monstrous love?" And suddenly the man turned round and said in a low and trembling voice: "Look here! If I give you twenty francs instead of ten, I suppose you could buy some flowers for her, as well?"

The unhappy woman's face brightened with pleasure and gratitude.

"Will you really give me twenty?"

"Yes," he replied, "and more perhaps. It quite depends upon yourself."

And with the quiet conscience of an honorable man who, at the same time, is not a fool he said gravely:

"You need only be a very complaisant."

And he added, mentally: "Especially as I deserve it, as in giving you twenty francs I am performing a good action."

# seventh night

*The hunter is himself hunted, by what appears to him a rather evil man. Luckily, he is lost, and the evil man turns out to be a quite different sort of an evil. . . .*

REALLY," PAUL REPEATED, "really!"

"I who sit here before you have been violated, and violated by! . . . But if I were to tell you immediately by whom, there would be no story, eh? And as you want a story I will tell you all about it from beginning to end, and begin at the beginning.

"I had been shooting for a week, over the waste land in the heart of Brittany which borders on the Black Mountain. It is a desolate and wild country, but it is full of game. One can walk for hours without meeting a human being, and when one meets anybody, it is just the same as if one had not, for the people are absolutely ignorant of French, and when I got to an inn at night, I had to employ signs to let the people know that I wanted supper and bed.

"As I happened to be in a sad frame of mind at the

time, that solitude delighted me, and my dog's companionship was quite enough for me, and so you may guess my irritation when I perceived one morning that I was being followed, absolutely followed, by another sportsman who seemed to wish to enter into conversation with me. The day before, I had already noticed him obstructing the horizon several times, and I had attributed it to the chances of sport, which brought us both to the same likely spots for game, but now I could not be mistaken! The fellow was evidently following me, and was stretching his little pair of compasses as much as he could, so as to keep up with my long strides, and took short cuts, so as to catch me up at the half circle.

"As he seemed bent upon the matter, I naturally grew obstinate also, and he spent his whole day in trying to catch me up, while I spent mine in trying to baffle him, and we seemed to be playing at *hide-and-seek;* the consequences were, that when it was getting dark, I had completely lost myself in the most deserted part of the moor. There was no cottage near, and not even a church spire in the distance. The only land-mark, was the hateful outline of that cursed man, about five hundred yards off.

"Of course he had won the game! I should have to put a good face on the matter, and allow him to join me, or rather I should have to join him myself, if I did not wish to sleep in the open air and with an empty stomach, and so I went up to him, and asked my way in a half-surly manner.

"He replied very affably, that there was no inn in

the neighborhood, as the nearest village was five leagues off, but that he lived only about an hour's walk off, and that he considered himself very fortunate in being able to offer me hospitality.

"I was utterly done up, and how could I refuse? So we went off through the heather and furze; I walking slowly because I was so tired, and he went tripping along merrily with his legs like a basset hound's, which seemed untirable.

"And yet he was an old man, and not strongly built, for I could have knocked him over by blowing on him; but how he could walk, the beast!

"But he was not a troublesome companion, as I imagined he would have been, and he did not at all seem to wish to enter into conversation with me, as I feared he would. When he had given his invitation, and I had accepted it and thanked him in a few words, he did not open his lips again, and we walked on in silence, and only his glances worried me, for I felt them on me, as if he wished to force me into an intimacy, which my closed lips refused. But on the whole, his tenacious looks, which I noticed furtively, appeared sympathetic and even admiring—yes; really admiring!

"But I could not give him as good as he brought, for he was certainly not handsome; his legs were short, and rather bandy and he was thin and narrow-chested. His face was like a bit of parchment, furrowed and wrinkled, without a hair on it to hide the folds in his skin. Hs hair resembled that of an *Ignorantin* brother, with its gray locks falling onto his greasy collar; he had a nose like a ferret, and rat's eyes, but he was able

47

to offer me food and quarters for the night, and it was not requisite that he should be handsome, in order to do that.

"Capital food, and very comfortable quarters! A manorial dwelling, a real old, well-furnished manorhouse; and in the large dining-room, in front of the huge fireplace, where a large fire was blazing, dinner was laid; I will say no more than that; A hotchpotch, which had been stewing since morning, no doubt! A *salmis* of woodcock, in defense of which angels would have taken up arms; buckwheat cakes, in cream, flavored with aniseed, and a cheese, which is a rare thing and hardly ever to be found in Brittany, a cheese to make anyone eat a four pound loaf if he only smelt the rind The whole washed down by Chambertin, and then brandy distilled by cider, which was so good that it made a man fancy that he had swallowed a deity in velvet breeches; not to mention the cigars, pure, smuggled havannahs; large, strong, not dry but green, on the contrary, which made a strong and intoxicating smoke.

"And how the little old gentleman stuffed, and drank and smoked! He was an ogre, a choirister, a sapper, and so was I, I must confess, and, upon my word, I cannot remember what we talked about during our Gargantuan feed! But we certainly talked, but what about? About shooting, certainly, and about women most probably. Confound it! Among men, after drinking! Yes, yes, about women, I am quite sure, and he told some funny stories, did the little old man; Especially about a portrait which was hanging over the large fireplace, and which represented his grandmother, a marchioness of the old régime. She was a woman who had certainly played some pranks, and they said that she was still frisky and had good legs and thighs when she was seventy.

" 'It is extraordinary,' I remarked, 'how like you are to that portrait.'

" 'Yes,' the old man replied with a smile; and then he added in his harsh, tremulous voice: 'I resemble her in everything. I am only sixty, and I feel as if I should have lusty, hot blood in me until I am seventy.'

"And then suddenly, very much moved, and looking at me admiringly, as he had done once before, he said to the portrait:

" 'I say, marchioness, what a pity that you did not know this handsome young fellow!'

"I remembered that apostrophe and that look very well, when I went to bed about an hour later, nearly drunk, in the large room papered in white and gold, to which I was shown by a tall, broad-shouldered footman, who wished me good-night in Breton.

"*Good-night*, yes! But that implied going to sleep, which was just what I could not do. The Chambertin, the cider brandy and the cigars had certainly made me drunk, but not so as to overcome me altogether. On the contrary, I was excited, my nerves were highly strung, my blood was heated, and I was in a half-sleep in which I felt that I was very much alive, and my whole being was in a vibration and expansion, just as if I had been smoking hasheesh.

"Of course, that was it; I was dreaming while I was awake; but I saw the door open and the marchioness

49

come in, who had stepped down, out of her frame. She had taken off her furbelows, and was in her nightgown. Her high head-dress was replaced by a simple knot of ribbon, which confined her powdered hair into a small chignon, but I recognized her quite plainly, by the trembling light of the candle which she was carrying. It was her face with its piercing eyes, its pointed nose and its smiling and sensual mouth. She did not look so young to me as she appeared in her portrait. Bah! Perhaps that was merely caused by the feeble, flickering light! But I had not even time to account for it, not to reflect on the strangeness of the sight, nor to discuss the matter with myself and to say: 'Am I dead drunk, or is it a ghost?'

"No, I had no time, and that is the fact, for the candle was suddenly blown out and the marchioness was in my bed and holding me in her arms, and one fixed idea, the only one that I had, haunted me, which was:

" 'Had the marchioness good limbs, and was she still frisky at seventy?' And I did not care much if she was seventy and if she was a ghost or not; I only thought of one thing: 'Has she really good limbs?' "

"By Jove, yes! She did not speak. Oh, marchioness! marchioness! And suddenly in spite of myself and to convince myself that it was not a mere fantastic dream, I exclaimed:

" 'Why, good heavens! I am not dreaming!'

" 'No, you are not dreaming,' two lips replied, trying to press themselves against mine.

"But, oh! horror! The mouth smelt of cigars and brandy! The voice was that of the little old man!

"With a bound I sent him flying on to the ground, and jumped out of bed, shouting:

" 'Beast! beast!'

"Then I heard the door slam, and bare feet pattering on the stairs as he ran away; so I dressed hastily in the dark and went downstairs, still shouting.

"In the hall below, where I could see through the upper windows that the dawn was breaking, I met the broad-shouldered footman, who was holding a great cudgel in his hand. He was bawling also, in Breton, and pointed to the open door, outside where my dog was waiting. What could I say to this savage who did not speak French? Should I face his cudgel? There was no reason for doing so; and besides, I was even more ashamed than furious; so I hastily took up my gun and my game-bag, which were in the hall, and went off without turning round.

"Disgusted with sport in that part of the country, I returned to Brest the same day, and there, timidly and with many precautions, I tried to find out something about the little old man. . . .

" 'Oh, I know!' somebody replied at last to my question; 'you are speaking of the manor-house at Hervénidozse, where the old countess lives, who dresses like a man and sleeps with her coachman.'

"And with a deep sigh of relief, and much to the astonishment of my informant, I replied:

" 'Oh! so much the better!' "

# *eighth night*

*He had given her twelve children, but after that he refused further congress with her. . . . How she tried for a thirteenth child, and failed, makes a story worth listening to.*

A<small>NYONE WHO ASSERTED</small>, or even insinuated, that the Reverend William Greenfield, Vicar of St. Sampson's, Tottenham, did not make his wife Anna perfectly happy, would have had to have a malicious motive. For in their twelve years of married life, he had honored her with twelve children, and could anybody decently ask more of a saintly man?

Saintly to heroism, that's what it was. For his wife Anna, who was endowed with invaluable virtues, which made her a model among wives and a paragon among mothers, had not been equally endowed physically; in one word, she was hideous. Her hair, which was coarse though it was thin, was the color of the national *half-and-half*, but of that thick *half-and-half* which looks as if it has been already swallowed several times, and her complexion, which was muddy and pimply, looked as if it were covered with sand mixed with brick-dust. Her teeth, which were long and protruding, seemed as if they were about to start out of their sockets in order to escape from that mouth with scarcely any lips, whose sulphurous breath had turned them yellow. They were evidently suffering from bile.

Her china-blue eyes stared vaguely, one very much to the right and the other very much to the left, with a divergent and frightened squint; no doubt in order that they might not see her nose, of which they felt ashamed. And they were quite right! Thin, soft, long, pendant, sallow, and ending in a violet knob, it irresistibly reminded those who saw it of something which cannot be mentioned except in a medical treatise. Her body, through the inconceivable irony of nature, was at the same time thin and flabby, wooden and chubby, without having either the elegance of slimness or the rounded gracefulness of stoutness. It might have been taken for a body which had formerly been adipose, but which had now grown thin, while the covering had remained floating on the framework.

She was evidently nothing but skin and bones, but then she had too many bones and too little skin.

It will be seen that the reverend gentleman had done his duty, his whole duty, more than his duty, in sacrificing a dozen times on this altar. Yes, a dozen times bravely and loyally! A dozen times, and his wife could not deny it nor dispute the number, because the children were there to prove it. A dozen times, and not one less!

And alas! not once more; and that was the reason why, in spite of appearances, Mrs. Anna Greenfield ventured to think, in the depths of her heart, that the Reverend William Greenfield, Vicar of St. Sampson's, Tottenham, had not made her perfectly happy; and she thought so all the more as, for four years now, she had been obliged to renounce all hope of that annual sacrifice, which was so easy and so fugitive formerly, but which had now fallen into disuse. In fact, at the birth of the twelfth child, the reverend gentleman had expressly said to her:

"God has greatly blessed our union, my dear Anna. We have reached the sacred number of the twelve tribes of Israel, and were we now to persevere in the works of the flesh, it would be mere debauchery, and I cannot suppose that you would wish me to end my exemplary life in lustful practices."

His wife blushed and looked down, and the holy man, with the legitimate pride of virtue which is its own reward, audibly thanked Heaven that he was "not as other men are."

A model among wives and the paragon of mothers, Anna lived with him for four years on those terms, without complaining to anyone, and contented herself by praying fervently to God that He would mercifully inspire her husband with the desire to begin a second series of the twelve tribes. At times even, in order to make her prayers more efficacious, she tried to compass that end by culinary means. She spared no pains, and gorged the reverend gentleman with highly-seasoned dishes. Hare soup, ox-tails stewed in sherry, the green fat in turtle soup, stewed mushrooms, Jerusalem arti-chokes, celery, and horse-radish; hot sauces, truffles, hashes with wine and cayenne pepper in them, curried lobsters, pies made of cocks' combs, oysters, and the soft roe of fish; and all these dishes were washed down by strong beer and generous wines, Scotch ale, Burgun-dy, dry champagne, brandy, whiskey and gin; in a word, by that numberless array of alcoholic drinks with which the English people love to heat their blood.

And, as a matter of fact, the reverend gentleman's blood became very heated, as was shown by his nose and cheeks, but in spite of this, the powers above were inexorable, and he remained quite indifferent as regards his wife, who was unhappy and thoughtful at the sight of that protruding nasal appendage, which, alas! was alone in its glory.

She became thinner, and at the same time, flabbier than ever, and almost began to lose her trust in God, when, suddenly, she had an inspiration. Was it not, perhaps, the work of the devil?

She did not care to inquire too closely into the matter, as she thought it a very good idea, and it was this:

"Go to the Universal Exhibition in Paris, and there, perhaps, you will discover the secret to make yourself loved."

Decidedly luck favored her, for her husband imme-diately gave her permission to go, and as soon as she got into the *Esplanade des Invalides*, she saw the Alger-ian dancers, and she said to herself.

"Surely this would inspire William with the desire to be the father of the thirteenth tribe!"

But how could she manage to get him to be present at such abominable orgies? For she could not hide from herself that it was an abominable exhibition, and she knew how scandalized he would be at their voluptuous movements. She had no doubt that the devil had led her there, but she could not take her eyes off the scene, and it gave her an idea; and so for nearly a fortnight you might have seen the poor, unattractive woman sitting, and attentively and curiously watching the swaying hips of the Algerian women. She was learning.

The very evening of her return to London, she rushed into her husband's bedroom, disrobed herself in an instant, except for a thin gauze covering, and for the first time in her life appeared before him in all the ugliness of her semi-nudity.

"Come, come," the saintly man stammered out, "are you—are you mad, Anna! What demon has possessed you? Why inflict the disgrace of such a scene on me?"

But she did not listen to him, and did not reply, but suddenly she also began to sway her hips about like an almah. The reverend gentleman could not believe his eyes, and in his stupefaction, he did not think of covering them with his hands or even of shutting them. He looked at her, stupefied and dumbfounded, a prey to the hypnotism of ugliness. He watched her as she came forward and retired, and went up and down, as she skipped and wriggled, and threw herself into extraordinary attitudes. For a long time he sat motionless and almost unable to speak. He only said in a low voice:

"Oh, Lord! To think that twelve times! . . . twelve times! . . . a whole dozen!"

However, she fell into a chair, panting and worn out, and said to herself:

"Thank Heaven! William looks like he used to do formerly on the days that he honored me. Thank Heaven! There will be a thirteenth tribe, and then a fresh series of tribes, for William is very methodical in all that he does!"

But William merely took a blanket off the bed and threw it over her, saying in a voice of thunder:

"Your name is no longer Anna, Mrs. Greenfield; for the future you shall be called Jezabel. I only regret that I have twelve times mingled my blood with your impure blood." And then, seized by pity, he added: "If you were only in a state of inebriety, of intoxication, I could excuse you."

"Well, yes, yes!" she exclaimed, repentantly, "yes, I am in that state . . . Forgive me, William—forgive a poor drunken woman!"

"I will forgive you, Anna," he replied, and he gave her a wash-hand basin, saying: "Cold water will do you good, and when your head is clear, remember the lesson which you must learn from this occurrence."

"What lesson?" she asked, humbly.

"That people ought never to depart from their usual habits."

"But why, then, William," she asked, timidly, "have you changed your habits?"

"Hold your tongue!" he cried—"hold your tongue, Jezabel! Have you not got over your intoxication yet? For twelve years I certainly followed the divine precept: *increase and multiply*, once a year. But since then, I have

57

grown accustomed to something else, and I do not wish to alter my habits."

And the Reverend William Greenfield, Vicar of St. Sampson's, Tottenham, the saintly man whose blood was inflamed by heating food and liquor, whose ears were like full-blown poppies and who had a nose like a tomato, left his wife and, as had been his habit for four years, went to make love to Polly, the servant.

"Now, Polly," he said, "you are a clever girl, and I mean, through you, to teach Mrs. Greenfield a lesson she will never forget. I will try and see what I can do for you."

And in order to this, he called her his little Jezabel, and said to her, with an unctuous smile:

"Call me Jeroboam! You don't understand why? Neither do I, but that does not matter. Take off all your things, Polly, and show yourself to Mrs. Greenfield."

The servant did as she was bidden, and the result was that Mrs. Greenfield never again hinted to her husband the desirability of laying the foundation of a thirteenth tribe.

# *ninth night*

*He was almost compromised in the arms of his best friend's wife when a miracle saved him, an ordinary, a commonplace miracle, but a miracle none the less. . . .*

IT WAS A LITTLE drawing-room, with heavy hangings, and with a faint, judicious smell of flowers and scents. A large fire burned in the grate, while one lamp, covered with a shade of old lace, on the corner of the mantelpiece threw a soft light onto the two persons who were talking.

The mistress of the house was an old lady with white hair, but one of those adorable old ladies whose unwrinkled skin is as smooth as the finest paper, and scented, impregnated with perfume as the delicate essences which she had used in her bath for so many years had penetrated through the epidermis.

The man with her was a very old friend, who had never married, a constant friend, a companion in the journey of life, but nothing else.

They had not exchanged words for about a minute,

and they were both looking at the fire, thinking no matter of what, in one of those moments of friendly silence between people who have no need to be constantly talking in order to be happy together, when suddenly a large log, a stump covered with burning roots, fell out. It fell over the fire-dogs into the drawing-room, and rolled onto the carpet, scattering great sparks all round. The old lady sprang up with a little scream, as if she was going to run away, while he kicked the log back onto the hearth and trod out all the burning sparks with his boots.

When the disaster was repaired, there was a strong smell of burning, and sitting down opposite to his friend, the man looked at her with a smile, and said, as he pointed to the log:

"That is the reason why I never married."

She looked at him in astonishment, with the inquisitive gaze of women who wish to know everything, that eye which women have who are no longer very young, in which complicated, and often malicious curiosity is reflected, and she asked:

"How so?"

"Oh! that is a long story," he replied; "a rather sad and unpleasant story.

"My old friends were often surprised at the coldness which suddenly sprang up between one of my best friends, whose Christian name was Julien, and myself. They could not understand how two such intimate and inseparable friends as we had been could suddenly become almost strangers to one another, and I will tell you the reason of it.

"He and I used to live together at one time. We were never apart, and the friendship that united us seemed so strong that nothing could break it.

"One evening when he came home, he told me that he was going to get married, and it gave me a shock as if he had robbed me or betrayed me. When a man's friend marries, it is all over between them. The jealous affection of a woman, that suspicious, uneasy, and carnal affection, will not tolerate that sturdy and frank attachment, that attachment of the mind, of the heart, and mutual confidence which exists between two men.

"You see, however great the love may be that unites them, a man and a woman are always strangers in mind and intellect; they remain belligerents, they belong to different races. There must always be a conqueror and a conquered, a master and a slave; now the one, now the other—they are never two equals. They press each other's hands, those hands trembling with amorous passion; but they never press them with a long, strong, loyal pressure, with that pressure which seems to open hearts and to lay them bare in a burst of sincere, strong, manly affection. Philosophers of old, instead of marrying and pro-creating children who would abandon them as a consolation for their old age, sought for a good, reliable friend, and grew old with him in that communion of thought which can only exist between men.

"Well, my friend Julien married. His wife was pretty, charming, a little, light, curly-haired, plump, bright woman, who seemed to worship him; and at first I went but rarely to their house, as I was afraid of interfering with their affection, and afraid of being in their way.

61

But somehow they attracted me to their house; they were constantly inviting me, and seemed very fond of me. Consequently, by degrees I allowed myself to be allured by the charm of their life. I often dined with them, and frequently, when I returned home at night, I thought that I would do as he had done, and get married, as I now found my empty house very dull.

"They seemed very much in love with one another, and were never apart.

"Well, one evening Julien wrote and asked me to go to dinner, and I naturally went.

" 'My dear fellow,' he said, 'I must go out directly afterwards on business, and I shall not be back until eleven o'clock, but I shall be at eleven precisely, and I reckon you to keep Bertha company.'

"The young woman smiled.

" 'It was my idea,' she said, 'to send for you.'

"I held out my hand to her.

" 'You are as nice as ever,' I said, and I felt a long, friendly pressure of her fingers, but I paid no attention to it; so we sat down to dinner, and at eight clock Julien went out.

"As soon as he had gone, a kind of strange embarrassment immediately seemed to rise between his wife and me. We had never been alone together yet, and in spite of our daily increasing intimacy, this *tête-à-tête* placed us in a new position. At first I spoke vaguely of those indifferent matters with which one fills up an embarrassing silence, but she did not reply, and remained opposite to me with her head down in an undecided manner, as if she were thinking over some difficult subject, and as I was at a loss for commonplace ideas, I held my tongue. It is surprising how hard it is at times to find anything to say.

"And then, again, I felt in the air, I felt in the unseen, something which is impossible for me to express, that mysterious premonition which tells you beforehand of the secret intentions, be they good or evil, of another person with respect to yourself.

"That painful silence lasted some time, and then Bertha said to me:

" 'Will you kindly put a log on the fire, for it is going out.'

"So I opened the box where the wood was kept, which was placed just where yours is, took out the largest log, and put it on the top of the others, which were three-parts burnt, and then silence reigned in the room again.

"In a few minutes the log was burning so brightly that it scorched our faces, and the young woman raised her eyes to me—eyes that had a strange look to me.

" 'It is too hot now,' she said; 'let us go and sit on the sofa over there.'

"So we went and sat on the sofa, and then she said suddenly, looking me full in the face:

" 'What should you do if a woman were to tell you that she was in love with you?'

" 'Upon my word,' I replied, very much at a loss for an answer, 'I cannot foresee such a case; but it would very much depend upon the woman.'

"She gave a hard, nervous, vibrating laugh; one of those false laughs which seem as if they must break thin glasses, and then she added: 'Men are never either venturesome nor acute.' And after a moment's silence, she continued: 'Have you ever been in love, Monsieur Paul?' I was obliged to acknowledge that I certainly had been, and she asked me to tell her all about it, whereupon I made up some story or other. She listened to me attentively with frequent sighs of approbation and contempt, and then suddenly she said:

" 'No, you understand nothing about the subject. It seems to me, that real love must unsettle the mind, upset the nerves and distract the head; that it must—how shall I express it?—be dangerous, even terrible, almost criminal and sacrilegious; that it must be a kind of treason; I mean to say that it is almost bound to break laws, fraternal bonds, sacred obstacles; when love is tranquil, easy, lawful and without dangers, is it really love?'

"I did not know what answer to give her, and I made this philosophical reflection to myself: 'Oh! female brain, here indeed you show yourself!'

"While speaking, she had assumed a demure, saintly air; and resting on the cushions, she stretched herself out at full length, with her head on my shoulder and her dress pulled up a little, so as to show her red silk stockings, which the firelight made look still brighter. In a minute or two she continued:

" 'I suppose I have frightened you?' I protested against such a notion, and she leant against my breast altogether, and without looking at me she said: 'If I were to tell you that I love you, what would you do?'

"And before I could think of an answer, she had

thrown her arms round my neck, had quickly drawn my head down and put her lips to mine.

"Oh! My dear friend, I can tell you that I did not feel at all happy! What! deceive Julien? become the lover of this little silly, wrong-headed, cunning woman, who was no doubt terribly sensual, and for whom her husband was already not sufficient! To betray him continually, to deceive him, to play at being in love merely because I was attracted by forbidden fruit, danger incurred and friendship betrayed! No, that did not suit me, but what was I to do? To imitate Joseph, would be acting a very stupid, and, moreover, difficult part, for this woman was maddening in her perfidy, inflamed by audacity, palpitating and excited. Let the man who has never felt on his lips, the warm kiss of a woman who is ready to give herself to him, throw the first stone at me . . .

" . . . Well, a minute more . . . you understand what I mean? I minute more and . . . I should have been . . . I beg your pardon, he would have been! . . . when a loud noise made us both jump up. The log had fallen into the room, knocking over the fire-irons and the fender, and onto the carpet which it had scorched, and had rolled under an arm-chair, which it would certainly set alight.

"I jumped up like a madman, and as I was replacing that log which had saved me, on the fire, the door opened hastily, and Julien came in.

" 'I have done,' he said, in evident pleasure. 'The business was over two hours sooner than I expected!'

"Yes, my dear friend, without that log, I should have

65

been caught in the very act, and you know what the consequences would have been!

"You may be sure that I took good care never to be overtaken in a similar situation again; never, never. Soon afterwards I saw that Julien was giving me the 'cold shoulder,' as they say. His wife was evidently undermining our friendship; by degrees he got rid of me, and we have altogether ceased to meet.

"I have not got married which ought not to surprise you, I think."

# *tenth night*

> *To keep her from her lover, the miller shut his daughter up in her room where she became a virtual prisoner, but she got out to see him, and strange were the fires which lit her way. . . .*

MARGOT FRESQUYL succumbed for the first time to the delicious intoxication of the mortal sin of loving, on the evening of Midsummer Day.

While most young people were holding each other's hands and dancing in a circle round the burning logs, the girl had slyly taken the deserted road which led to the wood, leaning on the arm of her partner, a tall, vigorous farm servant, whose Christian name was Tiennou, which, by the way, was the only name he had borne from his birth. For he was entered on the register of births with this curt note: *Father and mother unknown;* he having been found on St. Stephen's Day under a shed on a farm, where some poor, despairing wretch had abandoned him, perhaps even without turning her head round to look at him.

For months Tiennou had madly worshipped that fair, pretty girl, who was now trembling as he clasped her in his arms, under the sweet coolness of the leaves. He religiously remembered how she had dazzled him—like some ecstatic vision, the recollection of which always remains imprinted on his eyes—the first time that he saw her in her father's mill, where he had gone to ask for work. She stood out all rosy from the warmth of the day, amidst the impalpable clouds of flour, which diffused an indistinct whiteness through the air. With her hair hanging about her in untidy curls, as if she had just awakened from a profound sleep, she stretched herself lazily, with her bare arms clasped behind her head, and yawned so as to show her white teeth, which glistened like those of a young wolf, and her maiden nudity appeared beneath her unbuttoned bodice with innocent immodesty. He told her that he thought her adorable, so stupidly, that she made fun of him and scourged him with her cruel laughter; and, from that day he spent his life in Margot's shadow. He might have been taken for one of those wild beasts ardent with desire, which ceaselessly utter maddened cries to the stars on nights when the constellations bathe the dark coverts in warm light. Margot met him wherever she went, and seized with pity, and by degrees agitated by his sobs, by his dumb entreaties, by the burning looks which flashed from his large eyes, she had returned his love; she had dreamt restlessly that during a whole night she had been in his vigorous arms which pressed her like corn that is being crushed in the mill, that she was obeying a man who had subdued her, and learning strange things which the other girls talked about in a low voice when they were drawing water at the well.

She had, however, been obilged to wait until Midsummer Day, for the miller watched over his heiress very carefully.

The two lovers told each other all this as they were going along the dark road, and innocently giving utterance to words of happiness, which rise to the lips like the forgotten refrain of a song. At times they were silent, not knowing what more to say, and not daring to embrace each other any more. The night was soft and warm, the warmth of a half-closed alcove in a bedroom, and which had the effect of a tumbler of new wine.

The leaves were sleeping motionlessly in supreme peace, and in the distance they could hear the monotonous sound of the brooks as they flowed over the stones. Amidst the dull noise of the insects, the nightingales were answering each other from tree to tree, and everything seemed alive with hidden life, and the sky was bright with such a shower of falling stars, that they might have been taken for white forms wandering among the dark trunks of the trees.

"Why have we come?" Margot asked, in a panting voice. "Do you not want me any more, Tiennou?"

"Alas! I dare not," he replied. "Listen: you know that I was picked up on the high road, that I have nothing in the world except my two arms, and that Miller Fresquyl will never let you marry a poor devil like me."

She interrupted him with a painful gesture, and putting her lips to his, she said:

"What does that matter? I love you, and I want you
. . . Take me . . . "

And it was thus, on St. John's night, Margot Fresquyl
for the first time yielded to the mortal sin of love.

## II

D<small>ID</small> the miller guess his daughter's secret, when he
heard her singing merrily from dawn till dusk, and saw
her sitting dreaming at her window instead of sewing
as she was in the habit of doing?

Did he see it when she threw ardent kisses from the
tips of her fingers to her lover at a distance?

However that might have been, he shut poor Margot
in the mill as if it had been a prison. No more love
or pleasure, no more meetings at night at the verge of
the wood. When she chatted with the passers-by, when
she tried furtively to open the gate of the encslosure
and to make her escape ( her father beat her as if she had
been some disobedient animal, until she fell on her knees
on the floor with clasped hands, scarcely able to move
and her whole body covered with purple bruises.

She pretended to obey him, but she revolted in her
whole being, and the string of bitter insults which he
heaped upon her rang in her head. With clenched hands,
and a gesture of terrible hatred, she cursed him for
standing in the way of her love, and at night, she rolled
about on her bed, bit the sheets, moaned, stretched herself out for imaginary embraces, maddened by the
sensual heat with which her body was still palpitating.
She called out Tiennou's name aloud, she broke the
peaceful stillness of the sleeping house with her heart-

rending sobs, and her dejected voice drowned the monotonous sound of the water that was dripping under the arch of the mill, between the immovable paddles of the wheel.

III

THEN there came that terrible week in October when the unfortunate young fellows who had drawn bad numbers had to join their regiments. Tiennou was one of them, and Margot was in despair to think that she should not see him for five interminable years, that they could not even, at that hour of sad farewells, be alone and exchange those consoling words which afterwards alleviate the pain of absence.

Tiennou prowled about the house, like a starving beggar, and one morning, while the miller was mending the wheel, he managed to see Margot.

"I will wait for you in the old place tonight," he whispered, in terrible grief. "I know it is the last time . . . I shall throw myself into some deep hole in the river if you do not come! . . . "

"I will be there, Tiennou," she replied, in a bewildered manner. "I swear I will be there . . . even if I have to do something terrible to enable me to come!"

. . . . . .

The village was burning in the dark night, and the flames, fanned by the wind, rose up like sinister torches. The thatched roofs, the ricks of corn, the haystacks, and the barns fell in, and crackled like rockets, while the sky looked as if they were illuminated by an *aurora borealis*. Fresquyl's mill was smoking, and its calcined

71

ruins were reflected on the deep water. The sheep and cows were running about the fields in terror, the dogs were howling, and the women were sitting on the broken furniture, and were crying and wringing their hands; while during all this time Margot was abandoning herself to her lover's ardent caresses, and with her arms round his neck, she said to him, tenderly:

"You see that I have kept my promise . . . I set fire to the mill so that I might be able to get out. So much the worse if all have suffered. But I do not care as long as you are happy in having me, and love me!"

And pointing to the fire which was still burning fiercely in the distance, she added with a burst of savage laughter:

"Tiennou, we shall not have such beautiful tapers at our wedding Mass when you come back from your regiment!"

And thus it was that for the second time Margot Fresquyl yielded to the mortal sin of love.

# eleventh night

*The Marquis needed a girl to be caught with, for purposes of divorce. He got the girl, was caught at it, but it turned out to be a different kind of a catch. . . .*

"ONE THING IS SURE," Sulpice de Laurièr said, "and that is, that I had absolutely forgotten the date on which I was to allow myself to be taken in the very act, with some wench for the occasion. As neither my wife nor I had any serious or plausible reason for a divorce, not even the least incompatibility of temper, and as there is always the risk of not impressing the heart of even the most indulgent judge when he is told that the parties have agreed to drag their load separately, each for themselves, that they are too frisky, too fond of pleasure and of wandering about from place to place to continue the conjugal experiment, we got up between us the ingenious stage arrangement of, 'a serious wrong. . . .'

"This was really the funniest thing of all; and under any other circumstances it would have been repugnant

73

to me to mix up our servants in the affair like so many others do, or to distress that pretty little, fair and delicate Parisian woman, even though it were only in appearance and to pass as a common *Sganarelle* with the manners of a carter, in the eyes of some scoundrel of a footman, or of some lady's maid. And so when Maitre Le Chevrier, that kind lawyer who certainly knows more female secrets than the most fashionable confessor, gave a startled exclamation on seeing me still in my dressing-gown, and slowly smoking a cigar like an idler who has no engagements down on his tablets, and who is quietly waiting for the usual time for dressing and going to dine at his club, he exclaimed:

" 'Have you forgotten that this is the day, at the *Hôtel de Bade,* between five and six o'clock? In an hour, Madame de Laurière will be at the office of the Police Commissary in the Rue de Provence, with her uncle and Maitre Cantenac . ..'

"An hour; I only had an hour, sixty short minutes to dress in, to take a room, find a woman and persuade her to go with me immediately, and to excite her feelings, so that this extravagant adventure might not appear too equivocal to the Commissary of Police. One hour in which to carry out such a program was enough to make a man lose his head. And there were no possible means of putting off that obligatory entertainment, to let Madame Le Laurière know in time, and to gain a few minutes more.

" 'Have you found a woman, at any rate?" ' Maitre de Chevrier continued anxiously.

" 'No, my dear sir!'

"I immediately began to think of the whole string of my dear female friends. Should I choose Liline Ablette, who could refuse me nothing, Blanch Rebus, who was the best comrade a man ever had, or Lalie Spring, that luxurious creature, who was constantly in search of something new? Neither one nor the other of them, for it was ninety-nine chances to one that all these confounded girls were in the *Bois de Boulogne,* or at their dressmakers!"

" 'Bah! Just pick up the first girl you meet on the pavement.'

"And before the hour was up, I was bolting the door of a room, which looked out onto the boulevard.

"The woman whom I had picked up, as she was walking past the *cafés,* from the *Vaudeville* to *Tortoni's,* was twenty at the most. She had an impudent, snub nose, as if it had been turned up in fun by a fillip, large eyes with deep rims round them; her lips were too red, and she had the slow, indolent walk of a girl who goes in for debauchery too freely and who began too soon, but she was pretty, and her linen was very clean and neat. And she was evidently used to chance love-making, and had a way of undressing herself in two or three rapid movements, of throwing her toggery to the right and left, until she was extremely lightly clad, and of throwing herself onto the bed which astonished me as a sight that was well worth seeing.

"She did not talk much, though she began by saying: 'Pay up at once, old man . . . You don't look like a fellow who would bilk a girl, but it puts me into better trim when I have been paid.'

"I gave her two napoleons, and she eyed me with gratitude and respect at the same time, but also with that uneasy look of a girl who asks herself: 'What does this fool expect for it?'

"The whole affair began to amuse me, and I must confess that I was rather taken with her, for she had a beautiful figure and complexion, and I was hoping that the Commissary would not come directly, when there was a loud rapping at the door.

"She sat up with a start, and grew so pale that one would have said she was about to faint.

" 'What a set of pigs, to come and interrupt people like this!' she muttered between her teeth; while I affected the most complete calm.

" 'Somebody who has made a mistake in the room, my dear,' I said.

"But this noise increased, and suddenly I heard a man's voice saying clearly and authoritatively:

" 'Open the door, in the name of the law!'

"On hearing that, one would have thought that she had received a shock from an electric battery, by the nimble manner in which she jumped out of bed; and quickly putting on her stays and her dress anyhow, she endeavored to discover a way out in every corner of the room, like a wild beast, trying to escape from its cage. I thought that she was going to throw herself out of the window, so I seized hold of her to prevent her.

"The unfortunate creature acted like a madwoman, and when she felt my arm round her waist, she cried in a hoarse voice:

76

" 'I see it . . . You have sold me . . . You thought that I should expose myself. . . . Oh! you filthy brutes —you filthy brutes!'

"And suddenly, passing from abuse to entreaties, pale and with chattering teeth, she threw herself at my feet, and said, in a low voice:

" 'Listen to me, my dear: you don't look a bad sort of fellow, and you would not like them to lock me up. I have a kid and the old woman to keep. Hide me behind the bed, do, and please don't give me up. . . . I will make it up to you, and you shall have no cause for grumbling. . . . '

"At that moment however, the lock which they had unscrewed fell onto the floor with a metallic sound, and Madame de Laurière and the Police Commissary, wearing his tricolored scarf, appeared in the door, while behind them the heads of the uncle and of the lawyer could be seen indistinctly in the background.

"The girl had uttered a cry of terror and going up to the Commissary she said, panting:

" 'I swear to you that I am not guilty, that I was not . . . I will tell you everything if you will promise me not to tell them that I spilt, for they would pay me out. . . . '

"The Commissary, who was surprised, but who guessed that there was something which was not quite clear behind all this, forgot to draw up his report, and so the lawyer went up to him and said:

" 'Well, monsieur, what are we waiting for?'

"But he paid no attention to anything but the woman, and looking at her sharply and suspiciously through his gold-rimmed spectacles, he said to her in a hard voice:

" 'Your names and surnames?'

" 'Juliette Randal, or as I am generally called, Jujutte Pipehead.'

" 'So you will swear you were not—'

"She interrupted him eagerly:

" 'I swear it, monsieur, and I know that my little man had nothing to do with it either. He was only keeping a look-out while the others collared the swag. . . . I will swear that I can account for every moment of my time that night. Roquin was drunk, and told me everything. . . . They got five thousand francs from Daddy Zacharias, and of course Roquin had his share, but he did not work with his partners. It was Minon Ménilmuche, whom they call *Drink-without-Thirst*, who held the gardener's hands, and who bled him with a blow from his knife.'

"The Commissary let her run on, and when she had finished, he questioned me, as if I had belonged to Jujutte's band.

" 'Your name, Christian name, and profession?'

" 'Marquis Sulpice de Lauriér, living on my own private income, at 24, Rue de Galilee.'

" 'De Lauriér? Oh, very well. . . . Excuse me, monsieur, but at Madame de Lauriér's request, I declare formally before these gentlemen, who will be able to give evidence, that the girl Juliette Randal, whom they call *Jujutte Tête-de-Pipe*, is your mistress. You are at liberty to go, Monsieur le Marquis, and you, girl Randal, answer my questions.'

"Thus, by the most extraordinary chance, our divorce suit created a sensation which I had certainly never foreseen. I was obliged to appear in the Assize Court as a witness in the celebrated case of those burglars, when three of them were condemned to death, and to undergo the questioning of the idiotic Presiding Judge, who tried by all means in his power to make me acknowledge that I was Jujutte Tête-de-Pipe's regular lover; and in consequence, ever since then I have passed as an ardent seeker after novel sensations, and a man who wallows in the lowest depths of the Parisian dunghill.

"I cannot say that this unjust reputation has brought me any pleasant love affairs. Women are so perverse, so absurd, and so curious!"

# *twelfth night*

> *He got into the priest's confession-box by accident, and, as fate would have it, found himself listening to his own wife's outpourings. It was quite a confession for a husband to listen to.*

Monsieur de Champdelin had no cause to complain of his lot as a married man; nor could he talk of destiny having played him a bad turn, as it does so many others, for it would have been difficult for even a better man to find a more desirable, merrier, prettier little woman, or one easier to amuse and guide than his wife. To look at the large, limpid eyes which illuminated her fair, girlish face, one would think that her mother must have spent whole nights before her birth, in looking dreamily at the stars, and so had become, as it were, impregnated with their magic brightness. And one did not know which to prefer—her bright, silky hair, or her slightly *retroussé* nose, with its vibrating nostrils, her red lips, which looked as alluring as a ripe peach, her beautiful shoulders, her delicate ears, which resembled mother-of-pearl, or her slim waist and rounded figure, which would have delighted and tempted a sculptor.

Besides, she was always merry, overflowing with youth and life, never dissatisfied, only wishing to enjoy herself, to laugh, to love and be loved, and put all the house into a tumult, as if it had been a great cage full of birds. In spite of all this, however, that worn out fool, Champdelin, had never cared much about her, but had left that charming garden lying waste, and almost immediately after their honeymoon, he had resumed his usual bachelor habits, and had begun to lead the same fast life that he had done of old.

It was stronger than he, for his was one of those libertine natures which are constant targets for love, and which never resign themselves to domestic peace and happiness. The last woman who came across him, in a love adventure, was always the one whom he loved best, and the mere contact with a petticoat inflamed him, and made him commit the most imprudent actions.

As he was not hard to please, he fished, as it were, in troubled waters, went after the ugly ones and the pretty ones alike, was bold even to impudence, was not to be kept off by mistakes, nor anger, nor modesty, nor threats, through he sometimes fell into a trap and got a thrashing from some relative or jealous lover; he withstood all attempts to get hush-money out of him, and became only all the more enamored of vice and more ardent in his lures and pursuit of love affairs on that account.

But the work-girls and the shop-girls and all the tradesmen's wives in Saint Martéjoux knew him, and made him pay for their whims and their coquetry, and had to put up with his love-making. Many of them smiled or blushed when they saw him under the tall plane-trees in the public garden, or met him in the unfrequented, narrow streets near the Cathedral, with his thin, sensual face, whose looks had something satyr-like about them, and some of them used to laugh at him and make fun of him, though they ran away when he went up to them. And when some friend or other, who was sorry that he could forget himself so far, used to say to him, when he was at a loss for any other argument: "And your wife, Champdelin? Are you not afraid that she will have her revenge and pay you out in your own coin?" his only reply was a contemptuous and incredulous shrug of the shoulders.

She deceive him, indeed; she, who was as devout, as virtuous, and as ignorant of forbidden things as a nun, who cared no more for love than she did for an old slipper! She, who did not even venture on any veiled allusions, who was always laughing, who took life as it came, who performed her religious duties with edifying assiduity, she to pay him back, so as to make him look ridiculous, and to gad about at night? Never! Anyone who could think such a thing must have lost his senses.

However, one summer day, when the roofs all seemed red-hot, and the whole town appeared dead, Monsieur de Champdelin had followed two milliner's girls, with bandboxes in their hands from street to street, whispering nonsense to them, and promising beforehand to give them anything they asked him for, and had gone after them as far as the Cathedral. In their fright, they took refuge there, but he followed them in, and, emboldened by the solitude of the nave, and by the perfect silence in the building, he became more enterprising and bolder. They did not know how to defend themselves, or to escape from him, and were trembling at his daring attempts, and at his kisses, when he saw a confessional whose doors were open, in one of the side chapels. "We should be much more comfortable in there, my little dears," he said, going into it, as if to get such an unexpected nest ready for them.

But they were quicker than he, and throwing themselves against the grated door, they pushed it to before he could turn round, and locked him in. At first he thought it was only a joke, and it amused him; but when they began to laugh heartily and putting their tongues at him, as if he had been a monkey in a cage, and overwhelmed him with insults, he first of all grew angry, and then humble, offering to pay well for his ransom, and he implored them to let him out, and tried to escape like a mouse does out of a trap. They, however, did not appear to hear him, but naively bowed to him ceremoniously, wished him good night, and ran out as fast as they could.

Champdelin was in despair; he did not know what to do, and cursed his bad luck. What would be the end of it? Who would deliver him from that species of prison, and was he going to remain there all the afternoon and night, like a portmanteau that had been forgotten at the lost luggage office? He could not manage to force the lock, and did not venture to knock hard against the sides of the confessional, for fear of attracting the attention of some beadle or sacristan. Oh! those wretched girls, and how people would make fun of him and write verses about him, and point their fingers at him, if the joke were discovered and got noised abroad!

By and by, he heard the faint sound of prayers in the distance and through the green serge curtain that concealed him Monsieur Champdelin heard the rattle of the beads on the chaplets, as the women repeated their *Ave Maria's,* and the rustle of dresses and the noise of footsteps on the pavement.

Suddenly, he felt a tickling in his throat that nearly choked him, and he could not altogether prevent himself from coughing, and when at last it passed off, the unfortunate man was horrified at hearing some one come into the chapel and up to the confessional. Whoever it was, knelt down, and gave a discreet knock at the grating which separated the priest from his penitents, so he quickly put on the surplice and stole which were hanging on a nail, and covering his face with his handkerchief, and sitting back in the shade, he opened the grating.

It was a woman, who was already saying her prayers and he gave the responses as well as he could, from his boyish recollections, and was somewhat agitated by the delicious scent that emanated from her half-raised veil and from her bodice; but at her first words he started so, that he almost fainted. He had recognized his wife's voice, and it felt to him as if his seat were studded with sharp nails, that the sides of the confessional were closing in on him, and as if the air were growing rarified.

He now collected himself, however, and regaining his self-possession, he listened to what she had to say with increasing curiosity, and with some uncertain, and necessary interruptions. The young woman sighed, was evidently keeping back something, spoke about her unhappiness, her melancholy life, her husband's neglect, the temptations by which she was surrounded, and which she found it so difficult to resist; her conscience seemed to be burdened by an intolerable weight, though she hesitated to accuse herself directly. And in a low voice, with unctuous and coaxing tones, and mastering himself, Champdelin said:

"Courage, my child; tell me everything; the divine mercy is infinite; tell me all, without hesitation."

Then, all at once, she told him everything that was troubling her; how passion and desire had thrown her into the arms of one of her husband's best friends, the exquisite happiness that they felt when they met every day, his delightful tenderness, which she could no longer resist, the sin which was her joy, her only object, her consolation, her dream. She grew excited, sobbed, seemed enervated and worn out, as if she were still burning from her lover's kisses, hardly seemed to know what she was saying, and begged for temporary absolution from her sins; but then Champdelin, in his exasperation, and unable to restrain himself any longer, interrupted her in a furious voice:

"Oh; no! Oh! no; this is not at all funny . . . keep such sort of things to yourself, my dear!"

. . . . . .

Poor little Madame de Champdelin nearly went out of her mind with fright and astonishment, and they are now waiting for the decree which will break their chains and let them part.

# *thirteenth night*

*He married beautiful girls, in order to sell them into Eastern harems. But one of his victims became the wife of a Pasha, and eventually took a quaint revenge on him. . . .*

IN SENICHOU, a suburb of Prague, there lived, about twenty years ago, two poor but honest people, who earned their bread by the sweat of their brow; he worked in a large printing-establishment, and his wife employed her spare time as a laundress. Their pride, and only pleasure, was their daughter Viteska, a vigorous, voluptuous-looking, handsome lass of eighteen, whom they brought up very well and carefully. She worked for a dressmaker, and so was able to help her parents a little, and made use of her leisure moments to improve her education, and especially her music. She was a general favorite in the neighborhood on account of her quiet, modest habits, and was looked upon as a model by the whole suburb.

When she went to work in the town, the tall girl with her magnificent head, which resembled that of an ancient Bohemian Amazon, with its wealth of black hair, and her dark sparkling yet soft eyes, attracted the looks of passersby, in spite of her shabby dress, much more than the graceful, well-dressed ladies of the aristocracy. Frequently, some young wealthy lounger would follow her home; and even try to get into conversation with her, but she always managed to get rid of them and their importunities, and she did not require any protector, for she was quite capable of protecting herself from any insults.

One evening, however, she met a man on the suspension bridge, whose strange appearance made her give him a look which evinced some interest, but perhaps even more surprise. He was a tall, handsome man with bright eyes and a black beard; he was very sunburnt, and in his long coat, which was like a caftan, with a red fez on his head, he gave those who saw him the impression of an Oriental; he had noticed her look all the more as he himself had been so struck by her poor, and at the same time regal, appearance, that he remained standing and looking at her in such a way, that he seemed to be devouring her with his eyes, so that Viteska, who was usually so fearless, looked down. She hurried on and he followed her, and the quicker she walked, the more rapidly he followed her, and, at last, when they were in a narrow, dark street in the suburb, he suddenly said in an insinuating voice: "May I offer you my arm, my pretty girl?" "You can see that I am old enough to look after myself," Viteska replied hastily; "I am much obliged to you, and must beg you not to follow me any more; I am known in this neighborhood, and it might damage my reputation." "Oh! You are very much mistaken if you think you will get rid of me so easily," he replied. "I have just come from the East and am returning there soon. Come with me, and as I fancy that you are as sensible as you are beautiful, you will certainly make your fortune there, and I will bet that before the end of a year, you will be covered with diamonds, and be waited on by eunuchs and female slaves."

"I am a respectable girl, sir," she replied proudly, and tried to go on in front, but the stranger was immediately at her side again. "You were born to rule," he whispered to her. "Believe me, and I understand the matter, that you will live to be a Sultaness, if you have any luck." The girl did not give him any answer, but walked on. "But, at any rate, listen to me," the temper continued. "I will not listen to anything; because I am poor, you think it will be easy for you to seduce me," Viteska exclaimed: "but I am as virtuous as I am poor, and I should despise any position which I had to buy with shame." They had reached the little house where her parents lived, and she ran in quickly, and slammed the door behind her.

When she went into the town the next morning, the stranger was waiting at the corner of the street where she lived, and bowed to her very respectfully. "Allow me to speak a few words with you," he began. "I feel that I ought to beg your pardon for my behavior yesterday." "Please let me go on my way quietly," the girl replied. "What will the neighbors think of me?" "I did not know you," he went on, without paying any attention to her angry looks, "but your extraordinary beauty attracted me. Now that I know that you are as virtuous as you are charming, I wish very much to become better acquainted with you. Believe me, I have the most honorable intentions."

Unfortunately, the bold stranger had taken the girl's fancy, and she could not find it in her heart to refuse him. "If you are really in earnest," she stammered in charming confusion, "do not follow me about in the public streets, but come to my parents' house like a man of honor, and state your intentions there." "I will certainly do so, and immediately, if you like," the stranger replied, eagerly. "No, no," Viteska said; "but come this evening if you like."

The stranger bowed and left her, and really called on her parents in the evening. He introduced himself as Ireneus Krisapolis, a merchant from Smyrna, spoke of his brilliant circumstances, and finally declared that he loved Viteska passionately. "That is all very nice and right," the cautious father replied, "but what will it all lead to? Under no circumstances can I allow you to visit my daughter. Such a passion as yours often dies out as quickly as it arises, and a respectable girl is easily robbed of her virtue." "And suppose I make up my mind to marry your daughter?" the stranger asked, after a moment's hesitation. "Then I shall refer you to my child, for I shall never force Viteska to marry against her will," her father said.

The stranger seized the pretty girl's hand, and spoke in glowing terms of his love for her, of the luxury with which she would be surrounded in his house, of the wonders of the East, to which he hoped to take her, and at last Viteska consented to become his wife. Thereupon the stranger hurried on the arrangements for the wedding, in a manner that made the most favorable impression on them all, and during the time before their marriage he lay at her feet like her humble slave.

As soon as they were married, the newly-married couple set off on their journey to Smyrna and promised to write as soon as they got there, but a month, then two and three, passed without the parents, whose anxiety increased every day, receiving a line from them, until at last the father in terror applied to the police.

The first thing was to write to the Consul at Smyrna for information: his reply was to the effect that no merchant of the name of Ireneus Krisapolis was known in Smyrna, and that he had never been there. The police, at the entreaties of the frantic parents, continued their investigations, but for a long time without any result. At last, however, they obtained a little light on the subject, but it was not at all satisfactory. The police at Pestle said that a man, whose personal appearance exactly agreed with the description of Viteska's husband, had a short time before carried off two girls from the Hungarian capital, to Turkey, evidently intending to trade in that coveted, valuable commodity there, but that when he found that the authorities were on his track he had escaped from justice by a sudden flight.

.     .     .     .     .     .     .

Four years after Viteska's mysterious disappearance, two persons, a man and a woman, met in a narrow

91

street in Damascus, in a scarcely less strange manner, than when the Greek merchant met Viteska on the suspension bridge at Prague. The man with the black beard, the red fez, and the long, green caftan, was no one else than Ireneus Krisapolis; matters appeared to be going well with him; he had his hands comfortably thrust into the red shawl which he had round his waist, and a negro was walking behind him with a large parasol, while another carried his *Chiloque* after him. A noble Turkish lady met him in a litter borne by four slaves; she was wrapped like a ghost in a white veil, only that a pair of large, dark, threatening eyes flashed at the merchant.

He smiled, for he thought that he had found favor in the eyes of an Eastern houri, and that flattered him; but he soon lost sight of her in the crowd, and forgot her almost immediately. The next morning however, a eunuch of the pasha's came to him, to his no small astonishment, and told him to come with him. He took him to the Sultan's most powerful deputy, who ruled as an absolute despot in Damascus. They went through dark, narrow passages, and curtains were pushed aside, which rustled behind them again. At last they reached a large rotunda, the center of which was occupied by a beautiful fountain, while scarlet divans ran all around it. Here the eunuch told the merchant to wait, and left him. He was puzzling his brains what the meaning of it all could be, when suddenly a tall, commanding woman came into the apartment. Again a pair of large, threatening eyes looked at him through the veil, while he knew from her green, gold-embroidered caftan, that if it was not the pasha's wife, it was at least one of his favorites, who was before him, and so he hurriedly knelt down, and crossing his hands on his breast, he put his head on to the ground before her. But a clear, diabolical laugh made him look up, and when the beautiful Odalisque threw back her veil, he uttered a cry of terror, for his wife, his deceived wife, whom he had sold, was standing before him.

"Do you know me?" she asked with quiet dignity. "Viteska!" "Yes, that was my name when I was your wife," she replied quickly, in a contemptuous voice; "but now that I am the pasha's wife, my name is Sarema. I do not suppose you ever expected to find me again, you wretch, when you sold me in Varna to an old Jewish profligate, who was only half alive. You see I have got into better hands, and I have made my fortune, as you said I should do. Well? What do you expect of me; what thanks, what reward?"

The wretched man was lying overwhelmed, at the feet of the woman whom he had so shamefully deceived, and could not find a word to say; he had felt that he was lost, and had not even got the courage to beg for mercy. "You deserve death, you miscreant," Sarema continued. "You are in my hands, and I can do whatever I please with you, for the pasha has left your punishment to me alone. I ought to have you impaled, and to feast my eyes on your death agonies. That would be the smallest compensation for all the years of degradation that I have been through, and which I owe to you." "Mercy, Viteska! Mercy!" the wretched man cried, trembling all over.

The Odalisque's only reply was a laugh, in which rang all the cruelty of an insulted woman's deceived heart. It seemed to give her pleasure to see the man whom she had loved, and who had so shamefully trafficked in her beauty, in his mortal agony, as he cringed before her, whining for his life, as he clung to her knees, but at last she seemed to relent somewhat.

"I will give you your life, you poor wretch," she said, "but you shall not go unpunished." So saying, she clapped her hands, and four black eunuchs came in, and seized the favorite's unfortunate husband and in a moment bound his hands and feet.

"I have altered my mind, and he shall not be put to death," Sarema said, with a smile that made the traitor's blood run cold in his veins; "but give him a hundred blows with the bastinade, and I will stand by and count them." "For God's sake," the merchant screamed, "I can never endure it." "We will see about that," the favorite said, coldly, "and if you die under it, it was allotted you by fate; I am not going to retract my orders."

She threw herself down on the cushions, and began to smoke a long pipe, which a female slave handed to her on her knees. At a sign from her the eunuchs tied the wretched man's feet to the pole, by which the soles of the culprit were raised, and began the terrible punishment. Already at the tenth blow the merchant began to roar like a wild animal, but his wife whom he had betrayed, remained unmoved, carelessly blowing the blue wreaths of smoke into the air, and resting on her lovely arm, she watched his features, which were distorted by pain, with merciless enjoyment.

During the last blows he only groaned gently, and then he fainted.

.    .    .    .    .    .

A year later the dealer was caught with his female merchandise by the police in an Austrian town, and handed over to justice, when he made a full confession, and by that means the parents of the *Odalisque of Senichou* heard of their daughter's position. As they knew that she was happy and surrounded by luxury, they made no attempt to get her out of the Pasha's hands, who, like a thorough Mussulman, had become the slave of his slave.

The unfortunate husband was sent over to the frontier when he was released from prison. His shameful traffic, however, flourishes still, in spite of all the precautions of the police and of the consuls, and every year he provides the harems of the East with those voluptuous *Boxclanas*, especially from Bohemia and Hungary, who, in the eyes of a Mussulman, vie for the prizes of beauty, with the slender Circassian women.

# *fourteenth night*

*He was a hermaphrodite, quite rich, and a little sensitive about his horrible defect. . . .*

Y OU MAY BELIEVE ME, I laughed at it as much as the rest," Navarette assured us; "I laughed at it with that deep, cruel pitilessness which all of us, who are well made and vigorous, feel for those in whose making their stepmother, Nature, has suffered a serious miscalculation, involving sexual balance; for those laughable, feeble creatures who do, however, deserve our pity more than those other deformed wretches from whom we turn away in spite of ourselves.

"I had been the first to make fun of him at the club, to find those easy words which are remembered, and to turn that smooth, flabby, pink, ugly face, like that of an old woman, and of a Levantine eunuch in which the mouth is like a piece of inert flesh, and where the small eyes glisten with concentrated cunning, and remind us of the watchful, angry eyes of a gorilla, at the same time, into ridicule. I knew that he was selfish, without any affection, unreliable, full of whims, turning like a weathercock with every wind that blows, and caring for nothing in the world except gambling and old Dresden china.

"However, our intercourse was invariably limited to a careless, 'Good-morning,' and to the usual shake of the hands which men exchange when they meet at the theater or the club, and so I had neither to defend him, nor to uphold him as a friend. But I can swear to you that now I reproach myself for all these effusives jeers and bitter things, and they weigh on my conscience now that I have been told the other side, the equivocal enigma of that existence."

"A Punch and Judy secret," Bob Shelley said, throwing the end of his cigar into the fire.

"Oh! yes; we were a hundred miles from the truth when we merely supposed that he was unfit for service. This unhappy Lantosque, a well-born, clever man, and very rich to boot, might have exhibited himself in some traveling booth, for he was an hermaphrodite; do you understand? an hermaphrodite. And his whole life was one of long, incessant torture, of physical and moral suffering, which was more maddening than that which Tantalus endured on the banks of the river Acheron. He had nearly everything of the woman about him; he was a ridiculous caricature of our sex, with his shrill voice, his large hips, his bust concealed by a loose, wide coat, his cheeks, his chin, and upper lip without a vestige of hair, and he had to appear like a man, to restrain and stifle his instincts, his tastes, desires, and dreams, to fight ceaselessly against himself, and never to allow anything of that which he endured, nor what he longed for, nor that which was sapping his very life, to be discovered.

"Once only he was on the point of betraying himself, in spite of himself. He ardently loved a man, as Chloe must have loved Daphnis. He could not master himself, or calm his feverish passion, and went towards the abyss as if seized by mental giddiness. He could imagine nothing handsomer, more desirable, or more charming than that chance friend. He had sudden transports, fits of surprise, tenderness, curiosity, jealousy, the ardent longings of an old maid who is afraid of dying a virgin, who is waiting for love as for her deliverance, who attaches herself and devotes herself to a lover with her whole being, and who grows emaciated and dries up, and remains misunderstood and despised.

"And as they have both disappeared now, the lover dead from a sword thrust in the middle of the chest, at Milan, on account of some ballet girl, and as he certainly died without knowing that he had inspired such a passion, I may tell you his name.

"He was Count Sebinico, who used to deal at faro with such delicate, white hands, and who wore rings on nearly every finger, who had such a musical voice, and who, with his wavy hair, and his delicate profile, looked like a handsome, Florentine Condottiere.

"It must be very terrible to be thus ashamed of oneself, to have that longing for kisses which console the most wretched in their misery, which satisfy hunger and thirst, and assuage pain; that illusion of delicious, intoxicating kisses, the delight and the balm of which such a person can never know; the horror of that dishonor of being pointed at, made fun of, driven away like unclean creatures that prostitute their sex, and make love vile by unmentionable rites; oh! the constant bitterness of seeing that the person we love makes fun of us, ill-uses us, and does not show us even the slightest friendship!"

"Poor devil!" Jean d'Orthyse said, in a sad and moved voice. "In his place, I should have blown my brains out."

"Everybody says that, my dear fellow, but how few there are who venture to forestall that intruder, who always come too quickly."

Lantosque had splendid health, and declared that he had never put a penny into a doctor's pocket, and if he had allowed himself to have been looked after when he was confined to his bed two months before, by an attack of influenza, we should still be hearing him propose a game of poker before dinner, in his shrill voice. His death, however, was as tragic and mysterious as all those tales from beyond the grave are, on which the Invisible rests.

"Although he had a cough, which threatened to tear his chest to pieces, and although he was haunted by the fear of death, of that great depth of darkness in which we lose ourselves in the abyss of Annihilation and Oblivion, he obstinately refused to have his chest sounded, and repulsed Doctor Pertuzés almost furiously, who thought he had gone out of his mind.

"He cowered down, and covered himself with the bed-clothes up to his chin, and found strength enough to tear up the prescriptions, and to drive everyone, whether friend or relation, who tried to make him listen to reason, and who could not understand his attacks of rage and neurosis from his bedside. He seemed to be possessed by some demon, like those women in hysterical convulsions, whom the bishops used formerly to exorcise with much pomp. It was painful to see him.

"That went on for a week, during which time the pneumonia had ample opportunities for ravaging and giving the finishing stroke to his body, which had been so robust and free from ailments hitherto, and he died, trying to utter some last words which nobody understood, and endeavoring to point out one particular article of furniture in the room.

"His nearest relation was a cousin, the Marquis de Territet, a skeptic, who lived in Burgundy, and whom all this disturbance had upset in his habits, and whose only desire was to get it all over, the legal formalities, the funeral, and all the rest of it, as soon as possible.

"Without reflecting on the strange suggestiveness of that death-bed, and without looking to see whether there might not be, somehow or other, a will in which Lantosque expressed his last wishes, he wanted to spare his corpse the contact of mercenary hands, and to lay him out himself.

"You may judge of his surprise when, on throwing back the bed-clothes, he first of all saw that Lantosque was dressed from head to foot in tights, which accentuated, rather than otherwise, his female form.

"Much alarmed, feeling that he must have been violating some supreme order, and comprehending it all, he went to his cousin's writing-table, opened it, and successively searched every drawer, and soon found an envelope fastened with five seals, and addressed to him. He broke them and read as follows, written on a sheet of black-edged paper:

" 'This is my only will. I leave all that I possess to my cousin, Roland de Territet, on condition that he will undertake my funeral; that in his own presence, he will have me wrapped up in the sheets of the bed on which I die, and have me put into the coffin so, without any further preparations. I wish to be cremated at *Père-Lachaise,* and not to be subjected to any examination, or *post-mortem,* whatever may happen.' "

"And how came the marquis to betray the secret?" Bob Shelley asked.

"The marquis is married to a charming Parisian woman, and was any married man, who loved his wife, ever known to keep a secret from her?"

# fifteenth night

*No woman can love passionately until after she is married. Unfortunately people are not legally mated according to their proven abilities in matters amatory, as this story proves only too sadly. . . .*

THE AGED PHYSICIAN and his young patient were chatting by the side of the fire. There seemed to be not much the matter with her, except that she had one of those little feminine ailments from which pretty women frequently suffer; slight anaemia, nervous attack, and a suspicion of fatigue, of that fatigue from which newly married people often suffer at the end of the first month of their married life, when they have made a love match.

She was lying on the couch, telling him. "No, doctor, I shall never be able to understand a woman deceiving her husband. Even allowing that she does not love him, that she pays no heed to her vows and promises, how can she give herself to another man? How can she hide it from other people's eyes? How can she go on loving amidst lies and treason?"

102

The doctor smiled. "It is perfectly easy, I assure you," he replied; "take it from me, a woman does not think of all those little subtle details, when she has made up her mind to go astray. I even feel sure that no woman is ripe for true love until she has passed through all the promiscuousness and all the loathsomeness of married life, which, according to an illustrious man, is nothing but an exchange of ill-tempered words by day, and disagreeable odors at night. Nothing is more true, for no woman can love passionately until after she has married.

"As for dissimulation, all women have plenty of it on hand on such occasions, and the simplest of them are wonderful, and extricate themselves from the greatest dilemmas in an extraordinary way."

The young woman, however, seemed incredulous. . . . "No, doctor," she said, "one never thinks until after it has happened, of what one ought to have done in a dangerous affair, and women are certainly more liable than men to lose their heads on such occasions." The doctor raised his hands. "After it has happened, you say! Now, I will tell you something that happened to one of my female patients, whom I always considered as an immaculate woman.

"It happened in a provincial town, and one night when I was sleeping profoundly, in that deep, first sleep from which it is so difficult to arouse us, it seemed to me, in my dreams, as if the bells in the town were sounding a fire alarm, and I woke up with a start. It was my own bell, which was ringing wildly, and as my footman did not seem to be answering the door, I, in

103

turn, pulled the bell at the head of my bed, and soon I heard banging, and steps in the silent house, and then Jean came into my room, and handed me a letter which said: 'Madame Lelièvre begs Doctor Siméon to come to her immediately.'

"I thought for a few moments, and then I said to myself: 'A nervous attack, vapors, nonsense; I am too tired.' And so I replied: 'As Doctor Siméon is not at all well, he must beg Madame Lelièvre to be kind enough to call in his colleague, Monsieur Bonnet.' I put the note into an envelope, and went to sleep again, but about half an hour later the street bell rang again, and Jean came to me and said: 'There is somebody downstairs; I do not quite know whether it is a man or a woman, as the individual is so wrapped up, who wishes to speak to you immediately. He says it is a matter of life and death for two people.' Whereupon, I sat up in bed and told him to show the person in.

"A kind of black phantom appeared, who raised her veil as soon as Jean had left the room. It was Madame Berthe Lelièvre, quite a young woman, who had been married for three years to a large shopkeeper in the town, who was said to have married the prettiest girl in the neighborhood.

"She was terribly pale, her face was contracted like the faces of mad people are, occasionally, and her hands trembled violently. Twice she tried to speak, without being able to utter a sound, but at last she stammered out: 'Come . . . quick . . . quick, Doctor. . . . Come . . . my . . . my lover has just died in my bedroom.' She stopped, half suffocated with emotion, and then went on: 'My husband will . . . be coming home from the club very soon.'

"I jumped out of bed, without even considering that I was only in my night-shirt, and dressed myself in a few moments, and then I said: 'Did you come a short time ago?' 'No,' she said, standing like a statue petrified with horror. 'It was my servant . . . she knows.' And then, after a short silence, she went on: 'I was there . . . by his side.' And she uttered a sort of cry of horror, and after a fit of choking, which made her gasp, she wept violently, and shook with spasmodic sobs for a minute or two. Then her tears suddenly ceased, as if by an internal fire, and with an air of tragic calmness, she said: 'Let us make haste.'

"I was ready, but I exclaimed: 'I quite forgot to order my carriage.' 'I have one,' she said; 'it is his, which was waiting for him!' She wrapped herself up, so as to completely conceal her face, and we started.

"When she was by my side in the darkness of the carriage, she suddenly seized my hand, and crushing it in her delicate fingers, she said, with a shaking voice, that proceeded from a distracted heart: 'Oh! If you only knew, if you only knew what I am suffering! I loved him, I have loved him distractedly, like a mad woman, for the last six months.' 'Is anyone up in your house?' I asked. 'No, nobody except Rose, who knows everything.'

"We stopped at the door, and evidently everybody was asleep, and we went in without making any noise, by means of her latch-key, and walked upstairs on tiptoe. The frightened servant was sitting on the top of the stairs, with a lighted candle by her side, as she was afraid to stop by the dead man, and I went into the room, which was turned upside down, as if there had been a struggle in it. The bed, which was tumbled and open, seemed to be waiting for somebody; one of the sheets was hanging onto the floor, and wet napkins, with which they had bathed the young man's temples, were lying on the floor, by the side of a wash-stand basin and a glass, while a strong smell of vinegar pervaded the room.

"The dead man's body was lying at full length in the middle of the room, and I went up to it, looked at it, and touched it. I opened the eyes, and felt the hands, and then, turning to the two women, who were shaking as if they were frozen, I said to them: 'Help me to carry him onto the bed.' When we had laid him gently into it, I listened to his heart, and put a looking-glass to his lips, and then said: 'It is all over; let us make haste and dress him.' It was a terrible sight!

"I took his limbs one by one, as if they had belonged to some enormous doll, and held them out to the clothes which the women brought, and they put on his socks, drawers, trousers, waistcoat, and lastly the coat, but it was a difficult matter to get the arms into the sleeves.

"When it came to buttoning his boots, the two women knelt down, while I held the light, but as his feet were rather swollen, it was very difficult, and as they could not find a button-hook, they had to use their hairpins. When the terrible toilet was over, I looked at our work, and said: 'You ought to arrange his hair a little.' The girl went and brought her mistress's large-toothed comb and brush, but as she was trembling, and pulling out his long, matted hair in doing it, Madame Lelière took the comb out of her hand, and arranged his hair as if she were caressing him. She parted it, brushed his beard, rolled his moustachios gently round her fingers, as she must have done for him in life.

"Suddenly, however, letting go of his hair, she took her dead lover's inert head in her hands, and looked for a long time in despair at the dead face, which no longer could smile at her, and then, throwing herself onto him, she took him into her arms and kissed him ardently. Her kisses fell like blows onto his closed mouth and eyes, onto his forehead and temples, and then, putting her lips to his ear, as if he could still hear her, and as if she were about to whisper something to him, to make their embraces still more ardent, she said several times, in a heartrending voice: 'Adieu, my darling!'

"Just then the clock struck twelve, and I started up. 'Twelve o'clock!' I exclaimed. 'That is the time when the club closes. Come, Madame, we have not a moment to lose!' She started up, and I said: 'We must carry him into the drawing-room.' And when we had done this, I placed him on a sofa, and lit the chandeliers, and just then the front door was opened and shut noisily. He had come back, and I said: 'Rose, bring me the basin and the towels, and make the room look tidy. Make haste, for heaven's sake! Monsieur Lelièvre is coming in.'

"I heard his steps on the stairs, and then his hands feeling along the walls. 'Come here, my dear fellow,' I said, 'we have had an accident.'

"And the astonished husband appeared in the door

with a cigar in his mouth, and said: 'What is the matter? What is the meaning of this?' 'My dear friend,' I said, going up to him; 'you find us in great embarrassment. I had remained late, chatting with your wife and our friend, who had brought me in his carriage, when he suddenly fainted, and in spite of all we have done, he has remained unconscious for two hours. I did not like to call in strangers, and if you will now help me downstairs with him, I shall be able to attend to him better at his own house.'

"The husband, who was surprised, but quite unsuspicious, took off his hat, and then he took his rival, who would be quite inoffensive for the future, under his arms. I got between his two legs, as if I had been a horse between the shafts, and we went downstairs, while his wife lighted us. When we got outside, I held the body up, so as to deceive the coachman, and said: 'Come, my friend; it is nothing; you feel better already, I expect. Pluck up your courage, and make an attempt. It will soon be over.' But as I felt that he was slipping out of my hands, I gave him a slap on the shoulder, which sent him forward and made him fall into the carriage, and then I got in after him. Monsieur Lelièvre, who was rather alarmed, said to me: 'Do you think it is anything serious?' To which I replied, '*No*,' with a smile, as I looked at his wife, who had put her arm into that of her legitimate husband, and was trying to see into the carriage.

"I shook hands with them, and told the coachman to start, and during the whole drive the dead man kept falling against me. When we got to his house, I said that he had become unconscious on the way home, and helped to carry him upstairs, where I certified that he was dead, and acted another comedy to his distracted family, and at last I got back to bed, not without swearing at lovers."

The doctor ceased, though he was still smiling, and the young woman, who was in a very nervous state, said: "Why have you told me that terrible story?"

He gave her a gallant bow, and replied:

"So that I may offer you my services, if necessary."

# sixteenth night

*She decided to walk to her assigna-
tion with the Viscount. On the way,
along came the Baron in his carriage,
and would not take no for an answer. She disposed of the Viscount
quite handily. . . .*

ALTHOUGH SHE WORE her bonnet and jacket,
with a black veil over her face, and another in her
pocket, which she would put on over the other, as soon
as she got into the cab, she was tapping the top of her
little boot with the point of her parasol, and remained
sitting in her room, without being able to make up her
mind whether or not to keep this appointment.

And yet, how many times within the last two years
had she so dressed herself, when she knew that her
husband would be on the Stock Exchange, in order to
go to the bachelor chambers of her lover, the handsome
Viscount de Martelet.

The clock behind her ticked loudly, a book which
she had half read through lay open on a little rosewood
writing-table between the windows, and a strong, sweet

smell of violets from two bunches which were in a couple of Dresden china vases, mingled with a vague smell of verbena which came through the half-open door of her dressing-room.

The clock struck three, she got up from her chair, turned round to look at herself in the glass, and smiled. "He is already waiting for me, and will be getting tired."

Then she left the room, told her footman that she would be back in an hour, at the latest—which was a lie; went downstairs and ventured into the street on foot.

It was towards the end of May, that delightful time of the year, when the spring seems to be besieging Paris, and to conquer it over its roofs, invading the houses through their walls, and making it look gay, shedding brightness over its stone facades, the asphalt of its pavements, the stones on the roads, bathing it and intoxicating it with sap, like a forest putting on its spring verdure.

Madame Haggan went a few steps to the right, intending, as usual, to go along the Parade Provence, where she would hail a cab; but the soft air, that feeling of summer which penetrates our breast on some days, now took possession of her so suddenly that she changed her mind, and went down the Rue de la Chausée d'Antin, without knowing why, but vaguely attracted by a desire to see the trees in the *Square de la Trinité*.

"He may just wait ten minutes longer for me," she said to herself. And that idea pleased her also as she walked slowly through the crowd. She fancied that she saw him growing impatient, looking at the clock, opening the window, listening at the door, sitting down for a few moments, getting up again, and not daring to smoke, as she had forbidden him to do so when she was coming to him, and throwing despairing looks at his box of cigarettes.

She walked slowly, interested in what she saw, the shops and the people she met, walking slower and slower, and so little eager to get to her destination that she only sought for some pretext for stopping, and at the end of the street, in the little square, the verdure attracted her so much, that she went in, took a chair, and, sitting down, watched the hands of the clock as they moved.

Just then, the half hour struck, and her heart beat with pleasure when she heard the chimes. She had gained half-an-hour; then it would take her a quarter of an hour to reach the Rue Miromesnil, and a few minutes more in strolling along—an hour! a whole hour saved from her *rendez-vous!* She would not stop three-quarters of an hour, and that business would be finished once more.

Oh! she disliked going there! Just like a patient going to the dentist, so she had the intolerable recollection of all their past meetings, one a week on an average, for the last two years; and the thought that another was going to take place immediately made her shiver with misery from head to foot. Not that it was exactly painful, like a visit to the dentist, but it was wearisome, so wearisome, so complicated, so long, so unpleasant, that anything, even a visit to the dentist would have seemed preferable to her. She went on, however, but very slowly, stopping, sitting down, going hither and thither, but she went. Oh! how she would have liked to miss this meeting, but she had left the unhappy viscount in the lurch, twice following, during the last month, and she did not dare to do it again so soon. Why did she go to see him? Oh! why? Because she had acquired the habit of doing it, and had no reason to give poor Martelet when he wanted to know *the why!* Why had she begun it? Why? She did not know herself, any longer. Had she been in love with him? Very possibly! Not very much, but a little, a long time ago! He was very nice, sought after, perfectly dressed, most courteous, and after the first glance, he was a perfect lover for a fashionable woman. He had courted her for three months—the normal period, an honorable strife and sufficient resistances—and then she had consented, and with what emotion, what nervousness, what terrible, delightful fear, and that first meeting in his small, ground-floor bachelor rooms, in the Rue de Miromesnil. Her heart? What did her little heart of a woman who had been seduced, vanquished, conquered, feel when she for the first time entered the door of that house which was her nightmare? She really did not know! She had quite forgotten. One remembers a fact, a date, a thing, but one hardly remembers, after the lapse of two years, what an emotion, which soon vanished, because it was very slight, was like. But, oh! she had certainly not forgotten the others, that rosary of meetings, that road to the cross of love, and those stations, which were so monotonous, so fatiguing, so similar to each other, that she felt a nauseating taste in her mouth at what was going to happen so soon.

And the very cabs were not like the other cabs which one makes use of for ordinary purposes! Certainly, the cabmen guessed. She felt sure of it, by the very way they looked at her, and the eyes of these Paris cabmen are terrible! When one remembers they are constantly remembering, in the Courts of Justices, after a lapse of several years, faces of criminals whom they have only driven once, in the middle of the night, from some street or other to a railway station, and that they have to do with almost as many passengers as there are hours in the day, and that their memory is good enough for them to declare: "That is the man whom I took up in the Rues des Martyrs, and put down at the Lyons Railway Station, at 12 o'clock at night, on July 10, last year!" Is it not terrible when one risks what a young woman risks when she is going to meet her lover, and has to trust her reputation to the first cabman she meets? In two years she had employed at least a hundred to a hundred and twenty in that drive to the Rue Miromesnil, reckoning only one a week, and they were so many witnesses, who might appear against her at a critical moment.

As soon as she was in the cab, she took another veil, which was as thick and dark as a domino mask, out of her pocket, and put it on. That hid her face, but what about the rest, her dress, her bonnet, and her parasol? They might be remarked; they might, in fact, have been seen already. Oh! What misery she endured in this Rue de Miromesnil! She thought that she recognized all the foot-passengers, the servants, everybody, and almost before the cab had stopped, she jumped out and ran past the porter who was standing outside his lodge. He must know everything, everything!—her address, her name, her husband's profession—everything, for those porters are the most cunning of policemen! For two years she had intended to bribe him, to give him (to throw at him one day as she passed him) a hundred-franc bank-note, but she had never once dared to do it. She was frightened! What of? She did not know! Of his calling back, if he did not understand? Of a scandal? Of a crowd on the stairs? Of being arrested, perhaps? To reach the Viscount's door, she had only to ascend a half a flight of stairs, and it seemed to her as high as the tower of Saint Jacques' Church.

As soon as she had reached the vestibule, she felt as if she were caught in a trap, and the slightest noise before or behind her, nearly made her faint. It was impossible for her to go back, because of that porter who barred her retreat; and if anyone came down at that moment she would not dare to ring at Martelet's door, but would pass it as if she had been going elsewhere! She would have gone up, and up, and up! She would have mounted forty flights of stairs! Then, when everything would seem quiet again down below, she would run down, feeling terribly frightened, lest she would not recognize the lobby.

He was there in a velvet coat lined with silk, very stylish, but rather ridiculous, and for two years he had never altered his manner of receiving her, not in a single movement! As soon as he had shut the door, he used to say this: "Let me kiss your hands, my dear, dear friend!" Then he followed her into the room, when with closed shutters and lighted candles, out of refinement, no doubt, he knelt down before her and looked at her from head to foot with an air of adoration. On the first occasion that had been very nice and very successful; but now it seemed to her as if she saw Monsieur Delauney acting the last scene of a successful piece for the hundred and twentieth time. He might really change his manner of acting. But no, he never altered his manner of acting, poor fellow. What a good fellow he was, but very commonplace! . . .

And how difficult it was to undress and dress without a lady's maid! Perhaps that was the moment when she began to take a dislike to him. When he said: "Do you want me to help you?" she could have killed him. Certainly there were not many men as awkward as he was, or as uninteresting. Certainly, little Baron de Isombal would never have asked her in such a manner: "Do you want me to help you?" He would have helped her, he was so witty, so funny, so active. But there! He was a diplomatist, he had been about in the world, and had roamed everywhere, and, no doubt, dressed and undressed women arrayed in every possible fashion! . . .

The church clock struck the three-quarters, and she looked at the dial, and said: "Oh, how agitated he will be!" and then she quickly left the square; but she had not taken a dozen steps outside, when she found herself face to face with a gentleman who bowed profoundly to her.

"Why! Is that you, Baron?" she said, in surprise. She had just been thinking of him.

"Yes, Madame." And then, after asking how she was, and a few vague words, he continued: "Do you know that you are the only one—you will allow me to say of my lady friends, I hope? who has not yet seen my Japanese collection."

"But my dear Baron, a lady cannot go to a bachelor's room like this."

"What do you mean? That is a great mistake, when it is a question of seeing a rare collection!"

"At any rate, she cannot go alone."

"And why not? I have received a number of ladies alone, only for the sake of seeing my collection! They come every day. Shall I tell you their names? No— I will not do that; one must be discreet, even when one is not guilty; as a matter of fact, there is nothing improper in going to the house of a well-known serious man who holds a certain position, unless one goes for an unavoidable reason!"

"Well, what you have said is certainly correct, at bottom."

"So you will come and see my collection?"

"When?"

"Well, now, immediately."

"Impossible; I am in a hurry."

"Nonsense, you have been sitting in the square for this last half hour."

"You were watching me?"

"I was looking at you."

"But I am sadly in a hurry."

"I am sure you are not. Confess that you are in no particular hurry."

Madame Haggan began to laugh, and said: "Well, ... no ... not ... very. ... "

"A cab passed close to them, and the little Baron called out: "Cabman!" and the vehicle stopped, and opening the door, he said: "Get in, Madame."

"But, Baron! no, it is impossible today; I really cannot."

"Madame, you are acting very imprudently; get in! people are beginning to look at us, and you will collect a crowd; they will think I am trying to carry you off, and we shall both be arrested; please get in!"

She got in, frightened and bewildered, and he sat down by her side, saying to the cabman: "Rue de Provence."

But suddenly she exclaimed: "Good heavens! I have forgotten a very important telegram; please drive to the nearest telegraph office first of all."

The cab stopped a little farther on, in the Rue de Chateaudun, and she said to the Baron: "Would you kindly get me a fifty centimes telegraph form? I promised my husband to invite Martelet to dinner tomorrow, and had quite forgotten it."

When the Baron returned and gave her the blue telegraph form, she wrote in pencil:

"My Dear Friend: I am not at all well. I am suffering terribly from neuralgia, which keeps me in bed. Impossible to go out. Come and dine tomorrow night, so that I may obtain my pardon.

"JEANNE."

She wetted the gum, fastened it carefully, and addressed it to: "Viscount de Martelet, 240 Rue Miromesnil," and then, giving it back to the Baron, she said: "Now, will you be kind enough to throw this into the telegram box."

# seventeenth night

*Where debauchery is carried on in a very simple, and almost patriarchal fashion, and where one does not run the slightest risk . . . it is almost a pity to name it love. . . .*

Come! Come!" said Pierre Dufaille, shrugging his shoulders. "What do you mean by saying that there are no more adventures? Say that there are no more adventurous men, and you may be right! It is true that these days very few venture to trust to chance, and that as soon as there is any slight mystery, or a spice of danger, they draw back. If, however, a man is willing to go into adventure blindly, and run the risk of anything that may happen, he can still meet with adventures, and even I, who never look for them, met with one in my life, and a very startling one, let me tell you.

"I was staying in Florence, and was living very quietly, and all I indulged in, in the way of adventures, was to listen occasionally to the immoral proposals with which every stranger is beset at night on the *Piazzo de la Signoria,* by some worthy Pandarus or other, with a head like that of a venerable priest. These excellent fellows generally introduce you to their families, where debauchery is carried on in a very simple, and almost patriarchal fashion, and where one does not run the slightest risk.

"One day as I was looking over Benvenuto Cellini's wonderful Perseus, in front of the *Loggia dei Lanzi,* I suddenly felt my sleeve pulled somewhat roughly, and on turning round, I found myself face to face with a woman of about fifty, who said to me with a strong German accent: 'You are French, Monsieur, are you not?' 'Certainly, I am,' I replied. 'And would you like to go home with a very pretty woman?'

" 'Most certainly I should,' I replied, with a laugh.

"Nothing could have been funnier than the looks and the serious air of the procuress, or than the strangeness of the proposal, made to broad daylight, and in very bad French, but it was even worse when she added: 'Do you know everything they do in Paris?' 'What do you mean, my good woman?' I asked her, rather startled. 'What is done in Paris, that is so unusual?'

"However, when she explained her meaning, I replied that I certainly could not, and as I was not quite so immodest as the lady, I blushed a little. But not for long, for almost immediately afterwards I grew pale, when she said: 'I want to assure myself of it, personally.' And she said this in the same phlegmatic manner, which did not seem so funny to me now, but, on the contrary, rather frightened me. 'What!' I said. 'Personally! You! Explain yourself!'

121

"If I had been rather surprised before, I was altogether astonished at her explanation. It was indeed an adventure, and was almost like a romance. I could scarcely believe my ears, but this is what she told me.

"She was the confidential attendant on a lady moving in high society, who wished to be initiated into the most secret refinements of Parisian high life, and who had done me the honor of choosing me for her companion. But then, this preliminary test! 'By Jove!' I said to myself, 'this old German hag is not so stupid as she looks!' And I laughed in my sleeve, as I listened inattentively to what she was saying to persuade me.

" 'My mistress is the prettiest woman you can dream of; a real beauty; springtime! A flower!' 'You must excuse me, but if your mistress is really like springtime and a flower, you (pray excuse me for being so blunt) are not exactly that, and perhaps I should not exactly be in a mood to humor you, my dear lady, in the same way that I might her.'

"She jumped back, astonished in turn: 'Why, I only want to satisfy myself with my own eyes; not by injuring you.' And she finished her explanation, which had been incomplete before. All she had to do was to go with me to *Mother Patata*'s well-known establishment, and there to be present while I conversed with one of its fair and frail inhabitants.

" 'Oh!' I said to myself, 'I was mistaken in her tastes. She is, of course, an old, shriveled up woman, as I guessed, but she is a specialist. This is interesting, upon my word! I never met with such a one before!'

"Here, gentlemen, I must beg you to allow me to

hide my face for a moment. What I said was evidently not strictly correct, and I am rather ashamed of it; my excuse must be that I was young, that *Patata's* was a celebrated place, of which I had heard wonderful things said, but the entry to which was barred me, on account of my small means. Five napoleons was the price! Fancy! I could not treat myself to it, and so I accepted the good lady's offer. I do not say that it was not disagreeable, but what was I to do? And then, the old woman was a German, and so her five napoleons were a slight return for our five milliards, which we paid them as our war indemnity.

"Well, *Patata's* boarder was charming, the old woman was not too troublesome, and your humble servant did his best to sustain the ancient glory of Frenchmen.

"Let me drink my disgrace to the dregs! On the next day but one after, I was waiting at the statue of Perseus. It was shameful, I confess, but I enjoyed the partial restitution of the five milliards, and it is surprising how a Frenchman loses his dignity, when he travels.

"The good lady made her appearance at the appointed time. It was quite dark, and I followed her without a word, for, after all, I was not very proud of the part I was playing. But if you only knew how fair that little girl at *Patata's* was! As I went along, I thought only of her, and did not pay any attention to where we were going, and I was only roused from my reverie by hearing the old woman say: 'Here we are. Try and be as entertaining as you were the day before yesterday.'

"We were not outside *Patata's* house, but in a narrow street running by the side of a palace with high walls, and in front of us was a small door, which the old woman opened gently.

"For a moment I felt inclined to draw back. Apparently the old hag was also ardent on her own account! She had me in a trap! No doubt she wanted in her turn to make use of my small talents! But, no! That was impossible!

" 'Go in! Go in!' she said. 'What are you afraid of? My mistress is so pretty, so pretty, much prettier than the little girl of the other day.' So it was really true, this story out of *The Arabian Nights?* Why not? And after all, what was I risking? The good woman would certainly not injure me, and so I went in, though somewhat nervously.

"Oh! My friend, what an hour I spent then! Paradise! and it would be useless, impossible to describe it to you! Apartments fit for a princess, and one of those princesses out of fairy tales, a fairy herself. An exquisite German woman, exquisite as German women can be, when they try. An Undine of Heinrich Heine's, with hair like the Virgin Mary's, innocent blue eyes, and a skin like strawberries and cream.

"Suddenly, however, my Undine got up, and her face convulsed with fury and pride. Then, she rushed behind some hangings, where she began to give vent to a flood of German words, which I did not understand, while I remained standing, dumbfounded. But just then, the old woman came in, and said, shaking with fear: 'Quick, quick; dress yourself and go, if you do not wish to be killed.'

"I asked no questions, for what was the good of trying to understand? Besides, the old woman, who grew more and more terrified, could not find any French words, and chattered wildly. I jumped up and got into my shoes and overcoat and ran down to the street.

"Ten minutes later, I recovered my breath and my senses, without knowing what streets I had been through, nor where I had come from, and I stole furtively into my hotel, as if I had been a malefactor.

"In the *cafés* the next morning, nothing was talked of except a crime that had been committed during the night. A German baron had killed his wife with a revolver, but he had been liberated on bail, as he had appealed to his counsel, to whom he had given the following explanation, to the truth of which the lady companion of the baroness had certified.

"She had been married to her husband almost by force, and detested him, and she had some particular reasons (which were not specified) for her hatred of him. In order to have her revenge on him, she had had him seized, bound and gagged by four hired ruffians, who had been caught, and who had confessed everything. Thus, reduced to immobility, and unable to help himself, the baron had been obliged to witness a degrading scene, where his wife caressed a Frenchman, and thus outraged conjugal fidelity and German honor at the same time. As soon as he was set at liberty, the baron had punished his faithless wife, and was now seeking her accomplice."

"And what did you do?" someone asked Pierre Dufaille.

"The only thing I could do, by George!" he replied. "I put myself at the poor devil's disposal; it was his right, and so we fought a duel. Alas! It was with swords, and he ran me right through the body. That was also his right, but he exceeded his right when he called me her *ponce*. Then I gave him his chance, and as I fell, I called out with all the strength that remained to me: 'A Frenchman! A Frenchman! Long live France!' "

# *eighteenth night*

*Her husband only came every Sunday, and he was horrible! I understood her perfectly, and we laughed and danced together. . . . Until*

AH, MY DEAR FELLOW, what jades women are!"

"What makes you say that?"

"Because they have played me a nasty trick."

"You?"

"Yes, me."

"Women, or a woman?"

"Two women."

"Two women at once?"

"Yes."

"Serves you right for playing two of them at the same time. What was the trick?"

The two young men were lounging outside a *café* on the Boulevards, and drinking liquors mixed with water, those aperients which look like infusions of all the shades in a box of watercolors. They were nearly the same age, twenty-five to thirty. One was dark and the other fair, and they had the same semi-elegant look of stock-jobbers, of men who go to the Stock Exchange, and into drawing-rooms, who are to be seen everywhere, who live everywhere, and love everywhere. The dark one continued.

"I have told you of my connection with that little woman, a tradesman's wife, whom I met on the beach at Dieppe?"

"Yes."

"My dear fellow, you know what it is. I had a mistress in Paris, whom I loved dearly; an old friend, a good friend, and it has grown into a habit, in fact, and I value it very much."

"Your habit."

"Yes, my habit, and hers also. She is married to an excellent man, whom I also value very much, a very cordial fellow. A capital companion! I may say, I think that my life is bound up with that house."

"Well?"

"Well! they could not manage to leave Paris, and I found myself a widower at Dieppe."

"Why did you go to Dieppe?"

"For change of air. One cannot remain on the Boulevards the whole time."

"And then?"

"Then I met the little woman I mentioned to you on the beach there."

"The wife of that head of the public office?"

"Yes; she was dreadfully dull; her husband only came every Sunday, and he is horrible! I understand her perfectly, and we laughed and danced together."

"And the rest?"

"Yes, but that came later. However, we met, we liked each other. I told her I liked her, and she made me repeat it, so that she might understand it better, and she put no obstacles in my way."

"Did you love her?"

"Yes, a little; she is very nice."

"And what about the other?"

"The other was in Paris! Well, for six weeks it was very pleasant, and we returned here on the best of terms. Do you know how to break with a woman, when that woman has not wronged you in any way?"

"Yes, perfectly well."

"How do you manage it?"

"I give her up."

"How do you do it?"

"I do not see her any longer."

"But supposing she comes to you?"

"I am . . . not at home."

"And if she comes again?"

"I say I am not well."

"If she looks after you?"

"I play her some dirty trick."

"And if she puts up with it?"

"I write to her husband anonymous letters, so that he may look after her on the days that I expect her."

"That is serious! I cannot resist, and do not know how to bring about a rupture, and so I have a collection of mistresses. There are some whom I do not see more than once a year, others every ten months, others on those days when they want to dine at a restaurant, those whom I have put at regular intervals do not worry me, but I often have great difficulty with the fresh ones, so as to keep them at proper intervals."

"And then. . . . "

"And then . . . Then, this little woman was all fire and flame, without any fault of mine, as I told you! As her husband spends all the whole day at his office, she began to come to me unexpectedly, and twice she nearly met my regular one on the stairs."

"The devil!"

"Yes; so I gave each of them her days, regular days, to avoid confusion; Saturday and Monday for the old one, Tuesday, Friday and Sunday for the new one."

"Why did you show her the preference?"

"Ah! My dear friend, she is younger."

"So that only gave you two days to yourself in a week."

"That is enough for one."

"Allow me to compliment you on that."

"Well, just fancy that the most ridiculous and most annoying thing in the world happened to me. For four months everything had been going on perfectly; I felt perfectly safe, and I was really very happy, when suddenly, last Monday, the crash came.

"I was expecting my regular one at the usual time, a quarter past one, and was smoking a good cigar, and dreaming, very well satisfied with myself, when I suddenly saw that it was past the time, at which I was much surprised, for she is very punctual, but I thought that something might have accidentally delayed her. However, half-an-hour passed, then an hour, an hour and a half, and then I knew that something must have detained her; a sick headache, perhaps, or some annoying visitor. That sort of waiting is very vexatious, that . . . useless waiting . . . very annoying and enervating. At last, I made up my mind to go out, and not knowing what to do, I went to her and found her reading a novel."

"Well!" I said to her. And she replied quite calmly: "My dear, I could not come; I was hindered."

"How?"

"My . . . something else."

"What was it?"

"A very annoying visit."

"I saw that she would not tell me the true reason, and as she was very calm, I did not trouble myself any more about it, and hoped to make up for lost time with the other, the next day, and on the Tuesday, I was very . . . very excited, and amorous in expectation of the public official's little wife, and I was surprised that she had not come before the appointed time, and I looked at the clock every moment, and watched the hands impatiently, but the quarter past, then the half-hour, then two o'clock. I could not sit still any longer, and walked up and down very soon in great strides, putting my face against the window, and my ears to the door, to listen whether she was not coming upstairs."

"Half-past two, three o'clock! I seized my hat, and rushed to her house. She was reading a novel my dear fellow! 'Well!' I said, anixously, and she replied as calmly as usual: 'I was hindered, and could not come.'

" 'By what?'

" 'An annoying visit.'

"Of course, I immediately thought that they both knew everything, but she seemed so calm and quiet, that I set aside my suspicions, and thought it was only some strange coincidence, as I could not believe in such dissimulation on her part, and so, after half-an-hour's friendly talk, which was, however, interrupted a dozen times by her little girl coming in and out of the room. I went away, very much annoyed. Just imagine the next day. . . . "

"The same thing happened?"

"Yes, and the next also. And that went on for three weeks without any explanation, without anything explaining that strange conduct to me, the secret of which I suspected, however."

"They knew everything?"

"I should think so, by George. But how? Ah! I had a great deal of anxiety before I found it out."

"How did you manage it at last?"

"From their letters, for on the same day they both gave me their dismissal in identical terms."

"Well?"

"This is how it was. . . . You know that women always have an array of pins about them. I know hairpins, I doubt them, and look after them, but the others are much more treacherous; those confounded little black-headed pins which look all alike to us, great fools that we are, but which they can distinguish, just as we can distinguish a horse from a dog.

"Well, it appears that one day my minister's little wife left one of those tell-tale instruments pinned to the

132

paper, close to my looking-glass. My usual one had immediately seen this little black speck, no bigger than a flea, and had taken it out without saying a word, and then had left one of her pins, which was also black, but of a different pattern, in the same place.

"The next day, the minister's wife wished to recover her property, and immediately recognized the substitution. Then her suspicions were aroused, and she put in two and crossed them, and my original one replied to this telegraphic signal by three black pellets, one on the top of the other, and as soon as this method had begun, they continued to communicate with one another, without saying a word, only to spy on each other. Then it appears that the regular one, being bolder, wrapped a tiny piece of paper round the little wire point, and wrote upon it: *C. D., Poste Restante, Boulevards, Malherbes.*

"Then they wrote to each other. You understand that was not everything that passed between them. They set to work with precaution, with a thousand stratagems, with all the prudence that is necessary in such cases, but the regular one did a bold stroke, and made an appointment with the other. I do not know what they said to each other; all that I know is, that I had to pay the costs of their interview. There you have it all!"

"Is that all?"

"Yes."

"And you do not see them any more?"

"I beg your pardon. I see them as friends, for we have not quarreled altogether."

"And have they met again?"

"Yes, my dear fellow, they have become intimate friends."

"And has not that given you an idea?"

"No, what idea?"

"You great booby! The idea of making them put back the pins where they found them."

# nineteenth night

*The carter's wench knew dark mat-
ters which nobody besides herself
self should know . . . vowed herself
to passing kisses soon forgotten . . .
like a carter's wench, of course. . . .*

T HE DRIVER had jumped from his box, and
was now walking slowly by the side of his thin horses,
waking them up every moment by a cut of the whip,
or a coarse oath. Suddenly he pointed to the top of the
hill, where the windows of a solitary house, in which the
inhabitants were still up, although it was very late and
quite dark, were shining like yellow lamps, and said to
me: "One gets a good drop there, Monsieur, and well
served, by George."

His eyes flashed in his thin, sun-burnt face, which
was of a deep brickdust color, while he smacked his lips
like a drunkard, who remembers a bottle of good liquor
that he has lately drunk, and drawing himself up in a
blouse like a vulgar swell, he shivered like the back of
an ox, when it is sharply pricked with the goad. "Yes,

and well served by a wench who will turn your head for you before you have tilted your elbow and drunk a glass!" he added.

The moon was rising behind the snow-covered mountain peaks, which looked almost like blood under its rays, and which were crowned by dark, broken clouds, which whirled about and floated, and reminded the passenger of some terrible Medusa's head. The gloomy plains of Capsir, which were traversed by torrents, extensive meadows in which undefined forms were moving about, fields of rye, like huge golden table-covers, and here and there wretched villagers, and broad sheets of water, into which the stars seemed to look in a melancholy manner, opened out to the view. Damp gusts of winds swept along the road, bringing a strong smell of hay, of resin of unknown flowers, with them, and erratic pieces of rock, which were scattered on the surface like huge boundary stones, had spectral outlines.

The driver pulled his broad-brimmed felt hat over his eyes, twirled his large moustache, and said in an obsequious voice:

"Does Monsieur wish to stop here? This is the place!"

It was a wretched wayside public-house, with a reddish slate roof, that looked as if it were suffering from leprosy, and before the door there stood three wagons drawn by mules, and loaded with huge stems of trees, and which took up nearly the whole of the road; the animals, which were used to halting there, were dozing, and their heavy loads exhaled a smell of a pillaged forest.

Inside, three wagoners, one of whom was an old man,

while the other two were young, were sitting in front of the fire, which cackled loudly, with bottles and glasses on a large round-table by their side, and were singing and laughing boisterously. A woman with large round hips, and with a lace cap pinned onto her hair, in the Catalan fashion, who looked strong and bold, and who had a certain amount of gracefulness about her, and with a pretty, but untidy head, was urging them to undo the strings of their great leather purses, and replied to their somewhat indelicate jokes in a shrill voice, as she sat on the knee of the youngest, and allowed him to kiss her and to fumble in her bodice, without any signs of shame.

The coachman pushed open the door, like a man who knows that he is at home.

"Good evening, Glaizette, and everybody; there is room for two more, I suppose?"

The wagoners did not speak, but looked at us cunningly and angrily, like dogs whose food had been taken from them, and who showed their teeth, ready to bite, while the girl shrugged her shoulders and looked into their eyes like some female wild beast tamer; and then she asked us with a strange smile:

"What am I to get you?"

"Two glasses of cognac, and the best you have in the cupboard," Glaizette, the coachman replied, rolling a cigarette.

While she was uncorking the bottle I noticed how green her eyeballs were; it was a fascinating, tempting green, like that of the great green grasshopper; and also how small her hands were, which showed that she did not use them much; how white her teeth were, and how her voice, which was rather rough, though cooing, had a cruel, and at the same time, a coaxing sound. I fancied I saw her, as in a mirage, reclining triumphantly on a couch, indifferent to the fights which were going on about her, always waiting—longing for him who would prove himself the stronger, and who would prove victorious. She was, in short, the hospitable dispenser of love, by the side of that difficult, stony road, who opened her arms to poor men, and who made them forget everything in the profusion of her kisses. She knew dark matters, which nobody in the world besides herself should know, which her sealed lips would carry away inviolate to the other world. She had never yet loved, and would never really love, because she was vowed to passing kisses which were so soon forgotten.

I was anxious to escape from her as soon as possible; no longer to see her pale, green eyes, and her mouth that bestowed caresses from pure charity; no longer to feel the woman with her beautiful, white hands, so near one; so I threw her a piece of gold and made my escape without saying a word to her, without waiting for any change, and without even wishing her good-night, for I felt the caress of her smile, and the disdainful restlessness of her looks. . . .

The carriage started off at a gallop to Formiguéres, amidst a furious jingling of bells. I could not sleep any more; I wanted to know where that woman came from, but I was ashamed to ask the driver and to show any interest in such a creature, and when he began to talk, as we were going up another hill, as if he had guessed my sweet thoughts, he told me all he knew about Glaizette. I listened to him with the attention of a child, to whom somebody is telling some wonderful fairy tale.

She came from Fontpédrouze, a muleteers' village, where the men spend their time in drinking and gambling at the inn when they are not traveling on the high roads with their mules, while the women do all the field work, carry the heaviest loads on their back, and lead a life of pain and misery.

Her father kept an inn; the girl grew up very happy; she was courted before she was fifteen, and was so coquettish that she was certain to be almost always found in front of her looking-glass, smiling at her own beauty, arranging her hair, trying to make herself like a young lady on the *prado*. And now, as none of the family knew how to keep a halfpenny, but spent more than they earned, and were like cracked jugs, from which the water escapes drop by drop, they found themselves ruined one fine day, just as if they had been at the bottom of a blind alley. So on the "Feast of Our Lady of Succor," when people go on a pilgrimage to Font Romea, and the villages are consequently deserted, the inn-keeper set fire to the house. The crime was discovered through *la Glaizette*, who could not make up her mind to leave the looking-glass, with which her room was adorned, behind her, and so had carried it off under her petticoat.

The parents were sentenced to many years' imprisonment, and being let loose to live as best she could, the girl became a servant, passed from hand to hand, inherited some property from an old farmer, whom she had caught, as if she had been a thrush on a twig covered with bird-lime, and with the money she had built this public-house on the new road which was being built across the Capsir.

"A regular bad one, Monsieur," the coachman said in conclusion, "a vixen such as one does not see now in the worst garrison towns, and who would open the door to the whole fraternity, and not at all avaricious, but thoroughly honest. . . . "

I interrupted him in spite of myself, as if his words had pained me, and I thought of those pale green eyes, those magic eyes, eyes to be dreamt about, which were the color of grasshoppers, and I looked for them, and saw them in the darkness; they danced before me like phosphorescent lights, and I would have given then the whole contents of my purse to that man if he would only have been silent and urged his horses on to full speed, so that their mad gallop might carry me off quickly, quickly and far, and continually further from that girl.

# *twentieth night*

> *The Marquis might have been past his prime, and broke, but he was a gentleman, and paid up to his last forty-seven pennies, and so put little Sonia in her proper place. . . .*

IT WAS REALLY USELESS to argue when that obstinate little Sonia, with a Russian name and Russian caprices, once said: "That's how I want it." She was so delicate and pretty also, with her slightly turned-up nose, and her rosy and childish cheeks, while every female perversity was reflected in the depths of her strange eyes, which were the color of the sea on a stormy evening. Yes, she was very charming, very fantastic, and above all, so Russian, so deliciously and imperiously Russian, and all the more Russian, as she came from Montmartre, and in spite of this, not one of her seven lovers who composed her usual menagerie had laughed when their enslaver said one day:

"You know my feudal castle at Pludun-Herlouet, near Saint Jacut-de-la-Mer, which I bought two years ago, and in which I have not yet set foot? Very well, then! The day after to-morrow, which is the first of May, we will have a house-warming there."

The seven had not asked for any further explanation, but had accompanied little Sonia, and were now ready to sit down to dinner under her presidency in the dining-room of the old castle, which was situated ten hours from Paris. They had arrived there that morning; they were going to have dinner and supper together, and start off again at daybreak next morning; such were Sonia's orders, and nobody had made the slightest objection.

Two of her admirers, however, who were not yet used to her sudden whims, had felt some surprise, which was quickly checked by expressions of enthusiastic pleasure on the part of the others.

"What a delightful, original idea! Nobody else would have thought of such things! Positively, nobody else. Oh! these Russians!" But those who had known her for some time, and who had been consequently educated not to be surprised at anything, found it all quite natural.

It was half-past six in the evening, and the gentlemen were going to dress. Sonia had made up her mind to keep on her morning-gown, or if she dressed, she would do so later. Just then she was not inclined to move out of her great rocking-chair, from which she could see the sun setting over the sea. The sight always delighted her very much. It might have been taken for a large red billiard ball, rebounding from the green cloth. How funny it was! And how lucky that she was all alone to look at it, for those seven would not have understood it at all! Those men never have any soul, have they?

Certainly, the sunset was strange at first, but at length it made her sad, and just now Sonia's heart felt almost heavy, though the very sadness was sweet. She was congratulating herself more than ever on being alone, so as to enjoy that languor, which was almost like a gentle dream, when, in perfect harmony with that melancholy and sweet sensation, a voice rose from the road, which was overhung by the terrace; a tremulous, but fresh and pure voice sang the following words to a slow melody:

> "Walking in Paris,
> Having my drink,
> A friend of mine whispered:
> *What do you think?*
> *If love makes you thirsty,*
> *Then wine makes you lusty.*"

The sound died away, as the singer continued on his way, and Sonia was afraid that she should not hear the rest; it was really terrible; so she jumped out of the rocking-chair, ran to the balustrade of the terrace, and leaning over it, she called out: "Sing it again! I insist on it. The song, the whole song!"

On hearing this, the singer looked round and then came back, without hurrying, however, and as if he were prompted by curiosity, rather than by any desire to comply with her order, and holding his hand over his eyes, he looked at Sonia attentively, who, on her part, had plenty of time to look closely at him.

He was an old man of about sixty-five, and his rags

143

and the wallet over his shoulder denoted a beggar, but Sonia immediately noticed that there was a certain amount of affectation in his wretchedness. His hair and beard were not shaggy and ragged, like such men usually wear them, and evidently he had his hair cut occasionally, and he had a fine, and even *distinguished* face, as Sonia said to herself. But she did not pay much attention to that, as for some time she had noticed that old men at the seaside nearly all looked like gentlemen.

When he got to the foot of the terrace, the beggar stopped, and wagged his head and said: "Pretty! The little woman is very pretty!" But he did not obey Sonia's order, who repeated it, almost angrily this time, beating a violent tattoo on the stone-work. "The song, the whole song!"

He did not seem to hear, but stood there gaping, with a vacant smile on his face, and as his head was rather inclined towards his left shoulder, a thin stream of saliva trickled from his lips onto his beard, and his looks became more and more ardent. "How stupid I am!" Sonia suddenly thought. "Of course he is waiting for something." She felt in her pocket, in which she always carried some gold by way of half-pence, took out a twenty-franc piece and threw it down to the old man. He, however, did not take any notice of it, but continued looking at her ecstatically, and was only roused from his state of bliss by receiving a handful of gravel which she threw at him, right in his face.

"Do sing!" she exclaimed. "You must; I will have it; I have paid you." And then, still smiling, he picked up the napoleon and threw it back onto the terrace, and then he said proudly, though in a very gentle voice: "I do not ask for charity, little lady; but if it gives you pleasure, I will sing you the whole song, the whole of it, as often as you please." And he began the song again, in his tremulous voice, which was more tremulous than it had been before, as if he were much touched.

Sonia was overcome, and without knowing was moved into tears; delighted because the man had spoken to her so familiarly, and rather ashamed at having treated him as a beggar; and now her whole being was carried away by the slow rhythm of the melody, which related an old love story, and when he had done he again looked at her with a smile, and as she was crying, he said to her: "I dare say you have a beautiful horse, or a little dog that you are very fond of, which is ill. Take me to it, and I will cure it: I understand it thoroughly. I will do it *gratis*, because you are so pretty."

She could not help laughing. "You must not laugh," he said. "What are you laughing at? Because I am poor? But I am not, for I had work yesterday, and again today. I have a bag full. See, look here!" And from his belt he drew a leather purse in which coppers rattled. He poured them out into the palm of his hand, and said merrily: "You see, little one, I have a purse. Forty-seven sous; forty-seven!" "So you will not take my napoleon?" Sonia said. "Certainly not," he replied. "I do not want it; and then, I tell you again, I will not accept alms. So you do not know me?" "No, I do not." "Very well, ask anyone in the neighborhood. Everybody will tell you that the Marquis does not live on charity."

The Marquis! At that name she suddenly remembered

that two years ago she had heard his story. It was at the time that she bought the property, and the vendor had mentioned the *Marquis* as one of the curiosities of the soil. He was said to be half silly, at any rate an original, almost in his dotage, living by any lucky bits that he could make as horse-coper and veterinary. The peasants gave him a little work, as they feared that he might throw spells over anyone who refused to employ him. They also respected him on account of his former wealth and of his title, for he had been rich, very rich, and they said that he really was a marquis, and it was said that he had ruined himself in Paris by speculating. The reason, of course, *was women!*

At that moment the dinner bell began to ring, and a wild idea entered Sonia's head. She ran to the little door that opened onto the terrace, overtook the musician, and with a ceremonious bow she said to him: "Will you give me the pleasure and the honor of dining with me, Marquis?"

The old man left off smiling and grew serious; he put his hand to his forehead, as if to bring old recollections back, and then with a very formal, old-fashioned bow, he said: "With pleasure, my dear." And letting his wallet drop, he offered Sonia his arm.

When she introduced this new guest to them, all the seven, even to the best drilled, started. "I see what disturbs you," she said. "It is his dress. Well! It really leaves much to be desired. But wait a moment; that can soon be arranged."

She rang for her lady's maid and whispered something to her, and then she said: "Marquis, your bath is

146

ready in your dressing-room. If you will follow Sabina, she will show you to it. These gentlemen and I will wait dinner for you." And as soon as he had gone out, she said to the youngest there: "And now, Ernest, go upstairs and undress; I will allow you to dine in your morning coat, and you will give your dress coat and the rest to Sabina, for the Marquis."

Ernest was delighted at having to play a part in the piece, and the six others clapped their hands. "Nobody else could think of such things; nobody, nobody!"

Half an hour later they were sitting at dinner, the Marquis in a dress coat on Sonia's left, and it was a great deception for the seven. They had reckoned on having some fun with him, and especially Ernest, who set up as a wit, had intended to *draw* him. But at the first attempt of this sort, Sonia had given him a look which they all understood, and dinner began very ceremoniously for the seven, but merrily and without restraint between Sonia and the old man.

They cut very long faces, those seven, but inwardly, if one can say so, for of course they could not dream of showing how put out they were, and those inward long faces grew longer still when Sonia said to the old fellow, quite suddenly: "I say, how stupid these gentlemen are! Suppose we leave them to themselves?"

The Marquis rose, offered her his arm again, and said: "Where shall we go to?" But Sonia's only reply was to sing the couplet of that song which she had remembered:

"For three years I passed

The nights with my love,
In a beautiful bed
In a splendid alcove.
Though wine makes me sleepy,
Yet love keeps me frisky."

And the seven, who were altogether dumbfounded this time, and who could not conceal their vexation, saw the couple disappear out of the door which led to Sonia's apartments. "Hum!" Ernest ventured to say, "this is really rather strong!" "Yes," the eldest of the menagerie replied. "It certainly is rather strong, but it will do! You know, there is nobody like her for thinking of such things!"

The next morning, the *chateau* bell woke them up at six o'clock, when they had agreed to return to Paris, and the seven men asked each other whether they should go and wish Sonia good-morning, as usual, before she was out of her room. Ernest hesitated more than any of them about it, and it was not until Sabina, her maid, came and told them that her mistress insisted upon it, that they could make up their minds to do so, and they were surprised to find Sonia in bed by herself.

"Well!" Ernest asked boldly, "and what about the Marquis?" "He left very early," Sonia replied. "A queer sort of marquis, I must say!" Ernest observed contemptuously, and growing bolder. "Why, I should like to know?" Sonia replied, drawing herself up. "The man has his own habits, I suppose!" "Do you know, Madame," Sabina observed, "that he came back half an hour after he left?" "Ah!" Sonia said, getting up and walking about the room. "He came back? What did he want, I wonder?" "He did not say, Madame. He merely went upstairs to see you. He was dressed in his old clothes again."

And suddenly Sonia uttered a loud cry, and clapped her hands, and the seven came round to see what had caused her emotion. "Look here! Just look here!" she cried. "Do look on the mantel-piece! It is really charming! Do look!"

And with a smiling, and yet somewhat melancholy expression in her eyes, with a tender look which they could not understand, she showed them a small bunch of wild flowers, by the side of a heap of half-pennies. Mechanically she took them up and counted them, and then began to cry.

There were forty-seven of them.

# *twenty-first night*

*An adventure in Paris where the boulevards seemed abysses of human passion, and there could be no doubt that its houses concealed mysteries of prodigious love....*

Is THERE any feeling in a woman, stronger than curiosity? Oh; fancy seeing, knowing, touching what one has dreamed about! What would *any* woman not do for that? When once her eager curiosity is aroused, a woman will let herself in for any folly, commit any imprudence, venture upon anything, and recoil from nothing. I am speaking of women who are really women, women endowed with that triple-bottomed disposition, which appears to be reasonable and cold on the surface, but whose three secret compartments are filled. The first, with female uneasiness, which is always in a state of flutter; the next, with sly tricks which are colored in imitation of good faith, with those sophistical and formidable tricks of apparently devout women; and the last, with all those charming, improper acts, with that delightful deceit, exquisite

perfidy, and all those wayward qualities, which drive
lovers who are stupidly credulous, to suicide; but which
delight others.

The woman whose adventure I am about to relate,
was a little person from the provinces, who had been
insipidly chaste till then. Her life, which was apparently
so calm, was spent at home, with a busy husband and
two children, whom she brought up like an irreproachable woman. But her heart beat with unsatisfied curiosity, and some unknown longing. She was continually
thinking of Paris, and read the fashionable papers eagerly. The accounts of parties, of the dresses and various
entertainments, excited her longing; but, above all, she
was strangely agitated by those paragraphs which were
full of double meaning, by those veils which were half
raised by clever phrases, and which gave her a glimpse
of culpable and ravishing delights, and from her country home, she saw Paris in an apotheosis of magnificent
and corrupt luxury.

And during the long nights, when she dreamt, lulled
by the regular snores of her husband, who was sleeping
on his back by her side, with a silk handkerchief tied
round his head, she saw in her sleep those well-known
men whose names appeared on the first page of the
newspapers as great stars in the dark skies; and she pic-
tured to herself their life of continual excitement, of
constant debauches, of orgies such as they indulged in
in ancient Rome, which were horridly voluptuous, with
refinements of sensuality which were so complicated that
she could not even picture them to herself.

The boulevards seemed to her to be a kind of abyss

of human passions, and there could be no doubt that the houses there concealed mysteries of prodigious love. But she felt that she was growing old, and this, without having known life, except in those regular, horridly monotonous, every-day occupations, which constitute the happiness of the home. She was still pretty, for she was well preserved in her tranquil existence, like some winter fruit in a closed cupboard; but she was agitated and devoured by her secret ardor. She used to ask herself whether she should die without having experienced any of those damning, intoxicating joys, without having plunged once, just once into that flood of Parisian voluptuousness.

By dint of much perseverance, she paved the way for a journey to Paris, found a pretext, got some relations to invite her, and as her husband could not go with her, she went alone, and as soon as she arrived, she invented a reason for remaining two days, or rather for two nights, if necessary, as she told him that she had met some friends who lived a little way out of town.

And then she set out on a voyage of discovery. She went up and down the boulevards, without seeing anything except roving and numbered vice. She looked into the large *cafés*, and read the *Agony Column* of the *Figaro*, which every morning seemed to her like a tocsin, a summons to love. But nothing put her on the track of those orgies of actors and actresses; nothing revealed to her those temples of debauchery which she imagined opened at some magic word, like the cave in the *Arabian Nights*, or those catacombs in Rome, where the mysteries of a persecuted religion were secretly celebrated.

Her relations, who were quite middle-class people, could not introduce her to any of those well-known men with whose names her head was full, and in despair she was thinking of returning, when chance came to her aid. One day, as she was going along the *Rue de la Chaussée d'Antin,* she stopped to look into a shop full of those colored Japanese knick-nacks, which strike the eye on account of their color. She was looking at the little ivory buffoons, the tall vases of flaming enamel, and the curious bronzes, when she heard the shopkeeper dilating, with many bows, on the value of an enormous, pot-bellied, comical figure, which was quite unique, he said, to a little, bald-headed, gray-bearded man.

Every moment, the shopkeeper repeated his customer's name, which was a celebrated one, in a voice like a trumpet. The other customers, young women and well-dressed gentlemen, gave a swift and furtive, but respectful glance at the celebrated writer, who was looking admiringly at the china figure. They were both equally ugly.

"I will let you have it for a thousand francs, Monsieur Varin, and that is exactly what it cost me. I should ask anybody else fifteen hundred, but I think a great deal of literary and artistic customers, and have special prices for them. They all come to me, Monsieur Varin. Yesterday, Monsieur Busnach bought a large, antique goblet of me, and the other day I sold two candelabra like this (is it not handsome?) to Monsieur Alexander Dumas. If Monsieur Zola were to see that Japanese figure, he would buy it immediately, Monsieur Varin."

The author hesitated in perplexity, as he wanted to have the figure, but the price was above him, and he thought no more about her looking at him than if he had been alone in the desert. She came in trembling, with her eyes fixed shamelessly upon him, and she did not even ask herself whether he were good-looking, elegant or young. It was Jean Varin himself, Jean Varin. After a long struggle, and painful hesitation, he put the figure down onto the table. "No, it is too dear," he said. The shopkeeper's eloquence redoubled. "Oh! Monsieur Varin, too dear? It is worth two thousand francs, if it is worth a sou." But the man of letters replied sadly, still looking at the figure with the enameled eyes: "I do not say it is not; but it is too dear for me." And thereupon, she, seized by a kind of mad audacity, came forward and said: "What shall you charge me for the figure?" The shopkeeper, in surprise, replied: "Fifteen hundred francs, Madame." "I will take it."

The writer, who had not even noticed her till that moment, turned round suddenly; he looked at her from head to foot, with half-closed eyes, observantly, and then he took in the details, as a connoisseur. She was charming, suddenly animated by that flame which had hitherto been dormant in her. And then, a woman who gives fifteen hundred francs for a knick-knack is not to be met with every day.

But she was overcome by a feeling of delightful delicacy, and turning to him, she said in a trembling voice: "Excuse me, Monsieur; no doubt I have been rather hasty, as perhaps you had not finally made up your mind." He, however, only bowed, and said: "Indeed, I had, Madame." And she, filled with emotion, continued: "Well, Monsieur, if either today, or at any other time, you change your mind, you can have this Japanese figure. I only bought it because you seemed to like it."

He was visibly flattered, and smiled. "I should much like to find out how you know who I am?" he said. Then she told him how she admired him, and became quite eloquent as she quoted his works, and while they were talking he rested his arms on a table, and fixed his bright eyes upon her, trying to make out who and what she really was. But the shopkeeper, who was pleased to have that living puff of his goods, called out, from the other end of the shop: "Just look at this, Monsieur Varin; is it not beautiful?"

And then everyone looked round, and she almost trembled with pleasure at being seen talking so intimately with such a well-known man.

At last, however, intoxicated, as it were, by her feelings, she grew bold, like a general does, who is going to give the order for an assault. "Monsieur," she said, "will you do me a great, a very great pleasure? Allow me to offer you this funny Japanese figure, as a keepsake from a woman who admires you passionately, and whom you have seen for ten minutes."

Of course he refused, and she persisted, but still he resisted her offer, at which he was much amused, and at which he laughed heartily; but that only made her more obstinate, and she said: "Very well, then, I shall take it to your house immediately. Where do you live?"

He refused to give her his address, but she got it from the shopkeeper, and when she had paid for her purchase, she ran out to take a cab. The writer went after her, as he did not wish to accept a present for which he could not possibly account. He reached her just as she was jumping into the vehicle, and getting in after her, he almost fell onto her, and then tumbled onto the bottom of the cab as it started. He picked himself up, however, and sat down by her side, feeling very much annoyed.

It was no good for him to insist and to beg her; she showed herself intractable, and when they got to the door, she stated her conditions. "I will undertake not to leave this with you," she said, "if you will promise to do all I want today." And the whole affair seemed so funny to him that he agreed. "What do you generally do at this time?" she asked him; and after hesitating for a few moments, he replied: "I generally go for a walk." "Very well, then, we will go to the *Bois de Boulogne!*" she said, in a resolute voice, and they started.

He was obliged to tell her the names of all the well-known women, pure or impure, with every detail about them; their life, their habits, their private affairs, and their vices; and when it was getting dusk, she said to him: "What do you do every day at this time?" "I have some absinthe," he replied, with a laugh. "Very well, then, Monsieur," she went on, seriously, "let us go and have some absinthe."

They went into a large *café* on the boulevard which he frequented, and where he met some of his colleagues, whom he introduced to her. She was half mad with pleasure, and she kept saying to herself: "At last! At last!" But time went on, and she observed that she supposed it must be about his dinner time, and she suggested that they should go and dine. When they left *Bignon's*, after dinner, she wanted to know what he did in the evening, and looking at her fixedly, he replied: "That depends; sometimes I go to the theater." "Very well, then, Monsieur; let us go to the theater."

They went to the Vaudeville with an order, thanks to him, and, to her great pride, the whole house saw her sitting by his side, in the balcony stalls.

When the play was over, he gallantly kissed her hand, and said: "It only remains for me to thank you for this delightful day. . . . " But she interrupted him: "What do you do at this time, every night?" "Why . . . why . . I go home" She began to laugh, a little tremulous laugh. "Very well, Monsieur . . . let us go to your rooms."

They did not say anything more. She shivered occasionally, from head to foot, feeling inclined to stay, and inclined to run away, but with a fixed determination, after all, to see it out to the end. She was so excited that she had to hold onto the baluster as she went upstairs, and he came up behind her, with a wax match in his hand.

As soon as they were in the room, she undressed herself quickly, and retired without saying a word, and then she waited for him, cowering against the wall. But she was as simple as it was possible for a provincial lawyer's wife to be, and he was more exacting than a

157

pascha with three tails, and so they did not at all understand each other. At last, however, he went to sleep, and the night passed, and the silence was only disturbed by the *tick-tack* of the clock, and she, lying motionless, thought of her conjugal nights; and by the light of the Chinese lantern, she looked, nearly heart-broken, at the little fat man lying on his back, whose round stomach raised up the bed-clothes like a balloon filled with gas. He snored with the noise of a wheezy organ pipe, with prolonged snorts and comic chokings. His few hairs profited by his sleep, to stand up in a very strange way, as if they were tired of having been fastened for so long to that pate, whose bareness they were trying to cover, and a small stream of saliva was running out of one corner of his half-open mouth.

At last the daylight appeared through the drawn blinds; so she got up and dressed herself without making any noise, and she had already half opened the door, when she made the lock creak, and he woke up and rubbed his eyes. He was some moments before he quite came to himself, and then, when he remembered all that had happened, he said: "What! Are you going already?" She remained standing, in some confusion, and then she said, in a hesitating voice: "Yes, of course; it is morning. . . . "

Then he sat up, and said: "Look here, I have something to ask you, in my turn." And as she did not reply, he went on: "You have surprised me most confoundedly since yesterday. Be open, and tell me why you did it all, for upon my word I cannot understand it in the least." She went close up to him, blushing like as if she had been a virgin, and said: "I wanted to know . . . what . . . what vice . . . really was, . . . and . . . well . . . well, it is not at all funny."

And she ran out of the room, and downstairs into the street.

A number of sweepers were busy in the streets, brushing the pavements, the roadway, and sweeping everything on one side. With the same regular motion, the motion of mowers in a meadow, they pushed the mud in front of them in a semi-circle, and she met them in every street, like dancing puppets, walking automatically with their swaying motion. And it seemed her over-excited dreams had been pushed into the gutter, or into the drain, and so she went home, out of breath, and very cold, and all that she could remember was the sensation of the motion of those brooms sweeping the streets of Paris in the early morning.

As soon as she got into her room, she threw herself onto her bed and cried.

# *twenty-second night*

*Raped before she was nine, Mlle. Fontenelle was assaulted once more, after a respectable marriage. . . . Especially because the marriage was so respectable, and the young woman had been so fortunate. . . .*

ONCE IN THE WAITING-ROOM at the station at Loubain, I looked at the clock, and found that I had two hours and ten minutes to wait for the Paris express.

I felt suddenly tired, like one who had just walked twenty miles, and looked about me as if to find some means of killing the time on the station walls. At last I went out again, stopped outside the gates of the station, and began to rack my brains to find something to do. The street, which was a kind of a boulevard, planted with acacias, between two rows of houses of unequal shape and different styles of architecture, houses such as one only sees in a small town, ascended a slight hill, and at the extreme end of it, there were some trees, as if it ended in a park.

From time to time, a cat crossed the street, and jumped over the gutters, carefully. A cur sniffed at every tree, and hunted for fragments from the kitchens, but I did not see a single human being, and I felt listless and disheartened. What could I do with myself? I was already thinking of the inevitable and interminable visit to the small *café* at the railway station, where I should have to sit over a glass of undrinkable beer and the illegible newspaper, when I saw a funeral procession coming out of a side street into the one in which I was, and the sight of the hearse was a relief to me. It would, at any rate, give me something to do for ten minutes. Suddenly, however, my curiosity was aroused. The corpse was followed by eight gentlemen, one of whom was weeping, while the others were chatting together, but there was no priest, and I thought to myself:

"This is a non-religious funeral," but then I reflected that a town like Loubain must contain at least a hundred free-thinkers, who would have made a point of making a manifestation. What could it be then? The rapid pace of the procession clearly proved that the body was to be buried without ceremony, and, consequently, without the intervention of religion.

My idle curiosity framed the most complicated suppositions, and as the hearse passed me, a strange idea struck me, which was to follow it, with the eight gentlemen. That would take up my time for an hour, at least, and I, accordingly, walked with the others, with a sad look on my face, and on seeing this, the two last turned round in surprise, and then spoke to each other in a low voice.

161

No doubt they were asking each other whether I belonged to the town, and then they consulted the two in front of them, who stared at me in turn. This close attention which they paid me, annoyed me, and to put an end to it, I went up to them, and, after bowing, I said:

"I beg your pardon, gentlemen, for interrupting your conversation, but seeing a civil funeral, I have followed it, although I did not know the deceased gentleman whom you are accompanying."

"It is a woman," one of them said.

I was much surprised at hearing this, and asked:

"But it is a civil funeral, is it not?"

The other gentleman, who evidently wished to tell me all about it, then said: "Yes and no. The clergy have refused to allow us the use of the church."

On hearing that I uttered a prolonged *A—h!* of astonishment. I could not understand it at all, but my obliging neighbor continued:

"It is rather a long story. This young woman committed suicide, and that is the reason why she cannot be buried with any religious ceremony. The gentleman who is walking first, and who is crying, is her husband."

I replied with some hesitation:

"You surprise and interest me very much, Monsieur. Shall I be indiscreet if I ask you to tell me the facts of the case? If I am troubling you, think that I have said nothing about the matter."

The gentleman took my arm familiarly.

"Not at all, not at all. Let us stop a little behind the others, and I will tell it you, although it is a very sad story. We have plenty of time before getting to the cemetery, whose trees you see up yonder, for it is a stiff pull up this hill."

And he began:

"This young woman, Madame Paul Hamot, was the daughter of a wealthy merchant in the neighborhood, Monsieur Fontanelle. When she was a mere child of eleven, she had a terrible adventure; a footman violated her. She nearly died, in consequence, and the wretch's brutality betrayed him. A terrible criminal case was the result, and it was proved that for three months the poor young martyr had been the victim of that brute's disgraceful practices, and he was sentenced to penal servitude for life.

"The little girl grew up stigmatized by disgrace, isolated without any companions, and grown-up people would scarcely kiss her, for they thought that they would soil their lips if they touched her forehead, and she became a sort of monster, a phenomenon to all the town. People said to each other in a whisper: 'You know, little Fontanelle,' and everybody turned away in the streets when she passed. Her parents could not even get a nurse to take her out for a walk, as the other servants held aloof from her, as if contact with her would poison everybody who came near her.

"It was pitiable to see the poor child. She remained quite by herself, standing by her maid, and looking at the other children amusing themselves. Sometimes, yielding to an irresistible desire to mix with the other children, she advanced, timidly, with nervous gestures, and mingled with a group, with furtive steps, as if conscious of her own infamy. And, immediately, the mothers, aunts and nurses used to come running from every seat, who took the children entrusted to their care by the hand and dragged them brutally away.

"Little Fontanelle remained isolated, wretched, without understanding what it meant, and then she began to cry, nearly heart-broken with grief, and then she used to run and hide her head in her nurse's lap, sobbing.

"As she grew up, it was worse still. They kept the girls from her, as if she were stricken with the plague. Remember that she had nothing to learn, nothing; that she no longer had the right to the symbolical wreath of orange-flowers; that almost before she could read, she had penetrated that redoubtable mystery, which mothers scarcely allow their daughters to guess, trembling as they enlighten them, on the night of their marriage.

"When she went through the streets, always accompanied by her governess, as if her parents feared some fresh, terrible adventure, with her eyes cast down under the load of that mysterious disgrace, which she felt was always weighing upon her, the other girls, who were not nearly so innocent as people thought, whispered and giggled as they looked at her knowingly, and immediately turned their heads absently, if she happened to look at them. People scarcely greeted her; only a few men bowed to her, and the mothers pretended not to see her, whilst some young blackguards called her *Madame Baptiste,* after the name of the footman who had outraged and ruined her.

"Nobody knew the secret torture of her mind, for she hardly ever spoke, and never laughed, and her parents themselves appeared uncomfortable in her presence, as if they bore her a constant grudge for some irreparable fault.

"An honest man would not willingly give his hand to a liberated convict, would he, even if that convict were his own son? And Monsieur and Madame Fontanelle looked on their daughter as they would have done on a son who had just been released from the hulks. She was pretty and pale, tall, slender, distinguished-looking, and she would have pleased me very much Monsieur, but for that unfortunate affair.

"Well, when a new sub-prefect was appointed here eighteen months ago, he brought his private secretary with him. He was a queer sort of fellow, who had lived in the *Latin Quarter*, it appears. He saw Mademoiselle Fontanelle, and fell in love with her, and when told of what occurred, he merely said: 'Bah! That is just a guarantee for the future, and I would rather it should have happened before I married her, than afterwards. I shall sleep tranquilly with that woman.'

"He paid his addresses to her, asked for her hand, and married her, and then, not being deficient in boldness, he paid wedding-calls, as if nothing had happened. Some people returned them, others did not, but, at last, the affair began to be forgotten.

"She adored her husband as if he had been a god, for, you must remember, he had restored her to honor and to social life, he had braved public opinion, faced insults, and, in a word, performed such a courageous act, as few men would accomplish, and she felt the most exalted and uneasy love for him.

165

"When she became pregnant, and it was known, the most particular people and the greatest sticklers opened their doors to her, as if she had been definitely purified by maternity.

"It is funny, but so it is, and thus everything was going on as well as possible, when, the other day, was the feast of the patron saint of our town. The Prefect, surrounded by his staff and the authorities, presided at the musical competition, and when he had finished his speech, the distribution of medals began, which Paul Hamot, his private secretary, handed to those who were entitled to them.

"As you know, there are always jealousies and rivalries, which make people forget all propriety. All the ladies of the town were there on the platform, and, in his proper turn, the bandmaster from the village of Mourmillon came up. This band was only to receive a second-class medal, for one cannot give first-class medals to everybody, can one? But when the private secretary handed him his badge, the man threw it in his face and exclaimed:

" 'You may keep your medal for Baptiste. You owe him a first-class one, for a better reason than the one for which it is coming to me.'

"There were a number of people there who began to laugh. The common herd are neither charitable nor refined, and every eye was turned towards that poor lady. Have you ever seen a woman going mad, Monsieur? Well, we were present at the sight! She got up and fell back on her chair three times following, as if she had wished to make her escape, but saw that she could not make her way through the crowd, and then another voice in the crowd exclaimed:

" 'Oh! Oh! Madame Baptiste!'

"And a great uproar, partly laughter, and partly indignation, arose. The word was repeated over and over again; people stood on tip-toe to see the unhappy woman's face; husbands lifted their wives up in their arms, so that they might see the unhappy woman's face, and people asked:

" 'Which is she? The one in blue?'

"The boys crowed like cocks, and laughter was heard all over the place.

"She did not move now on her state chair, just as if she had been put there for the crowd to look at. She could not move, nor disappear, nor hide her face. Her eyelids blinked quickly, as if a vivid light were shining in her face, and she panted like a horse that is going up a steep hill, so that it almost broke one's heart to see it. Meanwhile, however, Monsieur Hamot had seized the ruffian by the throat, and they were rolling on the ground together, amidst a scene of indescribable confusion, and the ceremony was interrupted.

"An hour later, as the Hamots were returning home, the young woman, who had not uttered a word since the insult, but who was trembling as if all her nerves had been set in motion by springs, suddenly sprang on the parapet of the bridge, and threw herself into the river, before her husband could prevent her. The water is very deep under the arches, and it was two hours before her body was recovered. Of course, she was dead."

The narrator stopped, and then added:

167

"It was, perhaps, the best thing she could do in her position. There are some things which cannot be wiped out, and now you understand why the clergy refused to have her taken into church. Ah! If it had been a religious funeral, the whole town would have been present, but you can understand that her suicide added to the other affair, and made families abstain from attending her funeral; and then, it is not an easy matter, here, to attend a funeral which is performed without religious rites."

We passed through the cemetery gates and I waited, much moved by what I had heard, until the coffin had been lowered into the grave, before I went up to the poor fellow who was sobbing violently, to press his hand vigorously. He looked at me in surprise through his tears, and then said:

"Thank you, Monsieur." And I was not sorry that I had followed the funeral.

# twenty-third night

*She was married, could conceive of
only a chaste love, yet could go to
bed with one man even as she was
dreaming amorously of another.*

DURING THE THREE YEARS of her marriage,
she had not left the *Val de Ciré,* where her husband ran
two cotton-mills. She led a quiet life, and, although she
had no children, was quite happy in her house among
the trees, which her husband's work-people called the
*chateau.*

Monsieur Vasseur was considerably older than she
was, but he was very kind, she loved him, and no guilty
thought had ever entered her mind.

Her mother came and spent every Summer at Ciré,
and then returned to Paris for the winter, as soon as
the leaves began to fall.

Jeanne coughed a little every autumn, for the narrow valley through which the river wound, grew foggy
for five months. First of all, slight mists hung over the
meadows, making all the low-lying ground look like a
large pond, out of which the roofs of the houses rose.

Then that white vapor, which rose like a tide, enveloped everything, and turned the valley into a land of phantoms, through which men moved about like ghosts, without recognizing each other ten yards off, and the trees, wreathed in mist, and dripping with moisture, rose up through it.

But the people who went along the neighboring hills, and who looked down upon the deep, white depression of the valley, saw the two huge chimneys of Monsieur Vasseur's factories, rising above the mist below. Day and night they vomited forth two long trails of black smoke, and that alone indicated that people were living in that hollow, which looked as if it were filled with a cloud of cotton.

That year, when October came, the medical men advised the young woman to go and spend the winter in Paris with her mother, as the air of the valley was dangerous for her weak chest, and she went. For a month or so, she thought continually of the house which she had left, to which she seemed rooted, and whose well-known furniture and quiet ways she loved so much, but by degrees she grew accustomed to her new life, and got to liking entertainments, dinners and evening parties, and balls.

Till then, she had retained her girlish manners, she had been undecided and rather sluggish; she walked languidly, and had a tired smile, but now she became animated and merry, and was always ready for pleasure. Men paid her marked attentions, and she was amused at their talk, and made fun of their gallantries, as she felt sure that she could resist them, for she was rather disgusted with love, from what she had learned of it in marriage.

The idea of giving up her body to the coarse caresses of such bearded creatures, made her laugh with pity, and shudder a little with ignorance.

She asked herself how women could consent to those degrading contacts with strangers, as they were already obliged to endure them with their legitimate husbands. She would have loved her husband much more if they had lived together like two friends, and had restricted themselves to chaste kisses, which are the caresses of the soul.

But she was much amused by their compliments, by the desire which showed itself in their eyes, and which she did not share, by their declarations of love, which they whispered into her ear as they were returning to the drawing-room after some grand dinner, by their words, which were murmured so low that she almost had to guess them, and which left her blood quite cool, and her heart untouched, while they gratified her unconscious coquetry, while they kindled a flame of pleasure within her, and while they made her lips open, her eyes glow bright, and her woman's heart, to which homage was due, quiver with delight.

She was fond of those *tête-à-têtes* when it was getting dusk, when a man grows pressing, stammers, trembles and falls on his knees. It was a delicious and new pleasure to her to know that they felt that passion which left her quite unmoved, to say *no*, by a shake of the head, and with her lips, to withdraw her hands, to get up and calmly ring for lights, and to see the man who had been trembling at her feet, get up, confused and furious when he heard the footman coming.

She often had a hard laugh, which froze the most burning words, and said harsh things, which fell like a jet of icy water on the most ardent protestations, while the intonations of her voice were enough to make any man who really loved her, kill himself, and there were two especially who made obstinate love to her, although they did not at all resemble one another.

One of them, Paul Péronel, was a tall man of the world, gallant and enterprising, a man who was accustomed to successful love affairs, and who knew how to wait, and when to seize his opportunity.

The other, Monsieur d'Avancelle, quivered when he came near her, scarcely ventured to express his love, but followed her like a shadow, and gave utterance to his hopeless desire by distracted looks, and the assiduity of his attentions to her, and she made him a kind of slave who followed her steps, and whom she treated as if he had been her servant.

She would have been much amused if anybody had told her that she would love him, and yet she did love him, after a singular fashion. As she saw him continually, she had grown accustomed to his voice, to his gestures, and to his manner, as one grows accustomed to those with whom one meets continually. Often his face haunted her in her dreams, and she saw him as he really was; gentle, delicate in all his actions, humble, but passionately in love, and she awoke full of those dreams, fancying that she still heard him, and felt him near her, until one night (most likely she was feverish), she saw

172

herself alone with him in the small wood, where they were both of them sitting on the grass. He was saying charming things to her, while he pressed and kissed her hands.

She could feel the warmth of his skin and of his breath, and she was stroking his hair, in a very natural manner.

We are quite different in our dreams to what we are in real life. She felt full of love for him, full of calm and deep love, and was happy in stroking his forehead and in holding him against her. Gradually he put his arms round her, kissed her eyes and her cheeks without her attempting to get away from him; their lips met, and she yielded.

When she saw him again, unconscious of the agitation that he had caused her, she felt that she grew red, and while he was telling her of his love, she was continually recalling to mind their previous meeting, without being able to get rid of the recollection.

She loved him, loved him with refined tenderness, which arose chiefly from the remembrance of her dream, although she dreaded the accomplishment of the desires which had arisen in her mind.

At last, he perceived it, and then she told him everything, even to the dread of his kisses, and she made him swear that he would respect her, and he did so. They spent long hours of transcendental love together, during which their souls alone embraced, and when they separated, they were enervated, weak and feverish.

Sometimes their lips met, and with closed eyes they reveled in that long, yet chaste caress; she felt, however, that she could not resist much longer, and as she did not wish to yield, she wrote and told her husband that she wanted to come to him, and to return to her tranquil, solitary life. But in reply, he wrote her a very kind letter, and strongly advised her not to return in the middle of the winter, and so expose herself to a sudden change of climate, and to the icy mists of the valley, and she was thunderstruck, and angry with that confiding man, who did not guess, who did not understand, the struggles of her heart.

February was a warm, bright month, and although she now avoided being alone with Monsieur Avancelle, she sometimes accepted his invitation to drive round the lake in the *Bois de Boulogne* with him, when it was dusk.

On one of those evenings, it was so warm that it seemed as if the sap in every tree and plant were rising. Their cab was going at a walk; it was growing dusk, and they were sitting close together, holding each others' hands, and she said to herself:

"It is all over, I am lost!" for she felt her desires rising in her again, the imperious want for that supreme embrace, which she had undergone in her dream. Every moment their lips sought each other, clung together and separated, only to meet again immediately.

He did not venture to go into the house with her, but left her at her door, more in love with him than ever, and half fainting.

Monsieur Paul Péronel was waiting for her in the little drawing-room, without a light, and when he shook hands with her, he felt how feverish she was. He began to talk in a low, tender voice, lulling her worn-out mind with the charm of amorous words.

She listened to him without replying, for she was thinking of the other; she thought she was listening to the other, and thought she felt him leaning against her, in a kind of hallucination. She saw only him, and did not remember that any other man existed on earth, and when her ears trembled at those three syllables: "I love you," it was he, the other man, who uttered them, who kissed her hands, who strained her to his breast, like the other had done shortly before in the cab. It was he who pressed victorious kisses on her lips, it was his lips, it was he whom she held in her arms and embraced, whom she was calling to, with all the longings of her heart, with all the over-wrought ardor of her body.

When she awoke from her dream, she uttered a terrible cry. Paul Péronel was kneeling by her, and thanking her, passionately, while he covered her disheveled hair with kisses, and she almost screamed out: "Go away! go away! go away!"

And as he did not understand what she meant, and tried to put his arm round her waist again, she writhed, as she stammered out:

"You are a wretch, and I hate you! Go away; go away!" And he got up in great surprise, took up his hat, and went.

The next day she returned to *Val de Ciré*, and her husband, who had not expected her for some time, blamed her for a freak.

"I could not live away from you any longer," she said.

He found her altered in character, and sadder than formerly, but when he said to her:

"What is the matter with you? You seem unhappy. What do you want?" she replied:

"Nothing. Happiness exists only in our dreams, in this world."

Avancelle came to see her the next summer, and she received him without any emotion, and without regret, for she suddenly perceived that she had never loved him, except in a dream, from which Paul Péronel had brutally roused her.

But the young man, who still adored her, thought as he returned to Paris:

"Women are really very strange, complicated and inexplicable beings."

# *twenty-fourth night*

> *The pious widow and how she disposed of her love-life with the aid of two well-meaning dragoons.*

"Madame Bonderoi?"

"Yes, Madame Bonderoi."

"But that can't be."

"I tell you it is."

"Madame Bonderoi, the old lady in a lace cap, the devout, the holy, the honorable Madame Bonderoi, whose little false curls looked as if they were glued round her head?"

"That's the very woman."

"Oh! Come, you must be mad."

"I swear to you, it's Madame Bonderoi."

"In that case, you must give me the details."

"Here they are. During the life of Monsieur Bonderoi, the lawyer, people said that she utilized his clerks for her own partircular service. She is one of those respectable middle-class women, with secret vices, and inflexible principles, of whom there are so many. She liked good-looking young fellows, and I should like to know what is more natural than that? Do not we all like pretty girls?

"As soon as old Bonderoi was dead, his widow began to live the peaceful and irreproachable life of a woman with a fair, fixed income. She went to church assiduously, and spoke evil of her neighbors, but gave no handle to anyone for speaking ill of her, and when she grew old she became the little wizened, sour-faced, mischievous woman whom you know. Well, this adventure, which you would scarcely believe, happened last Friday.

"My friend, Jean d'Anglemare, is, as you know, a captain in a dragoon regiment, who is quartered in the barracks in the *Rue de la Rivette,* and when he got to his quarters the other morning, he found that two men of his squadron had had a terrible quarrel. The rules about military honor are very severe, and so a duel took place between them. After the duel they became reconciled, and when their officer questioned them, they told him what their quarrel had been about. They had fought on Madame Bonderoir's account."

"Oh!"

"Yes, my dear fellow, about Madame Bonderoi."

"But I will let Trooper Siballe speak."

"This is how it was, Captain. About a year and a half ago, I was lounging about the barrack-yard, between six and seven o'clock in the evening, when a woman came up and spoke to me, and said, just as if she had been asking her way: 'Soldier, would you like to earn ten francs a week, honestly?' Of course, I told her that I decidedly should, and so she said:

178

'Come and see me at twelve o'clock tomorrow morning. I am Madame Bonderoi, and my address is No. 6, *Rue de la Tranchée*.' 'You may rely upon my being there, Madame.' And then she went away, looking very pleased, and she added: 'I am very much obliged to you, soldier.' 'I am obliged to you, Madame,' I replied. But I plagued my head about the matter, until the time came, all the same.

"At twelve o'clock, exactly, I rang the bell, and she let me in herself. She had a lot of ribbons on her head.

" 'We must make haste,' she said; 'as my servant might come in.'

" 'I am quite willing to make haste,' I replied, 'but what am I to do?'

"But she only laughed, and replied: 'Don't you understand, you great knowing fellow?'

"I was no nearer her meaning, I give you my word of honor, Captain, but she came and sat down by me, and said:

" 'If you mention this to anyone, I will have you put in prison, so swear that you will never open your lips about it.'

"I swore whatever she liked, though I did not at all understand what she meant, and my forehead was covered with perspiration, so I took my pocket-handkerchief out of my helmet, and she took it and wiped my brow with it; then she kissed me, and whispered: 'Then you will?' 'I will do anything you like, Madame,' I replied, 'as that is what I came for.'

"Then she made herself clearly understood by her actions, and when I saw what it was, I put my helmet onto a chair, and showed her that in the dragoons a man never retires, Captain.

"Not that I cared much about it, for she was certainly not in her prime, but it is no good being too particular in such a matter, as ten francs are scarce, and then I have relations whom I like to help, and I said to myself: 'There will be five francs for my father, out of that.'

"When I had done my allotted task, Captain, I got ready to go, and said to her:

" 'To everyone their due, Madame. A small glass of brandy costs two sous, and two glasses cost four.'

"She understood my meaning, and put a gold ten-franc piece into my hand. I do not like that coin, because it is so small that if your pockets are not very well made, and come at all unsewn, one is apt to find it in one's boots, or not to find it at all, and so, while I was looking at it, she was looking at me. She got red in the face, as she had misunderstood my looks, and she said: 'Is not that enough?'

"I did not mean that, Madame,' I replied; 'but if it is all the same to you, I would rather have two five-franc pieces.' And she gave them to me, and I took my leave. This has been going on for a year and a half, Captain. I go every Tuesday evening, when you give me leave to go out of barracks; she prefers that, as her servant has gone to bed then, but last week I was not well, and I had to go into the infirmary. When Tuesday came, I could not get out, and I was very vexed, because of the ten francs which I had been receiving every week, and I said to myself:

180

" 'If anybody goes there, I shall be done; and she will be sure to take an artilleryman, and that made me very angry. So I sent for Paumelle, who comes from my part of the country, and told him about it:

" 'There will be five francs for you, and five for me,' I said. He agreed, and went, as I had given him full instructions. She opened the door as soon as he knocked, and let him in, and as she did not look at his face, she did not perceive that it was not I, for, you know, Captain, one dragoon is very like another, with their helmets on.

"Suddenly, however, she noticed the change, and she asked, angrily: 'Who are you? What do you want? I do not know you.'

"Then Paumelle explained matters; he told her that I was not well, and that I had sent him as my substitute; so she looked at him, made him also swear to keep the matter secret, and then she accepted him, as you may suppose, for Paumelle is not a bad-looking fellow, either. But when he came back, Captain, he would not give me my five francs. If they had been for myself, I should not have said a word, but they were for my father, and on that score, I would stand no nonsense, and I said to him:

" 'You are not particular in what you do, for a dragoon; you are a discredit to your uniform.'

"He raised his fist, Captain, saying that fatigue duty like that was worth double. Of course, everybody has his own ideas, and he ought not to have accepted it. You know the rest."

"Captain d'Anglemare laughed until he cried as he

told me the story, but he also made me promise to keep the matter a secret, just as he had promised the two soldiers. So, above all, do not betray me, but promise me to keep it to yourself."

"Oh! You may be quite easy about that. But how was it all arranged, in the end?"

"How? It is a joke in a thousand! . . . Mother Bonderoi keeps her two dragoons, and reserves his own particular day for each of them, and in that way everybody is satisfied."

"Oh! That is capital! Really capital!"

"And he can send his old father and mother the money as usual, and thus morality is satisfied."

# *twenty-fifth night*

*Love is disposed of very oddly in the army, so that the mistress of a cadet makes a very good match for a captain.*

S TRAUSS' BAND was playing in the salon of the Horticultural Society. It was so full that the young cadet Hussar-sergeant Max B., who had nothing better to do on an afternoon when he was off duty than to drink a glass of good beer and listen to a new waltz tune, had already been looking about for a seat for some time, when the head waiter, who recognized him, quickly took him to an unoccupied place, and without waiting for his orders, brought him a glass of beer. A very gentlemanly-looking man, and three elegantly dressed ladies were seated at the table.

The cadet saluted them with military politeness, and sat down, but almost before he could put the glass to his lips, he noticed that the two elder ladies, who appeared to be married, turned up their noses as if displeased at his taking a seat at their table, and even said a few words which he could not catch, but which no doubt referred unpleasantly to him. "I am afraid I am in the way here," the cadet said, and got up to leave, when he felt a pull at his sabre-tasch beneath the table, and at the same time the gentleman felt bound to say with some embarrassment: "Oh! not at all; on the contrary, we are very pleased that you have chosen this table."

Thereupon the cadet resumed his seat, not so much because he accepted the gentleman's invitation as sincere, but because the silent request to remain, which he had received under the table, and which was much more sincerely meant, had raised in him one of those charming illusions, which are so frequent in our youth, and which promised so much happiness, with electrical rapidity. He could not doubt for a moment, that the daring invitation came from the third, the youngest and prettiest of the ladies, into whose company a fortunate accident had thrown him.

From the moment that he had sat down by her, however, she did not deign to bestow even another look on him, much less a word, and to the young hussar, who was still rather inexperienced in such matters, this seemed rather strange; but he possessed enough natural tact not to expose himself to a rebuff by any hasty advances, but quietly to wait further developments of the adventure on the part of the heroine of it. This gave him the opportunity of looking at her more closely, and for this he employed the moments when their attention was diverted from him, and was taken up by conversation among themselves.

The girl, whom the others called Angelica, was a

thorough Viennese beauty, not exactly regularly beautiful, for her features were not Roman or Greek, and not
even strictly German, and yet they possessed every female charm, and were seductive, in the fullest sense of
the word. Her strikingly small nose, which in a lady's-
maid might have been called impudent, and her little
mouth with its voluptuously full lips, which would have
been called lustful in a street-walker, imparted an indescribable piquant charm to her small head, which was
surmounted by an imposing tower of that soft brown
hair which is so characteristic of Viennese woman. Her
bright eyes were full of good sense, and a merry smile
lurked continually in the most charming little dim-
ples near her mouth and on her chin.

In less than a quarter of an hour, our cadet was
fettered, with no more will of his own than a slave
has, to the triumphal chariot of this delightful little
creature, and as he hoped and believed—forever. And
he was a man worth capturing. He was tall and slim,
but muscular, and looked like an athlete, and at the
time he had one of those handsome, open faces which
women like so much. His honest, dark eyes showed
strength of will, courage and strong passions, and that,
women also like.

During an interval in the music, an elderly gentleman, with the ribbon of an order in his button-hole,
came up to the table, and from the manner in which
he greeted them, it was evident that he was an old
friend. From their conversation, which was carried on
in a very loud tone of voice, and with much animation,
in the bad, Viennese fashion, the cadet gathered that

the gentleman who was with the ladies, was a Councilor of Legation, and that the eldest lady was his wife, while the second lady was his married, and the youngest his unmarried, sister-in-law. When they at last rose to go, the pretty girl, evidently intentionally, put her velvet jacket, trimmed with valuable sable, very loosely over her shoulders; then she remained standing at the exit, and slowly put it on, so that the cadet had an opportunity to get close to her. "Follow us," she whispered to him, and then ran after the others.

The cadet was only too glad to obey her directions, and followed them at a distance, without being observed, to the house where they lived. A week passed without his seeing the pretty Angelica again, or without her giving him any sign of life. The waiter in the Horticultural Society's grounds, whom he asked about them, could tell him nothing more than that they were people of position, and a few days later the cadet saw them all again at a concert, but he was satisfied with looking at his ideal from a distance. She, however, when she could do so without danger, gave him one of those coquettish looks which inexperienced young men imagine express the innermost feelings of a pure, virgin heart. On that occasion she left the grounds with her sisters, much earlier, and as she passed the handsome cadet, she let a small piece of rolled-up paper fall, which only contained the words: "Come at ten o'clock tonight, and ring the bell."

He was outside the house at the stroke of ten and rang, but his astonishment knew no bounds when, instead of Angelica or her confidential maid, the house-keeper opened the door. She saw his confusion, and quickly put an end to it by taking his hand, and pulling him into the house. "Come with me," she whispered; "I know all about it. The young lady will be here directly, so come along." Then she lead him through the kitchen into a room which was shut off from the rest of the house, and which she had apparently furnished for similar meetings, on her own account, and left him there by himself, and the cadet was rather surprised to see the elegant furniture, a wide, soft couch, and some rather obscene pictures in broad, gilt frames. In a few minutes, the beautiful girl came in, and without any further ceremony, threw her arms round the young soldier's neck. In her *negligée,* she appeared to him much more beautiful than in her elegant outdoor dress, but the virginal fragrance which then pervaded her, had given way to that voluptuous atmosphere which surrounds a young newly-married woman.

Angelica, whose little feet were encased in blue velvet slippers lined with ermine, and who was wrapped in a richly embroidered, white dressing-gown, that was trimmed with lace, drew the handsome cadet down on to the couch with graceful energy, and almost before he exactly knew what he had come for, she was his, and the young soldier, who was half dazed at his unexpected victory and good fortune, did not leave her until after twelve o'clock. He returned every night at ten, rang the bell, and was admitted by the girl's slyly-smiling confidante, and a few moments later was clasping his little goddess, who used to wrap her delicate, white limbs sometimes in dark sable, and at others in princely ermine, in his arms. Every time they partook of a delicious supper, they laughed and joked and loved each other like only young, good-looking people do love, and frequently they entertained one another until morning.

Once the cadet attempted diffidently to pay the house-keeper for her services, and also for the supper, but she refused his money with a laugh, and said that everything was already settled; and the young soldier had reveled in this manner in boundless bliss for four months, when, by an unfortunate accident, he met his mistress in the street one day. She was alone, but in spite of this she contracted her delicate, finely-arched eyebrows angrily, when he was about to speak to her, and turned her head away. This hurt the honest young fellow's feelings, and when that evening she drew him to her bosom, that was rising and falling tempestuously under the black velvet that covered it, he remonstrated with her quietly, but emphatically.—She made a little grimace, and looking at him coldly and angrily, she at last said, shortly: "I forbid you to take any notice of me out of doors. I do not choose to recognize you; do you understand?"

The cadet was surprised and did not reply, but the harmony of his pleasures was destroyed by a harsh discord. For some time he bore his misery in silence and with resignation, but at last the situation became unendurable; his mistress's fiery kisses seemed to mock him, and the pleasure which she gave him to degrade him, so at last he summoned up courage, and in his open way, he came straight to the point.

"What do you think of our future, Angelica?" She wrinkled her brows a little. "Do not let us talk about it; at any rate not today." "Why not? We must talk about it sooner or later," he replied, "and I think it is high time for me to explain my intentions to you, if I do not wish to appear as a dishonorable scoundrel in your eyes." She looked at him in surprise. "I look upon you as one of the best and most honorable of men, Max," she said, soothingly, after a pause. "And do you trust me also?" "Of course I do." "Are you convinced that I love you honestly?" "Quite." "Then do not hesitate any longer to bestow your hand upon me," her lover said, in conclusion. "What are you thinking about?" she cried, quickly, in a tone of refusal. "What is to be the end of our connection? What is at any rate not permissible with a woman, is wrong and dishonorable with a girl. You yourself must feel lowered if you do not become my wife as soon as possible." "What a narrow-minded view," Angelica replied, angrily; "but as you wish it, I will give you my opinion on the subject, but . . . by letter." "No, no; now, directly."

The pretty girl did not speak for some time, and looked down, but suddenly she looked at her lover, and a malicious, mocking smile lurked in the corners of her mouth. "Well, I love you, Max, I love you really and ardently," she said, carelessly; "but I can never be your wife. If you were an officer, I might perhaps marry you; yes, I certainly would, but as it is, it is impossible." "Is that your last word?" the cadet said, in great excitement. She only nodded, and then put her full, white arms round his neck, with all the security of a mistress who is granting some favor to her slave; but on that occasion she was mistaken. He sprang up, seized his sword and hurried out of the room, and she let him go, for she felt certain that he would come back again, but he did not do so, and when she wrote to him, he did not answer her letters, and still did not come; so at last she gave him up.

It was a bad, a very bad, experience for the honorable young fellow; the highborn, frivolous girl had trampled on all the ideals and illusions of his life with her small feet, for he then saw only too clearly, that she had not loved him, but that he had only served her pleasures and her lusts, while he, he had loved her so truly!

. . . . . .

About a year after the catastrophe with charming Angelica, the handsome cadet happened to be in his captain's quarters, and accidentally saw a large photograph of a lady on his writing table, and on going up and looking at it, he recognized—Angelica.

"What a beautiful girl," he said, wishing to find out how the land lay. "That is the lady I am going to marry," the captain, whose vanity was flattered, said, "and she is as pure and as good as an angel, just as she is as beautiful as one, and into the bargain she comes of a very good and very rich family; in short, in the fullest sense of the word, she is 'a good match.'"

# *twenty-sixth night*

> *Women have never been very en-*
> *thusiastic ghouls, but a dead lover is*
> *better than a live one to a woman*
> *who is the beneficiary of his last will*
> *and testament.*

I‌T CAN EASILY be shown that Austria is richer in every kind of talent than North Germany, but while in the latter men are systematically drilled for the one vocation which is soldiery, the Austrians go in for everything, with the result that very few of them get beyond mere diletantism in anything. Leo Wolfram was one of those intellectual dilettantes, and the more pleasure one took in his materials and characters, which were usually boldly taken from real life, and in a certain political, and what is still more, in a plastic plot, the more he was obliged to regret that he had never learnt to compose or to mold his characters, or to write; in one word, that he had never become a literary artist, but how greatly he had in himself the materials for a master of narration, his "Dissolving Views," and still more his *Goldkind*, prove.

This Goldkind is a striking type of our modern society, and the novel of that name contains all the elements of a classic novel, although of course in a crude, unfinished state. What an exact reflection of our social circumstances Leo Wolfram gave in that story our present reminiscences will show, in which a lady of that race plays the principal part.

It may be ten years ago, that every day four very stylishly dressed persons went to dine in a corner of the small dining-room of one of the best hotels in Vienna, who, both there and elsewhere, gave occasion for a great amount of talk. They were an Austrian landowner, his charming wife, and two young diplomatists, one of whom came from the North, while the other was a pure son of the South. There was no doubt that the lady came in for the greatest share of the general interest.

The practiced observer and discerner of human nature easily recognized in her one of those characters which Goethe has so aptly named "problematical," for she was one of those individuals who are always dissatisfied and at variance with themselves and with the world, who are a riddle to themselves, and who can never be relied on, and with the interesting and captivating, though unfortunate contradictions in her nature, she made a strong impression on everybody, even by her mere outward appearance. She was one of those women who are called beautiful, without their being really so. Her face, as well as her figure, was wanting in æsthetic lines, but there was no doubt that, in spite of that, or perhaps on that very account, she was the most dangerous, infatuating woman that one could imagine.

She was tall and thin, and there was a certain hardness about her figure, which became a charm through the vivacity and grace of her movements; her features harmonized with her figure, for she had a high, clever, cold forehead, a strong mouth with sensual lips, and an angular, sharp chin, the effect of which was, however, diminished by her slightly turned-up, small nose, her beautifully arched eyebrows, and her large, animated, swimming blue eyes.

In her face, which was almost too full of expression for a woman, there was as much feeling, kindness and candor as there was calculation, coolness and deceit, and when she was angry and drew her upper lip up, so as to show her dazzlingly white teeth, it had even a devilish look of wickedness and cruelty, and at that time, when women still wore their own hair, the beauty of her long, chestnut plaits, which she fastened on the top of her head like a crown, was very striking. Besides this, she was remarkable for her elegant, tasteful dresses, and a bearing which united to the dignity of a lady of rank that undefinable something which makes actresses and women who belong to the higher classes of the *demi-monde* so interesting to us.

In Paris she would have been taken for a kept woman, but in Vienna the best drawing-rooms were open to her, and she was not looked upon as more respectable o ras less respectable than any other of the aristocratic beauties.

Her husband decidedly belonged to that class of men whom that witty writer, Balzac, so delightfully calls *les hommes prédestinés* in his *Physiologie du Mariage*.

Without doubt, he was a very good-looking man, but he bore that stamp of insignificance which so often conceals coarseness and vulgarity, and was one of those men who, in the long run, become unendurable to a woman of refined tastes. He had a good private income, but his wife understood the art of enjoying life, and so a deficit in the yearly accounts of the young couple became the rules, without causing the lively lady to check her noble passion in the least on that account; she kept horses and carriages, rode with the greatest boldness, had her box at the opera, and gave beautiful little suppers, which at that time was the highest aim of a Viennese woman of her class.

One of the two young diplomats who accompanied her, a young Count, belonging to a well-known family in North Germany, and who was a perfect gentleman in the highest sense of the word, was looked upon as her adorer, yet, in spite of his ancient name and his position as attaché to a foreign legation, gave people that distinct impression that he was an adventurer, which makes the police keep such a careful eye on some persons, and he had the reputation of being an unscrupulous and dangerous duellist. Short, thin, with a yellow complexion, with strongly-marked but engaging features, an aquiline nose and bright, dark eyes, he was the typical picture of a man who seduces women and kills men.

The handsome woman appeared to be in love with the Count, and to take an interest in his friend; at least, that was the construction that the others in the dining-room put upon the situation, as far as it could be made out from the behavior and looks of the people concerned, and especially from their looks, for it was strange how devotedly and ardently the beautiful woman's blue eyes rested on the Count, and with what wild, diabolical sympathy she gazed at the Italian from time to time, and it was hard to guess whether there was most love or hatred in that glance. None of the four, however, who were then dining and chatting so gaily together, had any presentiment at the time that they were amusing themselves over a mine, which might explode at any moment, and bury them all.

It was the husband of the beautiful woman who provided the tinder. One day he told her that she must make up her mind to the most rigid entrenchment, give up her box at the opera, and sell her carriage and horses, if she did not wish to risk her whole position in society. Her creditors had lost all patience, and were threatening to distrain on her property, and even to put her in prison. She made no reply to this revelation, but during dinner she said to the Count, in a whisper, that she must speak to him later, and would, therefore, come to see him at his house. When it was dark, she came thickly veiled, and after she had responded to his demonstrations of affection for some time, with more patience than amiableness, she began. Their conversation is extracted from his diary.

"You are so unconcerned and happy, while misery and disgrace are threatening me!" "Please explain what you mean!" "I have incurred some debts." "Again?" he said reproachfully, "why do you not come to me at once, for you must do it in the end, and then at least you would avoid any exposure?" "Please do not take me to task," she replied; "you know it only makes me angry. I want some money; can you give me some?" "How much do you want?" She hesitated, for she had not the courage to name the real amount, but at last she said, in a low voice: "Five thousand florins." It was evidently only a small portion of what she really required, so he replied: "I am sure you want more than that!" "No." "Really not?" "Do not make me angry."

He shrugged his shoulders, went to his strong box and gave her the money, whereupon she nodded, and giving him her hand, she said: "You are always kind, and as long as I have you, I am not afraid; but if I were to lose you, I should be the most unhappy woman in the world." "You always have the same fears; but I shall never leave you; it would be impossible for me to separate from you," the Count exclaimed. "And if you die?" The Count said, with a peculiar smile: "I have provided for you in that eventuality also." "Do you mean to say" . . . she stammered, flushed, and her large, lovely eyes rested on her lover with an indescribable expression in them. He, however, opened a drawer in his writing-table, and took out a document, which he gave her. It was his will. She opened it with almost indecent haste, and when she saw the amount—thirty thousand florins—she grew pale to her very lips.

It was a moment in which the germs of a crime were sown in her breast, but one of those crimes which cannot be touched by the Criminal Code. A few days after she had paid her visit to the Count, she herself received one from the Italian. In the course of conversation he took a jewel case out of his breast pocket and asked her opinion of the ornaments, as she was well-known for her taste in such matters, telling her at the same time, that it was intended as a present for an actress, with whom he was on intimate terms.—"It is a magnificent set!" she said, as she looked at it. "You have made an excellent selection." Then she suddenly became absorbed in thought, while her nostrils began to quiver, and that touch of cold cruelty played on her lips.

"Do you think that the lady for whom this ornament is intended will be pleased with it?" the Italian asked. "Certainly," she replied; "I myself would give a great deal to have it." "Then may I venture to offer it to you?" the Italian said.

She blushed, but did not refuse it, but the same evening she rushed into her lover's room in a state of the greatest excitement. "I am beside myself," she stammered; "I have been most deeply insulted." "By whom?" the Count asked, excitedly. "By your friend, who has dared to send me some jewelry today. I suppose he looks upon me as a lost woman; perhaps I am already looked upon as belonging to the *demimonde,* and this I owe to you, to you alone, and to my mad love for you, to which I have sacrificed my honor and everything. Everything!" She threw herself down and sobbed, and would not be pacified until the Count gave her his word of honor that he would set aside every consideration for his friend, and obtain satisfaction for her at any price. He met the Italian the same evening at a card party and questioned him.

"I did not, in the first place, send the lady the jewelry, but I gave it to her myself, not, however, until she had asked me to do so." "That is a shameful lie!" the Count shouted, furiously. Unfortunately, there were others present, and his friend took the matter seriously, so the next morning he sent his seconds to the Count.

Some of their real friends tried to settle the matter in another way, but his bad angel, his mistress, who required thirty thousand florins, drove the Count to his death. He was found in the Prater, with his friend's bullet in his chest. A letter in his pocket spoke of suicide, but the police did not doubt for a moment that a duel had taken place. Suspicion soon fell on the Italian, but when they went to arrest him, he had already made his escape.

The husband of the beautiful, problematical woman, called on the broken-hearted father of the man who had been killed in the duel, and who had hastened to Vienna on receipt of a telegraphic message, a few hours after his arrival, and demanded the money. "My wife was your son's most intimate friend," he stammered, in embarrassment, in order to justify his action as well as he could. "Oh! I know that," the old Count replied, "and female friends of that kind want to be paid immediately, and in full. Here are the thirty thousand florins."

And our *Goldkind*? She paid her debts, and then withdrew from the scene for a while. She had been compromised, certainly, but then, she had risen in value in the eyes of those numerous men who can only adore and sacrifice themselves for a woman when her foot is on the threshold of vice and crime.

I saw her last during the Franco-German war, in

the beautiful *Mirabell-garden* at Salzburg. She did not seem to feel any qualms of conscience, for she had become considerably stouter, which made her more attractive, more beautiful, and consequently, more dangerous, than she was before.

# *twenty-seventh night*

*She was a great and beautiful lady,
and so much the greater for being
able to satisfy all of her adorers—as
you will see.*

THE PRINCESS LEONIE was one of those beautiful, brilliant enigmas, who manage to allure everyone
like a Sphinx, for she was young, charming, and sin-
gularly lovely, and understood how to embellish her
charms not a little by carefully-chosen clothes. She was
a great lady of the right stamp, and was quite an intellectual into the bargain, which is not the case with all
aristocratic ladies; she took a genuine interest in art
and literature, and it was even said that she patronized
one of our poets in a manner worthy of the Medicis,
strewing the beautiful roses of continual female sympathy on his thorny path. All this was evident to everybody, and had nothing strange about it. But the world
likes to know the history of such a woman, to look
into the depths of her soul, and because people could
not do this in Princess Leonie's case, they thought it
very strange.

No one could read that face, which was always beautiful, always cheerful, and always the same; no one could fathom those large, dark, unfathomable eyes, which hid their secrets under the unvarying brilliancy of majestic repose, like a mountain lake, whose waters look black on account of their depth. For everybody was agreed that the beautiful princess had her secrets, interesting and precious secrets, like all other ladies of our fashionable world.

Most people looked upon her as a flirt who had no heart, and even no blood, and they asserted that she was only virtuous because the power of loving was denied her, but that she took all the more pleasure in seeing that she was loved, and that she set her trammels and enticed her victims, until they surrendered at discretion at her feet, so that she might leave them to their fate, and hurry off in pursuit of some fresh game.

Others declared that the beautiful woman had met with her romances in life, and was still having them, but, as a thorough Messalina, she knew how to conceal her adventures as cleverly as that French queen who had every one of her lovers thrown into the cold waters of the Seine, as soon as he quitted her soft, warm arms, and she was described thus to Count Otto F., a handsome cavalry officer, who had made the acquaintance of the beautiful, dangerous woman at that fashionable watering place, Karlsbad, and had fallen deeply in love with her.

Even before he had been introduced to her, the Princess had already exchanged fiery, encouraging glances with him, and when a brother officer took him to call on her, she welcomed him with a smile which appeared to promise him happiness, but after he had paid his court to her for a month, he did not seem to have made any progress, and as she possessed in a high degree the skill of being able to avoid even the shortest private interviews, it appeared as if matters would go no further than that delightful promise.

Night after night, the enamored young officer walked along the garden railings of her villa as close to her windows as possible, without being noticed by any one, and at last fortune seemed to favor him. The moon, which was nearly at the full, was shining brightly, and in its silvery light he saw a tall, female figure, with large plaits round her head, coming along the gravel path; he stood still, as he thought he recognized the Princess, but as she came nearer he saw a pretty girl, whom he did not know, and who came up to the railings and said to him with a smile: "What can I do for you, Count?" mentioning his name.

"You seem to know me, Fraulein." "Oh! I am only the Princess's lady's-maid." . . . "But you could do me a great favor." "How?" she asked quickly: "You might give the Princess a letter." . . . "I should not venture to do that," the girl replied, with a peculiar, half-mocking, half-pitying smile, and with a deep curtsey, she disappeared behind the raspberry bushes which formed a hedge along the railings.

The next morning, as the Count, with several other ladies and gentlemen, was accompanying the Princess home from the pump-room, the fair coquette let her pocket-handerkchief fall just outside her house. The young officer took this for a hint, so he picked it up, concealed the letter that he had written, which he always kept about him so as to be prepared for any event, in the folds of the soft cambric, and gave it back to the Princess, who quickly put it into her pocket. That also seemed to him to be a good augury, and, in fact, in the course of a few hours he received a note in disguised handwriting, by the post, in which his bold wooing was graciously entertained, and an appointment was made for the same night in the pavilion of the Princess's villa.

The happiness of the enamored young officer knew no bounds; he kissed the letter a hundred times, thanked the Princess when he met her in the afternoon where the band was playing, by his animated looks, which she either did not or could not understand, and at night was standing an hour before the appointed time behind the wall at the bottom of the garden.

When the church clock struck eleven he climbed over it and jumped on to the ground on the other side, and looked about him carefully; then he went up to the small, white-washed summer-house, where the Princess had promised to meet him, on tiptoe. He found the door ajar, went in, and at the same moment he felt two soft arms thrown round him. "Is it you, Princess?" he asked, in a whisper, for the pavilion was in total darkness, as the venetian blinds were drawn. "Yes, Count, it is I." . . . "How cruel." . . . "I love you, but I am obliged to conceal my passion under the mask of coldness because of my social position"

As she said this, the enamored woman, who was trem-

bling on his breast with excitement, drew him on to a
couch that occupied one side of the pavilion, and began
to kiss him ardently The lovers spent two blissful hours
in delightful conversation and intoxicating pleasures;
then she bade him farewell, and told him to remain
where he was until she had gone back to the house. He
obeyed her, but could not resist looking at her through
the venetian blinds, and he saw her tall, slim figure
as she went along the gravel path with an undulating
walk. She wore a white boumous, which he recognized
as having seen in the pump-room; her soft, black hair
fell down over her shoulders, and before she disappeared into the villa she stood for a moment and looked
back, but he could not see her face, as she wore a thick
veil.

When Count F. met the Princess the next morning in
company with other ladies, when the band was playing,
she showed an amount of unconstraint which confused
him, and while she was joking in the most unembar-
rassed manner, he turned crimson and stammered out
such a lot of nonsense that the ladies noticed it, and
made him the target for their wit. None of them was
bolder or more confident in their attacks on him than
the Princess, so that at last he looked upon the woman
who concealed so much passion in her breast, and who
yet could command herself so thoroughly, as a kind of
miracle, and at last said to himself: "The world is right;
woman is a riddle!"

The Princess remained there for some weeks longer,
and always maintained the same polite and friendly,
but cool and sometimes ironical, demeanor towards him,

but he easily endured being looked upon as her unfortunate adorer by the world, for at least every other day a small, scented note, stamped with her arms and signed *Leonie*, summoned him to the pavilion, and there he enjoyed the full, delightful possession of the beautiful woman. It, however, struck him as strange that she would never let him see her face. Her head was always covered with a thick, black veil, through which he could see her eyes, which sparkled with love, glistening; he passed his fingers through her hair, he saw her well-known dresses, and once he succeeded in getting possession of one of her pocket-handkerchiefs, on which the name *Leonie* and the princely coronet were magnificently embroidered.

When she returned to Vienna for the winter, a note from her invited him to follow her there, and as he had indefinite leave of absence from his regiment, he could obey the commands of his divinity. As soon as he arrived there he received another note, which forbade him to go to her house, but promised him a speedy meeting in his rooms, and so the young officer had the furniture elegantly renovated, and looked forward to a visit from the beautiful woman with all a lover's impatience.

At last she came, wrapped in a magnificent cloak of green velvet, trimmed with ermine, but still thickly veiled, and before she came in she made it a condition that the room in which he received her should be quite dark, and after he had put out all the lights she threw off her fur, and her coldness gave way to the most impetuous tenderness.

"What is the reason that you will never allow me to see your dear, beautiful face?" the officer asked. "It is a whim of mine, and I suppose I have the right to indulge in whims," she said, hastily. "But I so long once more to see your splendid figure and your lovely face in full daylight," the Count continued. "Very well then, you shall see me at the Opera this evening."

She left him at six o'clock, after stopping barely an hour with him, and as soon as her carriage had driven off he dressed and went to the opera. During the overture, he saw the Princess enter her box and looking dazzlingly beautiful; she was wearing the same green velvet cloak, trimmed with ermine, that he had had in his hands a short time before, but almost immediately she let it fall from her shoulders, and showed a bust which was worthy of the Goddess of Love. She spoke with her husband with much animation, and smiled with her usual cold smile, though she did not give her adorer even a passing look, but, in spite of this, he felt the happiest of mortals.

In Vienna, however, the Count was not as fortunate as he had been at Karlsbad, where he had first met her, for his beautiful mistress only came to see him once a week; often she only stopped a short time with him, and once nearly six weeks passed without her favoring him at all, and she did not even make any excuse for remaining away. Just then, however, Leonie's husband accidentally made the young officer's acquaintance at the Jockey Club, took a fancy to him, and asked him to go and see him at his house.

When he called and found the Princess alone his

heart felt as if it would burst with pleasure, and seizing her hand, he pressed it ardently to his lips. "What are you doing, Count?" she said, drawing back. "You are behaving very strangely." "We are alone," the young officer whispered, "so why this mask of innocence? Your cruelty is driving me mad, for it is six weeks since you came to see me last." "I certainly think you are out of your mind," the Princess replied, with every sign of the highest indignation, and hastily left the drawing-room. Nothing else remained for the Count but to do the same thing, but his mind was in a perfect whirl, and he was quite incapable of explaining to himself the Princess's enigmatical behavior. He dined at an hotel with some friends, and when he got home he found a note in which the Princess begged him to pardon her, and promised to justify her conduct, for which purpose she would see him at eight o'clock that evening.

Scarcely, however, had he read her note, when two of his brother-officers came to see him, and asked him, with well-simulated anxiety, whether he were ill. When he said that he was perfectly well, one of them continued, laughing: "Then please explain the occurrence that is in everybody's mouth today, in which you call on a lady like Princess Leonie, whom you do not know, to upbraid her for her cruelty, and most unceremoniously call her *thou*?"

That was too much; Count F. might pardon the Princess for pretending not to know him in society, but that she should make him a common laughing-stock, nearly drove him mad. "If I call the Princess *thou*," he exclaimed, "it is because I have the right to do so, as I will prove."—His comrades shrugged their shoulders, but he asked them to come again punctually at seven o'clock, and then he made his preparations.

At eight o'clock his divinity made her appearance, still thickly veiled, but on this occasion wearing a valuable sable cloak. As usual, Count F. took her into the dark-room and locked the outer door; then he opened that which led into his bedroom, and his two friends came in, each with a candle in his hand.—The lady in the sable cloak cried out in terror when Count F. pulled off her veil, but then it was his turn to be surprised, for it was not the Princess Leonie who stood before him, but her pretty lady's-maid, who, now she was discovered, confessed that love had driven her to assume her mistress's part, in which she had succeeded perfectly, on account of the similarity of their figure, eyes and hair. She had found the Count's letter in the Princess's pocket-handkerchief when they were at Karlsbad and had answered it. She had made him happy, and had heightened the illusion which her figure gave rise to by borrowing the Princess' dresses.

Of course the Count was made great fun of, and turned his back on Vienna hastily that same evening, but the pretty lady's-maid also disappeared soon after the catastrophe, and only by those means escaped from her mistress's well-merited anger; for it turned out that that gallant little individual had already played the part of her mistress more than once, and had made all those hopeless adorers of the Princess, who had found favor in her own eyes, happy in her stead.

# twenty-eighth night

*She was a ghost of flesh and blood,
and she haunted only where she
loved. . . . It also shows how enjoy-
able week-ending can be when a
bachelor chooses the right house to
be invited to. . . .*

FORTUNA, the goddess of chance and good
luck, has always been *Cupid's* best ally; and Arnold, a
lieutenant in a hussar regiment, was evidently a special
favorite of both these roguish deities.

This good-looking, well-bred young officer had been
an enthusiastic admirer of the two Countesses W.,
mother and daughter, during a tolerably long leave of
absence, which he spent with his relations in Vienna.
He had adored them from the *Prater,* and worshiped
them at the opera, but he had never had an opportunity
of making their acquaintance, and, back at his dull
quarters in Galicia, he liked to think intimately about
those two aristocratic beauties. Last summer his regiment was transferred to Bohemia, to a wildly romantic
district, that had been made illustrious by a talented

writer, which abounded in magnificent woods, lofty mountain-forests and castles, and which was a favorite summer resort of the neighboring aristocracy.

Who can describe his joyful surprise, when he and his men were quartered in an old, weatherbeaten castle in the middle of a wood, and he learnt from the house-steward who received him that the owner of the castle was the husband, and, consequently, also the father of his Viennese ideals. An hour after he had taken possession of his old-fashioned, but beautifully furnished, room in a side-wing of the castle, he put on his full-dress uniform, and throwing his dolman over his shoulders, he went to pay his respects to the Count and the ladies.

He was received with the greatest cordiality. The Count was delighted to have a companion when he went out shooting, and the ladies were no less pleased at having some one to accompany them on their walks in the forests, or on their rides, so that he felt only half on the earth, and half in the seventh heaven of Mohammedan bliss. Before supper he had time to inspect the house more closely, and even to take a sketch of the large, gloomy building from a favorable point. The ancient seat of the Counts of W. was really very gloomy; in fact it created a sinister, uncomfortable feeling. The walls, which were crumbling away here and there, and which were covered with dark ivy; the round towers, which harbored jackdaws, owls, and hawks; the Aeolian harp, which complained and sighed and wept in the wind; the stones in the castle yard, which were overgrown with grass; the cloisters, in which every

210

footstep re-echoed; the great ancestral portraits which hung on the walls, coated as it were with dark, mysterious veils by the centuries which had passed over them —all this recalled to him the legends and fairy tales of his youth, and he involuntarily thought of the *Sleeping Beauty in the Wood*, and of *Blue Beard*, of the cruel mistress of the Kynast, and that aristocratic tigress of the Carpathians, who obtained the unfading charms of eternal youth by bathing in human blood.

He came in to supper where he found himself for the first time in company with all the members of the family, just in the frame of mind that was suitable for ghosts, and was not a little surprised when his host told him, half smiling and half seriously, that the "White Lady" was disturbing the castle again, and that she had latterly been seen very often. "Yes, indeed," Countess Ida exclaimed: "You must take care, Baron, for she haunts the very wing where your room is." The hussar was just in the frame of mind to take the matter seriously, but, on the other hand, when he saw the dark, ardent eyes of the Countess, and then the merry blue eyes of her daughter fixed on him, any real fear of ghosts was quite out of the question with him. For Baron T. feared nothing in this world, but he possessed a very lively imagination, which could conjure up threatening forms from another world so plainly that sometimes he felt very uncomfortable at his own fancies. But on the present occasion that malicious apparition had no power over him; the ladies took care of that, for both of them were beautiful and amiable.

The Countess was a mature Venus of thirty-six, of

211

middle height, and with the voluptuous figure of a true Viennese, with bright eyes, thick dark hair, and beautiful white teeth, while her daughter Ida, who was seventeen, had light hair and the pert little nose of the china figures of shepherdesses in the dress of the period of Louis XIV., and was short, slim, and full of French grace. Besides them and the Count, a son of twelve and his tutor were present at supper. It struck the hussar as strange that the tutor, who was a strongly-built young man, with a winning face and those refined manners which the greatest plebeian quickly acquires when brought into close and constant contact with the aristocracy, was treated with great consideration by all the family except the Countess, who treated him very haughtily. She assumed a particularly imperious manner towards her son's tutor, and she either found fault with, or made fun of, everything that he did, while he put up with it all with smiling humility.

Before supper was over their conversation again turned on to the ghost, and Baron T. asked whether they did not possess a picture of the *White Lady*. "Of course we have one," they all replied at once; whereupon Baron T. begged to be allowed to see it. "I will show it you tomorrow," the Count said. "No, Papa, now, immediately," the younger lady said mockingly; "just before the ghostly hour, such a thing creates a much greater impression."

All who were present, not excepting the boy and his tutor, took a candle and then they walked as if they had formed a torchlight procession, to the wing of the house where the hussar's room was. There was a life-size picture of the *White Lady* hanging in a Gothic passage near his room, among other ancestral portraits, and·it by no means made a terrible impression on anyone who looked at it, but rather the contrary. The ghost, dressed in stiff, gold brocade and purple velvet, and with a hawk on her wrist, looked like one of those seductive Amazons of the fifteenth century, who exercised the art of laying men and game at their feet with equal skill.

"Don't you think that the *White Lady* is very like mamma?" Countess Ida said, interrupting the Baron's silent contemplation of the picture. "There is no doubt of it," the hussar replied, while the Countess smiled and the tutor turned red, and they were still standing before the picture, when a strong gust of wind suddenly extinguished all the lights, and they all uttered a simultaneous cry. The *White Lady,* the little Count whispered, but she did not come, and as it was luckily a moonlight night, they soon recovered from their momentary shock. The family retired to their apartments, while the hussar and the tutor went to their own rooms, which were situated in the wing of the castle which was haunted by the *White Lady;* the officer's being scarcely thirty yards from the portrait, while the tutor's were rather further down the corridor.

The hussar went to bed, and was soon fast asleep, and though he had rather uneasy dreams nothing further happened. But while they were at breakfast the next morning, the Count's body-servant told them, with every appearance of real terror, that as he was crossing the court-yard at midnight, he had suddenly heard a noise like bats in the open cloisters, and when he looked he distinctly saw the *White Lady* gliding slowly through them; but they merely laughed at the poltroon, and though our hussar laughed also, he fully made up his mind, without saying a word about it, to keep a look-out for the ghost that night.

Again they had supper alone, without any company, had some music and pleasant talk and separated at half-past eleven. The hussar, however, only went to his room for form's sake; he loaded his pistols, and when all was quiet in the castle, he crept down into the court-yard and took up his position behind a pillar which was quite hidden in the shade, while the moon, which was nearly at the full, flooded the cloisters with its clear, pale light.

There were no lights to be seen in the castle except from two windows, which were those of the Countess's apartments, and soon they were also extinguished. The clock struck twelve, and the hussar could scarcely breathe from excitement; the next moment, however, he heard the noise which the Count's body-servant had compared to that of bats, and almost at the same instant a white figure glided slowly through the open cloisters and passed so close to him, that it almost made his blood curdle, and then it disappeared in the wing of the castle which he and the tutor occupied.

The officer who was usually so brave, stood as though he was paralyzed for a few moments, but then he took heart, and feeling determined to make the nearer ac-quaintance of the spectral beauty, he crept softly up the broad staircase and took up his position in a deep recess in the cloisters, where nobody could see him.

He waited for a long time; he heard every quarter strike, and at last, just before the close of the *witching hour*, he heard the same noise like the rustling of bats, and then she came, he felt the flutter of her white dress, and she stood before him—it was indeed the Countess.

He presented his pistol at her as he challenged her, but she raised her hand menacingly. "Who are you?" he exclaimed. "If you are really a ghost, prove it, for I am going to fire." "For heaven's sake!" the White Lady whispered, and at the same instant two white arms were thrown round him, and he felt a full, warm bosom heaving against his own.

After that night the ghost appeared more frequently still. Not only did the *White Lady* make her appearance every night in the cloisters, only to disappear in the proximity of the hussar's rooms as long as the family remained at the castle, but she even followed them to Vienna.

Baron T., who went to that capital on leave of absence during the following winter, and who was the Count's guest at the express wish of his wife, was frequently told by the footman that although hitherto she had seemed to be confined to the old castle in Bohemia, she had shown herself now here, now there, in the mansion in Vienna, in a white dress and making a noise like the wings of a bat, and bearing a striking resemblance to the beautiful Countess.

# *twenty-ninth night*

*She deceived her husband by dress-
ing her lover in skirts; and that
would have been alright, if the husband had not also fallen for him....*

A CHARMING young lady, who was a member
of the Viennese aristocracy, went last summer, as young
and charming ladies usually do, to a fashionable Austrian watering place, Carlsbad, which is much frequented by foreigners, without her husband.

As is usually the case in their rank of life, she had
married from family considerations and for money;
and the short spell of *Love after Marriage* was not sufficient to take deep root, so that, having satisfied family
traditions and her husband's wishes by giving birth to a
son and heir, they both went their ways; the young,
handsome and fascinating man to his clubs, the race-
course, and behind the scenes at the theaters, and his
charming, coquettish wife to her box at the opera, to
the ice in winter, and to some fashionable watering place
in the summer.

This time, she brought a young very highly-connected Pole with her from one of the latter resorts, who enjoyed all the rights and the liberty of an avowed favorite, and, consequently, had to perform all the duties of a slave.

As is to be expected in such cases, the lady rented a small house in one of the suburbs of Vienna, had it beautifully furnished and received her lover there. She was always dressed very attractively, sometimes as *La Belle Hélène* in Offenbach's Opera, only rather more after the ancient Greek fashion; another time as an Odalisque in the Sultan's harem, and another time as a lighthearted Suabian girl, and so forth. In winter, however, she grew tired of such meetings, and she wanted to have matters more comfortable, so she took it into her head to receive her lover in her own house. But how was it to be done? That, however, gave her no particular difficulty, as is the case with every woman, when once she has made up her mind to a thing, and after thinking it over for a day or two she went to the next *rendez-vous,* with a fully prepared plan of war.

The Pole was one of those types of handsome men which are rare; he was almost womanly in his delicate features, of the middle height, slim and well-made, and he resembled a youthful Bacchus who might very easily be made to pass for a Venus by the help of false locks; the more so as there was not even the slightest down on his lips. The lady, therefore, who was very fertile in resources, suggested to the handsome Pole that he might just as well transform himself into a handsome Polish lady, so that he might, under the cover of the ever feminine, be able to visit her undisturbed, and as it was winter, the thick, heavy, capacious dress assisted the metamorphosis.

The lady, accordingly, bought a number of very beautiful costumes for her lover, and in the course of a few days she told her husband that a charming young Polish lady, whose acquaintance she had made in the summer at Carlsbad, was going to spend the winter in Vienna, and would very frequently come and see her. Her husband listened to her with the greatest indifference, for it was one of his fundamental rules never to make love to any of his wife's female friends, and he went to his club as usual at night, and the next day had forgotten all about the Polish lady.

And now, half an hour after the husband had left the house, a cab drove up and a tall, slim, heavily veiled lady got out and went up the thickly carpeted stairs, only to be metamorphosed into the most ardent lover in the young woman's *boudoir*. The young Pole grew accustomed to his female attire so quickly that he even ventured to appear in the streets in it, and when he began to make conquests, and aristocratic gentlemen and successful speculators on the Stock Exchange looked at him significantly, and even followed him, he took a real pleasure in the part he was playing, and began to understand the pleasure a coquette feels in tormenting men.

The young Pole became more and more daring, until at last one evening he went to a private box at the opera, wrapped in an ermine cloak, on to which his dark, false curls fell in heavy waves.

A handsome young man in a box opposite to him

ogled him incessantly from the first moment, and the young Pole responded in a manner which made the other bolder every minute. At the end of the third act, the box opener brought the fictitious Venus a small bouquet with a card concealed in it, on which was written in pencil: "You are the most lovely woman in the world, and I implore you on my knees to grant me an interview." The young Pole read the name of the man who had been captivated so quickly, and, with a peculiar smile, wrote on a card on which nothing but the name "Valeska" was printed: "After the theater," and sent Cupid's messenger back with it.

When the spurious Venus was about to enter her carriage after the performance, thickly veiled and wrapped in her ermine cloak, the handsome young man was standing by it with his hat off, and he opened the door for her. She was kind enough to allow him to get in with her and during their drive she talked to him in the most charming manner, but she was cruel enough to dismiss him without pity before they reached her house, and this she did every time. For she went to the theater each night now, and every evening she received an ardent note, and every evening she allowed the amorous swain to accompany her as far as her house, and men were beginning to envy him on account of his brilliant conquest, when a catastrophe happened which was very surprising for all concerned.

The husband of the lady in whose eyes the Pole had found favor, surprised the loving couple one day under circumstances which made any justification impossible. But while he, trembling with rage and jealousy, was drawing a small Circassian dagger which hung against the wall from its sheath, and as his wife threw herself, half-fainting, on to a couch, the young Pole had hastily put the false curls on to his head, and had slipped into the silk dress and the sable cloak which he had been wearing when he came into his mistress's boudoir. "What does this mean," the husband stammered, "Valeska?"— "Yes, sir," the young Pole replied; "Valeska, who has come here to show your wife a few love letters, which." . . . "No, no," the deceived, but nevertheless guilty, husband said in imploring accents; "no, that is quite unnecessary." And at the same time he put the dagger back into its sheath. "Very well then, there is a truce between us," the Pole observed coolly, "but do not forget what weapons I possess, and which I mean to retain against all contingencies."

Then the gentlemen bowed politely to each other, and the unexpected meeting came to an end.

From that time forward, the terms on which the young married couple lived together assumed the character of that everlasting peace, which President Grant once promised to the whole world in his message to all nations. The young woman did not find it necessary to make her lover put on petticoats, and the husband constantly accompanied the real Valeska a good deal further than he did the false one on that memorable occasion.

# thirtieth night

*The hero of this adventure liked fat
girls, and the one he picked to share
his Xmas dinner was fat enough,
only with a fatness which suddenly
gives way. . . .*

T HE CHRISTMAS-EVE supper! Oh! no, I shall
never go in for that again!" Big, fat Henri Templier
said that in a furious voice, as if some one had proposed
to him the commission of a crime, while the others
laughed and coaxed, "Why do you fly into a rage?"

"Because a Christmas-eve supper played me the dir-
tiest trick in the world, and ever since that time I have
felt mounting horror for that night of imbecile gayety,"
he confessed.

"Tell us about it!" they urged him.

"You want to know why? Very well then, just listen.

"You remember how cold it was two years ago at
Christmas; cold enough to kill poor people in the streets.
The Seine was covered with ice; the pavements froze
one's feet through the soles of one's boots, and the whole
world seemed to be at the point of going to pot.

"I had a big piece of work on, and so I refused every invitation to supper, as I preferred to spend the night at my writing table. I dined alone and then began to work. But about ten o'clock I grew restless at the thought of the gay and busy life all over Paris, at the noise in the streets which reached me in spite of everything at my neighbors' preparations for supper, which I heard through the walls. I hardly knew any longer what I was doing; I wrote nonsense, and at last I came to the conclusion that I had better give up all hope of producing any good work that night.

"I walked up and down my room; I sat down and got up again. I was certainly under the mysterious influence of the enjoyment outside, and I resigned mysel fto it. So I pulled the bell for my servant and said to her:

" 'Angela, go and get a good supper for two; some oysters, a cold partridge, some crayfish, hams and some cakes. Put out two bottles of champagne, lay the cloth and go to bed.'

"She obeyed in some surprise, and when all was ready, I put on my great coat and went out. A great question was to be solved: 'Whom was I going to bring in to supper?' My female friends had all been invited elsewhere, and if I had wished to have one, I ought to have seen about it beforehand, so I thought that I would do a good action at the same time, and I said to myself:

" 'Paris is full of poor and pretty girls who will have nothing on their table tonight, and who are on the look out for some generous fellow. I will act the part of Providence to one of them this evening; and I will find one if I have to go into every pleasure resort, and have to question them and hunt for one till I find one to my choice.' And I started off on my search.

"I certainly found many poor girls, who were on the look-out for some adventure, but they were ugly enough to give any man a fit of indigestion, or thin enough to freeze as they stood if they had stopped, and you all know that I have a weakness for stout women. The more flesh they have, the better I like them, and a female colossus would drive me out of my senses with pleasure.

"Suddenly, opposite the Théatre des Variétés, I saw a face to my liking. A good head, and then two protuberances, that on the chest very beautiful, and that on the stomach simply surprising; it was the stomach of a fat goose. I trembled with pleasure, and said:

" 'By Jove! What a find girl!'

"It only remained for me to see her face. A woman's face is the dessert, while the rest is . . . the joint.

"I hastened on, and overtook her, and turned round suddenly under a gas lamp. She was charming, quite young, dark, with large, black eyes, and I immediately made my proposition, which she accepted without any hesitation, and a quarter of an hour later, we were sitting at supper in my lodgings. 'Oh! how comfortable it is here,' she said as she came in, and she looked about her with evident satisfaction at having found a supper and a bed, on that bitter night. She was superb; so beautiful that she astonished me, and so stout that she fairly captivated me.

"She took off her cloak and hat, sat down and began to eat; but she seemed in low spirits, and sometimes her pale face twitched as if she were suffering from some hidden sorrow.

" 'Have you anything troubling you?' I asked her.

" 'Bah! Don't let us think of troubles!'

"And she began to drink. She emptied her champagne glass at a draught, filled it again, and emptied it again, without stopping, and soon a little color came into her cheeks, and she began to laugh.

"I adored her already, kissed her continually, and discovered that she was neither stupid, nor common, nor coarse as ordinary street-walkers are. I asked her for some details about her life, but she replied:

" 'My little fellow, that is no business of yours!'

"At last it was time to go to bed, and while I was clearing the table, which had been laid in front of the fire, she undressed herself quickly, and got in. My neighbors were making a terrible din, singing and laughing like lunatics, and so I said to myself:

" 'I was qiute right to go out and bring in this girl; I should never have been able to do any work.'

"At that moment, however, a deep groan made me look round, and I said:

" 'What is the matter with you, my dear?'

"She did not reply, but continued to utter painful sighs, as if she were suffering horribly, and I continued:

" 'Do you feel ill?' " And suddenly she uttered a cry, a heartrending cry, and I rushed up to the bed, with a candle in my hand.

"Her face was distorted with pain, and she was

wringing her hands, panting and uttering long, deep groans, which sounded like a rattle in the throat, and which are so painful to hear, and I asked her in consternation:

" 'What is the matter with you? Do tell me what is the matter.'

" 'Oh! my stomach! my stomach!' she said. I pulled up the bed-clothes, and I saw . . . My friends, she was in labor.

"Then I lost my head, and I ran and knocked at the wall with my fists, shouting: 'Help! help!'

"My door was opened almost immediately, and a crowd of people came in, men in evening dress, women in low necks, harlequins, Turks, Musketeers, and this inroad startled me so, that I could not explain myself, and they, who had thought that some accident had happened, or that a crime had been committed, could not understand what was the matter. At last, however, I managed to say:

" 'This . . . this . . . woman . . . is being confined.'

"Then they looked at her, and gave their opinion, and a Friar, especially, declared that he knew all about it, and wished to assist nature, but as they were all as drunk as pigs, I was afraid that they would kiss her, and I rushed downstairs without my hat, to fetch an old doctor, who lived in the next street. When I came back with him, the whole house was up; the gas on the stairs had been relighted, the lodgers from every floor were in my room, while four boatmen were finishing my champagne and lobsters.

"As soon as they saw me they raised a loud shout, and a milkmaid presented me with a horrible little wrinkled specimen of humanity, that was mewing like a cat, and said to me:

" 'It is a girl.'

"The doctor examined the woman, declared that she was in a dangerous state, as the event had occurred immediately after supper, and he took his leave, saying he would immediately send a sick nurse and a wet nurse, and an hour later, the two women came, bringing all that was requisite with them.

"I spent the night in my armchair, too distracted to be able to think of the consequences, and almost as soon as it was light, the doctor came again, who found his patient very ill, and said to me:

" 'Your wife, Monsieur. . . . '

" 'She is not my wife,' I interrupted him.

" 'Very well then, your mistress; it does not matter to me.'

"He told me what must be done for her, what her diet must be, and then wrote a prescription.

"What was I to do? Could I send the poor creature to the hospital? I should have been looked upon as a brute in the house and in all the neighborhood, and so I kept her in my rooms, and she had my bed for six weeks.

"I sent the child to some peasants at Poissy to be taken care of, and she still costs me fifty francs a month, for as I had paid at first, I shall be obliged to go on paying as long as I live, and later on, she will believe that I am her father. But to crown my misfortunes, when the girl had recovered . . . I found that she was in love with me, madly in love with me, the baggage!"

"Well?"

"Well, she had grown as thin as a homeless cat, and I turned the skeleton out of doors, but she watches for me in the streets, hides herself, so that she may see me pass, stops me in the evening when I go out, in order to kiss my hand, and, in fact, worries me enough to drive me mad; and that is why I never keep Christmas eve now."

# thirty-first night

*In demanding a divorce for his woman-client, this lawyer named the most amazing co-respondents in juristic history.*

M. CHASSEL, ATTORNEY for the defense, rises to speak: Mr. President and gentlemen of the jury. The cause I am charged to defend before you, requires medicine rather than justice; and is much more a case of pathology than one of ordinary law. At first blush the facts seem very simple.

A young man, very rich, with a noble and cultivated mind, and a generous heart, falls in love with a young lady, who is the perfection of beauty, more than beautiful, in fact; she is adorable, besides being as gracious as she is charming, as good and true as she is tender and pretty; and he marries her. For some time he comports himself towards her not only as a devoted husband, but as a man full of solicitude and tenderness. Then he neglects her, misuses her, seems to entertain for her an insurmountable aversion, an irresistible disgust. One day he even strikes her, not only without any cause, but also without the faintest pretext. Gentlemen, I am not going to draw a picture of silly allurements, which no one would understand. I shall not paint for you the wretched life of those two beings, and the horrible grief of this young woman, in particular. It will be sufficient to convince you, if I read some fragments from a journal set down every day by that poor young man, by that poor fool! For it is in the presence of a fool, gentlemen, that we now find ourselves, and the case is all the more curious, all the more interesting, seeing that, in many points, it recalls the insanity of the unfortunate prince who recently died, of the witless king who reigned platonically over Bavaria. I shall hence designate this case—poetic folly.

You will readily call to mind all that has been told of that most singular prince. He caused to be erected amid the most magnificent scenery his kingdom afforded, veritable fairy castles. The reality even of the beauty of the things themselves, as well as of the places, did not satisfy him. He invented, he created, in these improbable manors, fictitious horizons, obtained by means of theatrical artifices, changes of view, painted forests, fabled empires, in which the leaves of the trees became precious stones. He had the Alps, and glaciers, steppes, deserts of sand made hot by a blazing sun; and at nights, under the rays of the real moon, lakes which sparkled from below by means of fantastic electric lights. Swans floated on the lakes which glistened with skiffs, while an orchestra, composed of the finest executants in the world, inebriated with poetry the soul of the royal fool. That man was chaste, that man was a virgin. He lived only to dream, his dream, his dream divine. One evening he took out with him in his boat, a lady, young and beautiful, a great artiste, and he begged her to sing. Intoxicated herself by the magnificent scenery, by the languid softness of the air, by the perfume of flowers, and by the ecstasy of that prince, both young and handsome, she sang, she sang as women sing who have been touched by love; then, overcome, trembling, she falls on the bosom of the king in order to seek out his lips. But he throws her into the lake, and seizing his oars, rows back to the shore, without concerning himself, whether anybody has saved her or not.

Gentlemen of the jury, we find ourselves in presence of a case similar in every way to that. I shall say no more now, except to read some passages from the journal which we unexpectedly came upon in the drawer of an old secretary.

.    .    .    .    .    .

How sad and weary is everything; always the same, always hateful. How I dream of a land more beautiful, more noble, more varied. What a poor conception they have of their God, if their God existed, or if he had not created other things, elsewhere. Always woods, little woods, waves which resemble waves, plains which resemble plains, everything is sameness and monotony. And Man? Man? What a horrible animal! wicked, haughty and repugnant!

.    .    .    .    .    .

It is essential to love, to love perdition, without seeing that which one loves. For, to see is to comprehend, and to comprehend is to embrace. It is necessary to love, to become intoxicated by it, just as one gets drunk with wine, even to the extent that one knows no longer what one is drinking. And to drink, to drink, to drink,

.    .    .    .    .    .

without drawing breath, day and night!

I have found her, I believe. She has about her something ideal which does not belong to this world, and which furnishes wings to my dream. Ah! my dream! How it reveals to me beings different from what they really are! She is a blonde, a delicate blonde, with hair whose delicate shade is inexpressible. Her eyes are blue! Only blue eyes can penetrate my soul. All women, the woman who lives in my heart, reveal themselves to me in the eye, only in the eyes. Oh! what a mystery, what a mystery is the eye! The whole universe lives in it, inasmuch as it sees, inasmuch as it reflects. It contains the universe, both things and beings, forests and oceans, men and beasts, the settings of the sun, the stars, the arts—all, all, it sees; it collects and absorbs all; and there is still more in it; the eye of itself has a soul; it has in it the man who thinks, the man who loves, the man who laughs, the man who suffers! Oh! regard the blue eyes of women, those eyes that are as deep as the sea, as changeful as the sky, so sweet, so soft, soft as the breezes, sweet as music, luscious as kisses; and transparent, so clear that one sees behind them, discerns the soul, the blue soul which colors them, which animates them, which electrifies them. Yes, the soul has the color of the looks. The blue soul alone contains in itself that which dreams; it bears its azure to the floods and into space. The eye! Think of it, the eye! It imbibes the visible life, in order to nourish thought. It drinks in the world, color, movement, books, pictures, all that is beautiful, all that is ugly, and weaves ideas out of them. And when it regards us, it gives us the sensation of a happiness that is not of this earth. It informs us of that of which we have always been ignorant; it makes us comprehend that the realities of our dreams are but noisome ordures.

. . . . . .

I love her too for her walk. "Even when the bird walks one feels that it has wings," as the poet has said. When she passes one feels that she is of another race from ordinary women, of a race more delicate, and more divine. I shall marry her tomorrow. But I am afraid, I am afraid of so many things!

Two beasts, two dogs, two wolves, two foxes, cut their way through the plantation and encounter one another. One of each two is male, the other female. They couple. They couple in consequence of an animal instinct, which forces them to continue the race, their race, the one from which they have sprung, the hairy coat, the form, movements and habitudes. The whole of the animal creation do the same without knowing why.

We human beings, also.

It is for this I have married; I have obeyed that insane passion which throws us in the direction of the female.

. . . . . .

She is my wife. In accordance with my ideal desires, she comes very nearly to realize my unrealizable dream.

232

But in separating from her, even for a second, after I have held her in my arms, she becomes no more than the being whom nature has made use of, to disappoint all my hopes.

Has she disappointed them? No. And why have I grown weary of her, become loath even to touch her; she cannot graze even the palm of my hand, or the tip of my lips, but my heart throbs with unutterable disgust, not perhaps disgust of her, but a disgust more potent, more widespread, more loathsome; the disgust, in a word, of carnal love so vile in itself that it has become for all refined beings, a shameful thing, which it is necessary to conceal, which one never speaks of save in a whisper, nor without blushing.

. . . . . . .

I can no longer bear the idea of my wife coming near me, calling me by name, with a smile: I cannot look at her, nor touch even her arm, I cannot do it any more. At one time I thought to be kissed by her would be to transport me to St. Paul's seventh heaven. One day, she was suffering from one of those transient fevers, and I smelled in her breath, a subtle, slight, almost imperceptible puff of human putridity; I was completely overthrown.

Oh! the flesh, with its seductive and eager smell, a putrefaction which walks, which thinks, which speaks, which looks, which laughs, in which nourishment ferments and rots, which, nevertheless, is rose-colored, pretty, tempting, deceitful as the soul itself.

. . . . . . .

Why flowers alone, which smell so sweet, those large

flowers, glittering or pale, whose tones and shades make my heart tremble and trouble my eyes. They are so beautiful, their structure is so finished, so varied and sensual, semi-opened like human organs, more tempting than mouths, and streaked with turned up lips, teeth, flesh, seed of life powders, which, in each, gives forth a distinct perfume.

They reproduce themselves, they alone, in the world, without polluting their inviolable race, shedding around them the divine influence of their love, the odoriferous incense of their caresses, the essence of their incomparable body, of their body adorned with every grace, with every elegances of every shape and form; who have likewise the coquetry of every hue of color, and the inebriating seduction of every variety of perfume.

·     ·     ·     ·     ·     ·

FRAGMENTS WHICH WERE SELECTED SIX MONTHS LATER.

I love flowers, not as flowers, but as material and delicious beings; I pass my days and my nights in beds of flowers, where they have been concealed from the public view like the women of a harem.

Who knows, except myself, the sweetness, the infatuation, the quivering, carnal, ideal, superhuman ecstasy of these tendernesses; and those kisses upon the bare flesh of a rose, upon the blushing flesh, upon the white skin, so miraculously different, delicate, rare, subtle, unctuous, of these adorable flowers!

I have flower-beds that no one has seen except myself, and which I tend myself.

I enter there as one would glide into a place of secret pleasure. In the lofty glass gallery, I pass first through a collection of enclosed carollas, half open or in full bloom, which incline towards the ground, or towards the roof. This is the first kiss they have given me.

The flowers just mentioned, these flowers which adorn the vestibule of my mysterious passions, are my servants and not my favorites.

They salute me by the change of their color and by their first inhalations. They are darlings, coquettes, arranged in eight rows to the right, eight rows the left, and so laid out that they look like two gardens springing up from under my feet.

My heart palpitates, my eyes flash at the sight of them; my blood rushes through my veins, my soul is elated, and my hands tremble from desire as soon as I touch them. I pass on. There are three closed doors at the bottom of that gallery. I can make my choice of them. I have three harems.

But I enter most often the habitation of the orchids, my little wheedlers, by preference. Their chamber is low, suffocating. The humid and hot air make the skin moist, takes away the breath and causes the fingers to quiver. They come, these strange girls, from a country marshy, burning and unhealthy. They draw you towards them as do the sirens, are as deadly as poison, admirably fantastic, enervating, dreadful. The butterflies here would also seem to have enormous wings, tiny feet, and eyes! Yes! they have also eyes! They look at me, they seem, prodigious, incomparable beings, fairies, daughters of the sacred earth, of the impalpable air, and of hot sun rays, that mother bountiful of the universe. Yes, they have wings, they have eyes, and nuances that no painter could imitate, every charm, every grace, every form that one could dream of. These wombs are transverse, odoriferous and transparent, ever open for love and more tempting than all the flesh of women. The unimaginable designs of their little bodies inebriates the soul, and transports it to a paradise of images and of voluptuous ideals. They tremble upon their stems as though they would fly. When they do fly do they come to me? No, it is my heart that hovers o'er them, like a mystic male, tortured by love.

No wing of any animal can keep pace with them. We are alone, they and I, in the lighted prison which I have constructed for them. I regard them, I contemplate them, I admire them, I adore them, the one after the other.

How healthy, strong and rosy, a rosiness that moistens the lips of desire! How I love them! The border is frizzled, paler than their throat, where the carolla hides itself away; a mysterious mouth, seductive sugar under the tongue, exhibiting and unveiling the delicate, admirable and sacred organs of these divine little creatures which smell so exquisitely and do not speak.

I sometimes have a passion for some of them that lasts as long as their existence, which only embraces a few days and nights. I then have them taken away from the common gallery and enclosed in a pretty glass cabin, in which there murmurs a jet of water over against a tropical gazon, which has been brought from one of the Pacific Islands. And I remain close to it, ardent, feverish and tormented, knowing that its death is near, and watch it fading away, while that in thought, I possess it, aspire to its love, drink it in, and then pluck its short life with an inexpressible caress.

.　　.　　.　　.　　.　　.　　.

When he had finished the reading of these fragments, the advocate continued:

"Decency, gentlemen of the jury, hinders me from communicating to you the extraordinary avowals of this shameless, idealistic fool. The fragments that I have just submitted to you will be sufficient, in my opinion, to enable you to appreciate this instance of mental malady, less rare in our epoch of hysterical insanity and of corrupt decadence than most of us believe.

I think, then, that my client is more entitled than any women whatever to claim a divorce, in the exceptional circumstances in which the disordered senses of her husband has placed her.

# *thirty-second night*

*Adoultery based on reason is still adultery, but there might have been something more than reason in the curious conduct of the rabbi's beautiful wife in her husband's absence. . . .*

Some years ago there lived in Braniza, a celebrated Talmudist, who was renowned no less on account of the beauty of his wife, than for his wisdom, his learning, and his fear of God. The Venus of Braniza deserved that name thoroughly, not only on account of her singular beauty, but even more for having chosen to be the wife of a man who devoted his whole life to study. The wives of such men are usually the very opposite, homely if not downright ugly, and often even cripples.

The Talmud explains this, in the following manner. It is well known that marriages are made in heaven, and at the birth of a boy a divine voice calls out the name of his future wife, and *vice versa*. But just as a good father tries to get rid of his good wares out of doors, and only uses the damaged stuff at home for his children, so God bestows those women whom other men would not care to have, on the Talmudists.

Well, God made an exception in the case of our Talmudist, and had bestowed a Venus on him, perhaps only in order to confirm the rule by means of this exception, and to make it appear less hard. His wife was a woman who would have done honor to any king's throne, or to the pedestal in any sculpture gallery. Tall, and with a wonderful, voluptuous figure, she carried a strikingly beautiful head, surmounted by thick, black plaits, on her proud shoulders, while two large, dark eyes languished and glowed beneath her long lashes, and her beautiful hands looked as if they were carved out of ivory.

This beautiful woman, who seemed to have been designed by nature to rule, to see slaves at her feet, to provide occupation for the painter's brush, the sculptor's chisel and the poet's pen, lived the life of a rare and beautiful flower, which is shut up in a hot house, for she sat the whole day long wrapped up in her costly fur jacket and looked down dreamily into the street.

She had no children; her husband, the philosopher, studied, and prayed, and studied again from early morning until late at night; his mistress was *the Veiled Beauty*, as the Talmudists call the Kabbalah. She paid no attention to her house, for she was rich and everything went of its own accord, just like a clock, which has only to be wound up once a week; nobody came to see her, and she never went out of the house; she sat and dreamed and brooded and—yawned.

One day when a terrible storm of thunder and lightning had spent all its fury over the town, and all windows had been opened in order to let the Messiah in, the Jewish Venus was sitting as usual in her comfortable easy chair, shivering in spite of her fur jacket, and was thinking, when suddenly she fixed her glowing eyes on the man who was sitting before the Talmud, swaying his body backwards and forwards, and said suddenly:

"Just tell me, when will Messias, the Son of David, come?"

"He will come," the philosopher replied, "when all the Jews have become either altogether virtuous or altogether vicious, say the Talmud."

"Do you believe that all the Jews will ever become virtuous," the Venus continued.

"How am I to believe that!"

"So Messias will come, when all the Jews have become vicious?"

The philosopher shrugged his shoulders and lost himself again in the labyrinth of the Talmud, out of which, so it is said, only one man returned unscathed, and the beautiful woman at the window again looked dreamily out onto the heavy rain, while her white fingers played unconsciously with the dark fur of her splendid jacket.

• • • • •

One day the Jewish philosopher had gone to a neighboring town, where an important question of ritual was to be decided. Thanks to his learning, the question was settled sooner than he had expected, and instead of returning the next morning, as he had intended, he came back the same evening with a friend, who was no less learned than himself. He got out of the carriage at his friend's house, and went home on foot, and was not a little surprised when he saw his windows brilliantly illuminated, and found an officer's servant comfortably smoking his pipe in front of his house.

"What are you doing here?" he asked in a friendly manner, but with some curiosity, nevertheless.

"I am looking out, in case the husband of the beautiful Jewess should come home unexpectedly."

"Indeed? Well, mind and keep a good look out."

Saying this, the philosopher pretended to go away, but went into the house through the garden entrance at the back. When he got into the first room, he found a table laid for two, which had evidently only been left a short time previously. His wife was sitting as usual at her bed room window wrapped in her fur jacket, but her cheeks were suspiciously red, and her dark eyes had not got their usual languishing look, but now rested on her husband with a gaze which expressed at the same time satisfaction and mockery. At that moment he kicked against an object on the floor, which emitted a strange sound, which he picked up and examined in the light. It was a pair of spurs.

"Who has been here with you?" the Talmudist said.

The Jewish Venus shrugged her shoulders contemptuously, but did not reply.

"Shall I tell you? The Captain of Hussars has been with you."

"And why should he not have been here with me?"

she said, smoothing the fur on her jacket with her white hand.

"Woman! are you out of your mind?"

"I am in full possession of my senses," she replied, and a knowing smile hovered round her red voluptuous lips. "But must I not also do my part, in order that Messias may come and redeem us poor Jews?"

# *thirty-third night*

> *From the time that she was twelve,
> she had been the mistress of every
> fellow in the village, had corrupted
> boys of her own age in every con-
> ceivable manner and place . . . and
> when she grew up . . .*

THEY CALLED HER *La Morillonne* (Black Grapes) because of her black hair and complexion, which resembled autumnal leaves, and because of her mouth whose thick purple lips were like blackberries, when she curled them.

That she should be born so dark in a district where everybody was fair, the issue of a father and mother with tow-colored hair and a complexion like butter, is one of the mysteries of atavism. One of her female ancestors must have had an intimacy with one of those traveling tinkers who, have gone about the country from time immemorial, with faces the color of bistre and indigo, crowned by a wisp of light hair.

From that ancestor she derived, not only her dark complexion, but also her dark soul, her deceitful eyes, whose depths were at times illuminated by flashes of every vice, her eyes of an obstinate and malicious animal.

Handsome? Certainly not, nor even pretty. Ugly, yes, and with such an ugliness! Such a false look! Her nose was flat, and had been smashed by a blow, while her unwholesome looking mouth was always slobbering with greediness, or uttering something vile. Her hair was thick and untidy, and a regular nest for vermin, to which may be added a thin, feverish body, with a limping walk. In short, she was a perfect monster, and yet all the young men of the neighborhood had made love to her, and whoever had been so honored, longed for her society again.

From the time that she was twelve, she had been the mistress of every fellow in the village. She had corrupted boys of her own age in every conceivable manner and place.

Young men at the risk of imprisonment, and even steady, old, notable and venerable men, such as the farmer at Eclausiaux, Monsieur Martin, the ex-mayor, and other highly respectable men, had been taken by the manners of that creature, and the reason why the rural policeman was not severe upon them, in spite of his love for summoning people before the magistrates, was, so people said, that he would have been obliged to take out a summons against himself.

The consequence was, that she had grown up without being interfered with, and was the mistress of every fellow in the village, as the schoolmaster said; who had himself been one of *the fellows*. But the most curious part of the business was, that no one was jealous. They handed her on from one to the other, and when someone expressed his astonishment at this to her one day, she said to this unintelligent stranger:

"Is everybody not satisfied?"

And then, how could any one of them, even if he had been jealous, have monopolized her? They had no hold on her. She was not selfish, and though she accepted all gifts, whether in kind or in money, she never asked for anything and she even appeared to prefer paying herself after her own fashion, by stealing. All she seemed to care about as her reward was pilfering, and a crown put into her hand, gave her less pleasure than a halfpenny which she had stolen. Neither was it any use to dream of ruling her as the sole male, or as the proud master of the hen roost, for which of them, no matter how broad shouldered he was, would have been capable of it? Some had tried to vanquish her, but in vain.

How then, could any of them claim to be her master? It would have been the same as wishing to have the sole right of baking their bread in the common oven, in which the whole village baked.

But there was one man who formed the exception, and that was Bru, the shepherd.

He lived in the fields in his movable hut, on cakes made of unleavened dough, which he kneaded on a stone and baked in the hot ashes, now here, now there, is a hole dug out in the ground, and heated with dead wood. Potatoes, milk, hard cheese, blackberries, and a small cask of old gin that he had distilled himself, were his daily pittance; but he knew nothing about love, although he was accused of all sorts of horrible things, and therefore nobody dared abuse him to his face; in the first place, because Bru was a spare and sinewy man, who handled his shepherd's crook like a drum-major does his staff; next, because of his three sheep dogs, who had teeth like wolves, and who knew nobody except their master; and lastly, for fear of the evil eye. For Bru, it appeared, knew spells which would blight the corn, give the sheep foot rot, the cattle the *rinder pest,* make cows die in calving, and set fire to the ricks and stacks.

But as Bru was the only one who did not loll out his tongue after La Morillonne, naturally one day she began to think of him, and she declared that she, at any rate, was not afraid of his evil eye, and so she went after him.

"What do you want?" he said, and she replied boldly: "What do I want? I want you."

"Very well," he said, "but then you must belong to me alone."

"All right," was her answer, "if you think you can please me."

He smiled and took her into his arms, and she was away from the village for a whole week. She had, in fact, become entirely Bru's exclusive property.

The village grew excited. They were not jealous of each other, but they were of him. What! Could she not resist him. Of course he had charms and spells against every imaginable thing. And they grew furious. Next they grew bold, and watched from behind a tree. She was still as lively as ever, but he, poor fellow, seemed to have become suddenly ill, and required the most tender nursing at her hands. The villagers, however, felt no compassion for the poor shepherd, and so, one of them, more courageous than the rest, advanced towards the hut with his gun in his hand:

"Tie up your dogs," he cried out from a distance; "fasten them up, Bru, or I shall shoot them."

"You need not be frightened of the dogs," *La Morillonne* replied; "I will be answerable for it that they will not hurt you," and she smiled as the young man with the gun went towards her.

"What do you want?" the shepherd said.

"I can tell you," she replied. "He wants me and I am very willing. There!"

Bru began to cry, and she continued:

"You are a good for nothing."

And she went off with the lad, while Bru seized his crook, seeing which the young fellow raised his gun.

"Seize him! seize him!" the shepherd shouted, urging on his dogs, while the other had already got his finger on the trigger to fire at them. But *La Morillonne* pushed down the muzzle and called out:

"Here, dogs! here! *Prr, prr,* my beauties!"

And the three dogs rushed up to her, licked her hands and frisked about as they followed her, while she called to the shepherd from the distance:

"You see, Bru, they are not at all jealous!"

And then, with a short and evil laugh, she added:

"They are my property now."

# *thirty-fourth night*

*For years he had been in love with
his best friend's wife. One day, after
a picnic at which the wine made
her husband sleep and her merry, his
chance came . . .*

Monsieur Savel, who was called in Mantes,
"Father Savel," got out of bed, and looked sadly about
him. It was a dull autumn day; the leaves were falling.
They fell slowly in the rain, resembling another rain,
but heavier and slower. M. Savel was not in good spirit.
He walked from the fireplace to the window, and from
the window to the fireplace. Life has its somber days.
Worse, it will no longer have any but somber days for
him now, for he has reached the age of sixty-two. He
is alone, an old bachelor, with nobody about him. How
sad it is to die alone, all alone, without the disinterested
affection of anyone!

He pondered on his life, so barren, so empty. He recalled the days gone by, the days of his infancy, the
house, the house of his parents; his college days, his fol-
lies, the time of his probation in Paris, the illness of his

father, his death. He then returned to live with his mother. They lived together, the young man and the old woman very quietly, and desired nothing more. At last the mother died. How sad a thing is life! He has lived always alone, and now in his turn, he, too, will soon be dead. He will disappear, and that will be his finish. There will be no more Saval upon the earth. What a frightful thing! Other people will live, they will live, they will laugh. Yes, people will go on amusing themselves, and he will no longer exist! Is it not strange that people can laugh, amuse themselves, be joyful under that eternal certainty of death! If this death were only probable, one could then have hope; but no, it is inevitable.

If, however, his life had been complete! If he had done something; if he had had adventures, grand pleasures, successes, satisfaction of some kind or another. But now, nothing. He had done nothing, never anything but rise from bed, eat, at the same hours, and go to bed again. And he has gone on like that, to the age of sixty-two years. He had not even taken unto himself a wife, as other men do. Why? Yes, why was it that he was not married? He might have been, for he possessed considerable means. Was it an opportunity which had failed him? Perhaps! But one can create opportunities. He was indifferent; that was all. Indifference had been his greatest drawback, his defect, his vice. Have some men missed their lives through indifference! To certain natures, it is so difficult for them to get out of bed, to move about, to take long walks, to speak, to study any question.

He had not even been in love. No woman had reposed on his bosom, in a complete abandon of love. He knew nothing of this delicious anguish of expectation, of the divine quivering of the pressed hand, of the ecstasy of triumphant passion.

What superhuman happiness must inundate your heart, when lips encounter lips for the first time, when the grasp of four arms makes one being of you, a being unutterably happy, two beings infatuated with one another.

M. Savel was sitting down, his feet on the fender, in his dressing gown. Assuredly his life had been spoiled, completely spoiled. He had, however, loved. He had loved secretly, dolorously and indifferently, just as was characteristic of him in everything. Yes, he had loved his old friend, Madame Saudres, the wife of his old companion, Saudres. Ah! if he had known her as a young girl! But he had encountered her too late; she was already married. Unquestionably he would have asked her hand; that he would! How he had loved her, nevertheless, without respite, since the first day he had set eyes on her!

He recalled, without emotion, all the times he had seen her, his grief on leaving her, the many nights that he could not sleep, because of his thinking of her.

In the mornings he always got up somewhat less amorous than in the evening.

Why?

Seeing that she must have once been so pretty, blonde and joyous, Saudres was not the man she should have selected. She was now fifty-two years of age.

She seemed happy. Ah! if she had only loved him in days gone by; yes, if she had only loved him! And why should she not have loved him, he, Savel, seeing that he loved her so much, yes, she, Madame Saudres!

If only she could have divined something— Had she not divined anything, had she not seen anything, never comprehended anything? But! Then what would she have thought? If he had spoken what would she have answered?

And Savel asked himself a thousand other things. He reviewed his whole life, seeking to grasp again a multitude of details.

He recalled all the long evenings spent at the house of Saudres, when the latter's wife was young and so charming.

He recalled many things that she had said to him, the sweet intonations of her voice, the little significant smiles that meant so much.

He recalled the walks that the three of them had had, along the banks of the Seine, their lunches on the grass on the Sundays, for Saudres was employed at the sub-prefecture. And all at once the distant recollection came to him, of an afternoon spent with her in a little plantation on the banks of the river.

They had set out in the morning, carrying their provisions in baskets. It was a bright spring morning, one of those days which inebriate one. Everything smelt fresh, everything seemed happy. The voices of the birds sounded more joyous, and the flapping of their wings more rapid. They had lunch on the grass, under the willow trees, quite close to the water, which glittered in the sun's rays. The air was balmy, charged with the odors of fresh vegetation; they had drunk the most delicious wines. How pleasant everything was on that day!

After lunch, Saudres went to sleep on the broad of his back, "The best nap he had in his life," said he, when he woke up.

Madame Saudres had taken the arm of Savel, and they had started to walk along the river's bank.

She leaned tenderly on his arm. She laughed and said to him: "I am intoxicated, my friend, I am quite intoxicated." He looked at her, his heart going pitty-pat. He felt himself grow pale, fearful that he had not looked too boldly at her, and that the trembling of his hand had not revealed his passion.

She had decked her head with wild flowers and water-lilies, and she had asked him: "Do you not like to see me appear thus?"

As he did not answer—for he could find nothing to say, he should rather have gone down on his knees—she burst out laughing, a sort of discontented laughter, which she threw straight in his face, saying: "Great goose, what ails you? You might at least speak!"

He felt like crying, and could not even yet find a word to say.

All these things came back to him now, as vividly as on the day when they took place. Why had she said this to him, "Great goose. What ails you! You might at least speak!"

And he recalled how tenderly she had leaned on his arm. And in passing under a shady tree he had felt her ear leaning against his cheek, and he had tilted his head abruptly, for fear that she had not meant to bring their flesh into contact.

When he had said to her: "Is it not time to return?" she darted at him a singular look. "Certainly," she said, "certainly," regarding him at the same time in a curious manner. He had not thought of anything then; and now the whole thing appeared to him quite plain.

"Just as you like, my friend. If you are tired let us go back."

And he had answered: "It is not that I am fatigued; but Saudres has perhaps woke up now."

And she had said: "If you are afraid of my husband's being awake, that is another thing. Let us return."

In returning she remained silent and leaned no longer on his arm. Why?

At that time it had never occurred to him to ask himself "why." Now he seemed to apprehend something that he had not then understood.

What was it?

M. Savel felt himself blush, and he got up at a bound, feeling thirty years younger, believing that he now understood Madame Saudres then to say, "I love you."

Was it possible! That suspicion which had just entered his soul, tortured him. Was it possible that he could not have seen, not have dreamed!

Oh! if that could be true, if he had rubbed against such good fortune without laying hold of it!

He said to himself: "I wish to know. I cannot remain in this state of doubt. I wish to know!" He put on his clothes quickly, dressed in hot haste. He thought: "I am sixty-two years of age, she is fifty-eight; I may ask her that now without giving offense."

He started out.

The Saudres's house was situated on the other side of the street, almost directly opposite his own. He went up to it, knocked, and a little servant came to open the door.

"You there at this hour, ill, Savel! Has some accident happened to you?"

M. Savel responded:

"No, my girl; but go and tell your mistress that I want to speak to her at once."

"The fact is, Madame is preparing her stock of pear-jams for the winter, and she is standing in front of the fire. She is not dressed, as you may well understand."

"Yes, but go and tell her that I wish to see her on an important matter."

The little servant went away, and Savel began to walk, with long, nervous strides, up and down the drawing-room. He did not feel himself the least embarrassed, however. Oh! he was merely going to ask her something, as he would have asked her about some cooking receipt, and that was: "Do you know that I am sixty-two years of age!"

The door opened; and Madame apepared. She was now a gross woman, fat and round, with full cheeks, and a sonorous laugh. She walked with her arms away from her body, and her sleeves tucked up to the shoulders, her bare arms all smeared with sugar juice. She asked, anxiously:

"What is the matter with you, my friend; you are not ill, are you?"

"No, my dear friend; but I wish to ask you one thing, which to me is of the first importance, something which is torturing my heart, and I want you to promise that you will answer me candidly."

She laughed, "I am always candid. Say on."

"Well, then. I have loved you from the first day I ever saw you. Can you have any doubt of this?"

She responded, laughing, with something of her former tone of voice.

"Great goose! what ails you? I knew it well from the very first day!"

Savel began to tremble. He stammered out: "You knew it? Then—"

He stopped.

She asked:

"Then? . . . What?"

He answered:

"Then . . . what would you think? . . . what . . . what. . . . What would you have answered?"

She broke forth into a peal of laughter, which made the sugar juice run off the tips of her fingers on to the carpet.

"I? But you did not ask me anything. It was not for me to make a declaration."

He then advanced a step towards her.

"Tell me . . . tell me. . . . You remember the day when Saudres went to sleep on the grass after lunch . . . when we had walked together as far as the bend of the river, below. . . . "

He waited, expectantly. She had ceased to laugh, and looked at him, straight in the eyes.

"Yes, certainly, I remember it."

He answered, shivering all over.

"Well . . . that day . . . if I had been . . . enterprising . . . what would you have done?"

She began to laugh as only a happy woman can laugh, who has nothing to regret, and responded frankly, in a voice tinged with irony:

"I would have yielded, my friend."

She then turned on her heels and went back to her jam-making.

Savel rushed into the street, cast down, as though he had encountered some great disaster. He walked with giant strides, through the rain, straight on, until he reached the river, without thinking where he was going. When he reached the bank he turned to the right and followed it. He walked a long time, as if urged on by some instinct. His clothes were running with water, his hat was bashed in, as soft as a piece of rag, and dripping like a thatched roof. He walked on, straight in front of him. At last, he came to the place where they had lunched so long, long ago, the recollection of which had tortured his heart. He sat down under the leafless trees, and he wept.

# *thirty-fifth night*

*One of six sailors on ship-leave, he led his companions into one of the better of Marseilles' houses of pleasure, where his companion for the night turned out to be his little . . .*

Having sailed from Havre on the 3rd of May, 1882, for a voyage in the China seas, the square-rigged three-master, *Notre Dame des Vents*, made her way back into the port of Marseilles, on the 8th of August, 1886, after an absence of four years. When she had discharged her first cargo in the Chinese port for which she was bound, she had immediately found a new freight for Buenos Ayres, and from that place had conveyed goods to Brazil.

Other passages, then damage repairs, calms ranging over several months, gales which knocked her out of her course—all the accidents, adventures, and misadventures of the sea, in short—had kept far from her country, this Norman three-master, which had come back to Marseilles with her hold full of tin boxes containing American preserves.

At her departure, she had on board, besides the captain and the mate, fourteen sailors, eight Normans and six Britons. On her return, there were left only five Britons and four Normans; the other Briton had died while on the way; the four Normans having disappeared under various circumstances, had been replaced by two Americans, a negro, and a Norwegian carried off, one evening, from a tavern in Singapore.

The big vessel, with reefed sails and yards crossed over her masts, drawn by a tug from Marseilles, rocking over a sweep of rolling waves which subsided gently on becoming calm, passed in front of the Chateau d'If, then under all the gray rocks of the roadstead, which the setting sun covered with a golden vapor; and she entered the ancient port, in which are packed together, side by side, ships from every part of the world, pell mell, large and small, of every shape and every variety of rigging, soaking like a "bouillabaise" of boats in this basin too limited in extent, full of putrid water, where shells touch each other, rub against each other, and seem to be pickled in the juice of the vessels.

*Notre Dame des Vents* took up her station between an Italian brig and an English schooner, which made way to let this comrade slip in between them; then, when all the formalities of the custom-house and of the port had been complied with, the captain authorized the two-thirds of his crew to spend the night on shore.

It was already dark. Marseilles was lighted up. In the heat of this summer's evening a flavor of cooking with garlic floated over the noisy city, filled with the clamor of voices, of rolling vehicles, of the crackling of whips, and of all the clamors of southern mirth.

As soon as they felt themselves on shore, the ten men, whom the sea had been tossing about for some months past, proceeded along quite slowly with the hesitating steps of persons who are out of their element, unaccustomed to cities, two by two, procession.

They swayed from one side to another as they walked, looked about them, smelling out the lanes opening out on the harbor, rendered feverish by the amorous appetite which had been growing to maturity in their bodies during their last sixty-six days at sea. The Normans strode on in front, led by Célestin Duclos, a tall young fellow, sturdy and waggish, who served as a captain for the others every time they set forth on land. He divined the places worth visiting, found out by-ways after a fashion of his own, and did not take much part in the squabbles so frequent among sailors in seaport towns. But, once he was caught in one, he was afraid of nobody.

After some hesitation as to which of the obscure streets which lead down to the waterside, and from which arise heavy smells, a sort of exhalation from closets, they ought to enter, Célestin gave the preference to a kind of winding passage, where gleamed over the doors projecting lanterns bearing enormous numbers on their rough colored glass. Under the narrow arches at the entrance to the houses, women wearing aprons like servants, seated on straw chairs, rose up on seeing them coming near, taking three steps towards the gutter which separated the street into two halves, and which cut off the path from this file of men, who sauntered along at their leisure, humming and sneering, already getting excited by the vicinity of those dens of prostitutes.

Sometimes, at the end of a hall, appeared, behind a second open door, which presented itself unexpectedly, covered over with dark leather, a big wench, undressed, whose heavy thighs and fat calves abruptly outlined themselves under her coarse white cotton wrapper. Her short petticoat had the appearance of a puffed out girdle; and the soft flesh of her breast, her shoulders, and her arms, made a rosy stain on a black velvet corsage with edgings of gold lace. She kept calling out from her distant corner, "Will you come here, my pretty boys?" and sometimes she would go out herself to catch hold of one of them, and to drag him towards her door with all her strength, fastening on to him like a spider drawing forward an insect bigger than itself. The man, excited by the struggle, would offer a mild resistance, and the rest would stop to look on, undecided between the longing to go in at once and that of lengthening this appetizing promenade. Then when the woman, after desperate efforts, had brought the sailor to the threshold of her abode, in which the entire band would be swallowed up after him, Célestin Duclos, who was a judge of houses of this sort, suddenly exclaimed: "Don't go in there, Marchand! That's not the place."

The man, thereupon, obeying this direction, freed himself with a brutal shake; and the comrades formed themselves into a band once more, pursued by the filthy insults of the exasperated wench, while other women, all along the alley, in front of them, came out past their doors, attracted by the noise, and in hoarse voices threw out to them invitations coupled with promises. They went on, then, more and more stimulated, from the combined effects of the coaxings and the seductions held out as baits to them by the choir of portresses of love all over the upper part of the street, and the ignoble maledictions hurled at them by the choir at the lower end —the despised choir of disappointed wenches. From time, they met another band—soldiers marching along with spurs jingling at their heels—sailors again—isolated citizens—clerks in business houses. On all sides might be seen fresh street, narrow, and studded all over with those equivocal lanterns. They pursued their way still through this labyrinth of squalid habitation, over those greasy pavements through which putrid water was oozing, between those walls filled with women's flesh.

At last, Duclos made up his mind, and, drawing up before a house of rather attractive exterior, made all his companions follow him in there.

## II

THEN followed a scene of thorough going revelry. For four hours the six sailors gorged themselves with love and wine. Six months' pay was thus wasted.

In the principal room in the tavern they were installed as masters, gazing with malignant glances at the ordinary customers, who were seated at the little tables in the corners, where one of the girls, who was left free to come and go, dressed like a big baby or a singer at a café-concert, went about serving them, and then seated herself near them. Each man, on coming in, had selected his partner, whom he kept all the evening, for the vulgar taste is not changeable. They had drawn three tables close up to them; and, after the first bumper, the procession divided into two parts, increased by as many women as there were seamen, had formed itself anew on the staircase. On the wooden steps, the four feet of each couple kept tramping for some time, while this long file of lovers got swallowed up behind the narrow doors leading into the different rooms.

Then they came down again to have a drink, and, after they had returned to the rooms descended the stairs once more.

Now, almost intoxicated, they began to howl. Each of them, with bloodshot eyes, and his chosen female companion on his knee, sang or bawled, struck the table with his fist, shouted while swilling wine down his throat, set free the human brute. In the midst of them, Célestin Duclos, pressing close to him, a big damsel with red cheeks, who sat astride over his legs, gazed at her ardently. Less tipsy than the others, not that he had taken less drink, he was as yet occupied with other thoughts, and, more tender than his comrades, he tried to get up a chat. His thoughts wandered a little, escaped him, and then came back, and disappeared again, without allowing him to recollect exactly what he meant to say.

"What time—what time—how long are you here?"

"Six months," the girl answered.

He seemed to be satisfied with her, as if this were a proof of good conduct, and he went on questioning her:

"Do you like this life?"

She hesitated, then in a tone of resignation.

"One gets used to it. It is not more worrying than

any other kind of life. To be a servant-girl or else a scrub is always a nasty occupation."

He looked as if he also approved of the truthful remark.

"You are not from this place?" said he.

She answered merely by shaking her head.

"Do you come from a distance?"

She nodded, still without opening her lips.

"Where is it you come from?"

She appeared to be thinking, to be searching her memory, then said falteringly:

"From Perpignan."

He was once more perfectly satisfied, and said:

"Ah! yes."

In her turn she asked:

"And you, are you a sailor?"

"Yes, my beauty."

"Do you come from a distance?"

"Ah! yes. I have seen countries, ports, and everything."

"You have been round the world, perhaps?"

"I believe you, twice rather than once."

Again she seemed to hesitate, to search in her brain for something that she had forgotten, then, in a tone somewhat different, more serious:

"Have you met many ships in your voyages?"

"I believe you, my beauty."

"You did not happen to see the *Notre Dame des Vents?*"

He chuckled:

"No later than last week."

She turned pale, all the blood leaving her cheeks, and asked: "Is that true, perfectly true?"

" 'Tis true as I tell you."

"Honor bright! you are not telling me a lie?"

He raised his hand.

"Before God, I'm not!" said he.

"Then do you know whether Célestin Duclos is still on her?"

He was astonished, uneasy, and wished, before answering, to learn something further.

"Do you know him?"

She became distrustful in turn.

"Oh! 'tis not myself—'tis a woman who is acquainted with him."

"A woman from this place?"

"No, from a place not far off."

"In the street?"

"No, not in the street."

"What sort of a woman?"

"Why, then, a woman—a woman like myself."

"What has she to say to him, this woman?"

"I believe she is a country-woman of his."

They stared into one another's hand, watching one another, feeling, divining that something of a grave nature was going to arise between them.

He resumed:

"I could see her there, this woman."

"What would you say to her?"

"I would say to her—I would say to her—that I had seen Célestin Duclos."

"He is quite well—isn't he?"

"As well as you or me—he is a strapping young fellow."

She became silent again, trying to collect her ideas; then slowly:

"Where has the *Notre Dame des Vents* gone to?"

"Why, just to Marseilles."

She could not repress a start.

"Is that really true?"

" 'Tis really true."

"Do you know Duclos?"

"Yes, I do know him."

She still hesitated; then in a very gentle tone:

"Good! That's good!"

"What do you want with him?"

"Listen!—you will tell him—nothing!"

He stared at her, more and more perplexed. At last, he put this question to her:

"Do you know him, too, yourself?"

"No," said she.

"Then what do you want with him?"

Suddenly, she made up her mind what to do, left her seat, rushed over to the bar where the landlady of the tavern presided, seized a lemon, which she tore open, and shed its juice into a glass, then she filled this glass with pure water, and carrying it across to him:

"Drink this!"

"Why?"

"To make it pass for wine. I will talk to you afterwards."

He drank it without further protest, wiped his lips with the back of his hand, then observed:

"That's all right. I am listening to you."

"You will promise not to tell him you have seen me, or from whom you learned what I am going to tell you. You must swear not to do so."

He raised his hand.

"All right. I swear I will not."

"Before God?"

"Before God."

"Well, you will tell him that his father died, that his mother died, that his brother died, the whole three in one month, of typhoid fever, in January, 1883—three years and a half ago."

In his turn, he felt all his blood set in motion through his entire body, and for a few seconds he was so much overpowered that he could make no reply; then he began to doubt what she had told him, and asked:

"Are you sure?"

"I am sure."

"Who told it to you?"

She laid her hands on his shoulders, and looking at him out of the depths of her eyes:

"You swear not to blab?"

"I swear that I will not."

"I am his sister!"

He uttered that name in spite of himself:

"Francoise?"

She contemplated him once more with a fixed stare, then, excited by a wild feeling of terror, a sense of profound horror, she faltered in a very low tone, almost speaking into his mouth:

"Oh! oh! it is you, Célestin."

They no longer stirred, their eyes riveted in one another.

Around them, his comrades were still yelling. The sounds made by glasses, by fists, by heels keeping time to the choruses, and the shrill cries of the women, mingled with the roar of their songs.

He felt her leaning on him, clasping him, ashamed and frightened, his sister. Then, in a whisper, lest anyone might hear him, so hushed that she could scarcely catch his words:

"What a misfortune! I have made a nice piece of work of it!"

The next moment, her eyes filled with tears, and she faltered:

"Is that my fault?"

But, all of a sudden, he said:

"So then, they are dead?"

"They are dead."

"The father, the mother, and the brother?"

"The three in one month, and I told you. I was left by myself with nothing but my clothes, for I was in debt to the apothecary and the doctor and for the funeral of the three, and had to pay what I owed with the furniture.

"After that I went as a servant to the house of Mait'e Cacheux—you know him well—the cripple. I was just fifteen at the time, for you went away when I was not quite fourteen. I tripped with him. One is so senseless when one is young. Then I went as a nursery-maid to the notary who debauched me also, and brought me to Havre, where he took a room for me.

After a little while, he gave up coming to see me. For three days I lived without eating a morsel of food; and then, not being able to get employment, I went to a house, like many others. I, too, have seen different places—ah! and dirty places! Rouen, Evreux, Lille, Bordeaux, Perpignan, Nice, and then Marseilles, where I am now!"

The tears started from her eyes, flowed over her nose, wet her cheeks, and trickled into her mouth.

She went on:

"I thought you were dead, too?—my poor Célestin."

He said:

"I would not have recognized you myself—you were such a little thing then, and here you are so big!—but how is it that you did not recognize me?"

She answered with a despairing movement of her hands:

"I see so many men that they all seem to me alike."

He kept his eyes still fixed on her intently, oppressed by an emotion that dazed him, and filled him with such pain as to make him long to cry like a little child that has been whipped. He still held her in his arms, while she sat astride on his knees, with his open hands against the girl's back; and now by sheer dint of looking continually at her, he at length recognized her, the little sister left behind in the country with all those whom she had seen die, while he had been tossing on the seas. Then, suddenly taking between his big seaman's paws this head found once more, he began to kiss her, as one kisses kindred flesh. And after that, sobs, a man's deep sobs, heaving like great bellows, rose up in his throat, resembling the hiccoughs of drunkenness.

He stammered:

"And this is you—this is you, Francoise—my little Francoise!"—

Then, all at once, he sprang up, began swearing in an awful voice, and struck the table such a blow with his fists that the glasses were knocked down and smashed. After that, he advanced three steps, staggered, stretched out his arms, and fell on his face. And he rolled on the ground, crying out, beating the floor with his hands and feet, and uttering such groans that they seemed like a death-rattle.

All those comrades of his stared at him, and laughed.

"He's not a bit drunk," said one.

"He ought to be put to bed," said another. "If he goes out, we'll all be run in together."

Then, as he had money in his pockets, the landlady offered to let him have a bed, and his comrades, themselves so much intoxicated that they could not stand upright, hoisted him up the narrow stairs to the apartment of the woman who had just been in his company, and who remained sitting on a chair, at the foot of that bed of crime, weeping quite as freely as he had wept, until the morning dawned.

# *thirty-sixth night*

*A gay bachelor, he picked up a young thing to help him celebrate his fortieth birthday, and the next morning found his own portrait, as he was twenty years ago, on her mantlepiece— After that the bachelor became a hermit.*

W E HAD GONE with some friends, to see the old hermit installed on an antique mound covered with tall trees, in the midst of the great plain which extends from Cannes to La Napoule.

On our return we discussed those strange lay solitaries, numerous in former times, but now a vanished race. We tried to find out the moral causes, and sought to determine the nature of the griefs which in bygone days had driven men into solitudes.

All of a sudden one of our companions said:

"I have known two solitaries—a man and a woman. The woman must be living still. She dwelt, five years ago, on the ruins of a mountain top absolutely deserted on the coast of Corsica, fifteen or twenty kilometers away from every house. She lived there with a maid-servant. I went to see her. She had certainly been a distinguished woman of the world. She received me with politeness and even in a gracious manner, but I know nothing about her, and I could find out nothing about her.

"As for the man, let me tell you about him: Look round! You see over there that peaked woody mountain which stands by itself behind La Napoule in front of the summits of the Esterel; it is called in the district Snake Mountain. There is where my solitary lived within the walls of a little antique temple about a dozen years ago.

Having heard about him, I resolved to make his acquaintance, and I set out for Cannes on horseback one March morning. Leaving my steed at the inn at La Napoule, I commenced climbing on foot that singular cave, about one hundred and fifty perhaps, or two hundred meters in height, and covered with aromatic plants, especially cysti, whose odor is so sharp and penetrating that it irritates you and causes you discomfort. The soil is stony, and you can see gliding over the pebbles long adders which disappear in the grass. Hence this well-deserved appellation of Snake Mountain. On certain days, the reptiles seem to spring into existence under your feet when you climb the declevity exposed to the rays of the sun. They are so numerous that you no longer venture to go on, and experience a strange sense of uneasiness, not fear, for those creatures are harmless, but a sort of mysterious terror. I had several times the peculiar sensation of climbing a sacred mountain of antiquity, a fantastic hill perfumed and mysterious, covered with cysti and inhabited by serpents and crowned with a temple.

This temple still exists. They told me, at any rate, that it was a temple; for I did not seek to know more about it so as not to destroy the illusion.

So then, one March morning, I climbed up there under the pretext of admiring the country. On reaching the top, I perceived, in fact, walls and a man sitting on a stone. He was scarcely more than forty years of age, though his hair was quite white; but his beard was still almost black. He was fondling a cat which had cuddled itself upon his knees, and did not seem to mind me. I took a walk around the ruins, one portion of which covered over and shut in by means of branches, straw, grass and stones, was inhabited by him, and I made my way towards the place which he occupied.

The view here is splendid. On the right is the Esterel with its peaked summit strangely carved, then the boundless sea stretching as far as the distant coast of Italy with its numerous capes, facing Cannes, the Lerins Islands green and flat, which look as if they were floating, and the last of which shows in the direction of the open sea an old castellated fortress with battlemented towers built in the very waves.

Then, commanding a view of green mountain-side where you could see, at an equal distance, like innumerable eggs laid on the edge of the shore the long chaplet of villas and white villages built among the trees rose the Alps, whose summits are still shrouded in a hood of snow.

I murmured:

"Good heavens, this is beautiful!"

The man raised his head, and said:

"Yes, but when you see it every day, it is monstrous."

Then he spoke, he chatted, and tired himself with talking—my solitary, I detained him.

I did not tarry long that day, and only endeavored to ascertain the color of misanthropy. He created on me especially the impression of being bored with other people, weary of everything, hopelessly disillusioned and disgusted with himself as well as the rest.

I left him after a half-hour's conversation. But I came back, eight hours later, and once again in the following week, then every week, so that before two months we were friends.

Now, one evening at the close of May, I decided that the moment had arrived, and I brought provisions in order to dine with him on Snake Mountain.

It was one of those evenings of the South so odorous in that country where flowers are cultivated just as wheat is in the North, in that country where every essence that perfumes the flesh and the dress of women is manufactured, one of those evenings when the breath of the innumerable orange-trees with which the gardens and all the recesses of the dales are planted, excite and cause languor so that old men have dreams of love.

My solitary received me with manifest pleasure. He willingly consented to share in my dinner.

I made him drink a little wine, to which he had ceased to be accustomed. He brightened up and began to talk about his past life. He had always resided in Paris, and

273

had, it seemed to me, lived a gay bachelor's life.

I asked him abruptly:

"What put into your head this funny notion of going to live on the top of a mountain?"

"Her! it was because I got the most painful shock that a man can experience. But why hide from you this misfortune of mine? It will make you pity me, perhaps! And then—I have never told anyone—never—and I would like to know, for once, what another thinks of it, and how he judges it."

"Born in Paris, brought up in Paris, I grew to manhood and spent my life in that city. My parents had left me an income of some thousands of francs a year, and I procured as a shelter, a modest and tranquil place which enabled me to pass as wealthy for a bachelor.

"I had, since my youth, led a bachelor's life. You know what that is. Free and without family, resolved not to take a legitimate wife, I passed at one time three months with one, at another time six months with another, then a year without a companion, taking as my prey the mass of women who are either to be had for the asking or bought.

"This every day, or, if you like the phrase better, commonplace, existence agreed with me, satisfied my natural tastes for changes and silliness. I lived on the boulevards, in theaters and cafés, always out of doors, always without a regular home, though I was comfortably housed. I was one of those thousands of beings who let themselves float like corks, through life, for whom the walls of Paris are the walls of the world, and who have no care about anything, having no passion for anything. I was what is called a good fellow, without accomplishments and without defects. That is all. And I judge myself correctly.

"Then, from twenty to forty years, my existence flowed along slowly or rapidly without any remarkable event. How quickly they pass, the monstrous years of Paris, when none of those memories worth fixing the date of find way into the soul, these long and yet hurried years, trivial and gay, when you eat, drink and laugh without knowing why, your lips stretched out towards all they can taste and all they can kiss, without having a longing for anything. You are young, and you grow old without doing any of the things that others do, without any attachment, any root, any bond, almost without friends, without family, without wife, without children.

"So, gently and quickly, I reached my fortieth year; and in order to celebrate this anniversary, I invited myself to take a good dinner all alone in one of the principal cafés.

"After dinner, I was in doubt as to what I would do. I felt disposed to go to a theater; and then the idea came into my head to make a pilgrimage to the Latin quarters, where I had in former days lived as a law-student. So I made my way across Paris, and without premeditation went in to one of those public-houses where you are served by girls.

"The one who attended at my table was quite young, pretty, and merry-looking. I asked her to take a drink, and she at once consented. She sat down opposite me, and gazed at me with a practiced eye, without knowing

275

with what kind of a male she had to do. She was a fair-haired woman, or rather a fair-haired girl, a fresh, quite fresh young creature, whom you guessed to be rosy and plump under her swelling bodice. I talked to her in that flattering and idiotic style which we always adopt with girls of this sort; and as she was truly charming, the idea suddenly occurred to me to take her with me—always with a view to celebrating my fortieth year. It was neither a long nor difficult task. She was free, she told me, for the past fortnight, and she forthwith accepted my invitation to come and sup with me in the Halles when her work would be finished.

"As I was afraid lest she might give me the slip—you never can tell what may happen, or who may come into those drink-shops, or what wind may blow into a woman's head—I remained there all the evening waiting for her.

"I, too, had been free for the past month or two, and watching this pretty debutante of love going from table to table, I asked myself the question whether it would not be worth my while to make a bargain with her to live with me for some time. I am here relating to you one of those ordinary adventures which occur every day in the lives of men in Paris.

"Excuse me for such gross details. Those who have not loved in a poetic fashion take and choose women, as you choose a chop in a butcher's shop without caring about anything save the quality of their flesh.

"Accordingly, I took her to her own house—for I had a regard for my own sheets. It was a little working-girl's lodgings in the fifth story, clean and poor, and I spent two delightful hours there. This little girl had a certain grace and a rare attractiveness.

"When I was about to leave the room, I advanced towards the mantelpiece in order to place there the stipulated present, after having agreed on a day for a second meeting with the girl, who remained in bed, I got a vague glimpse of a clock without a globe, two flower-vases and two photographs, one of them very old, one of those proofs on glass called daguerreotypes. I carelessly bent forward towards this portrait, and I remained speechless at the sight, too amazed to comprehend. . . . It was my own, the first portrait of myself, which I had got taken in the days when I was a student in the Latin Quarter.

"I abruptly snatched it up to examine it more closely. I did not deceive myself—and I felt a desire to burst out laughing, so unexpected and queer did the thing appear to me.

"I asked:

" 'Who is this gentleman?'

"She replied:

" ' 'Tis my father, whom I did not know. Mamma left it to me, telling me to keep it, as it might be useful to me, perhaps, one day—'

"She hesitated, began to laugh, and went on:

" 'I don't know in what way, upon my word. I don't think he'll care to acknowledge me.'

"My heart went beating wildly, like the mad gallop of a runaway horse. I replaced the portrait, laying it down flat on the mantelpiece. On top of it I placed, without even knowing what I was doing, two notes for a hundred francs, which I had in my pocket, and I rushed away, exclaiming:

" 'We'll meet again soon—by-bye, darling—by-bye.'

"I heard her answering:

" 'Till Tuesday.'

"I was on the dark staircase, which I descended, groping my way down.

"When I got into the open air, I saw that it was raining, and I started at a great pace down some street or other.

"I walked straight on, stupefied, distracted, trying to jog my memory! Was this possible? Yes. I remembered all of a sudden a girl who had written to me, about a month after our rupture, that she was going to have a child by me. I had torn or burned the letter, and had forgotten all about the matter. I should have looked at the woman's photograph over the girl's mantelpiece. But would I have recognized it? It was the photograph of an old woman, it seemed to me.

"I reached the quay. I saw a bench, and sat down on it. It went on raining. People passed from time to time under umbrellas. Life appeared to me odious and revolting, full of miseries, of shames, of infamies deliberate or unconscious. My daughter! . . . I had just perhaps possessed my own daughter! . . . And Paris, this vast Paris, somber, mournful, dirty, sad, black, with all those houses shut up, was full of such things, adulteries, incests, violated children, I recalled to mind what I had been told about bridges haunted by the infamous votaries of vice.

"I had acted, without wishing it, without being aware

278

of it, in a worse fashion than these ignoble beings. I had entered my own daughter's bed!

"I was on the point of throwing myself into the water. I was mad! I wandered about till dawn, then I came back to my own house to think.

"I thereupon did what appeared to me the wisest thing. I desired a notary to send for this little girl, and to ask her under what conditions her mother had given her the portrait of him whom she supposed to be her father, stating that he was intrusted with this duty by a friend.

"The notary executed my commands. It was on her death-bed that this woman had designated the father of her daughter, and in the presence of a priest, whose name was given to me.

"Then, still in the name of this unknown friend, I got half of my fortune sent to this child, about one hundred and forty thousand francs, of which she could only get the income. Then I resigned my employment— and here I am.

"While wandering along this shore, I found this mountain, and I stopped there—up to what time I am unable to say!

"What do you think of me, and of what I have done?"

I replied as I extended my hand towards him:

"You have done what you ought to do. Many others would have attached less importance to this odious fatality."

He went on:

"I know that, but I was nearly going mad on account of it. It seems I had a sensitive soul without ever suspecting it. And now I am afraid of Paris, as believers are bound to be afraid of Hell. I have received a blow on the head—that is all—a blow resembling the fall of a tile when one is passing through the street. I am getting better for some time past."

I quitted my solitary. I was much disturbed by his narrative.

I saw him again twice, then I went away, for I never remain in the South after the month of May.

When I came back in the following year the man was no longer on Snake Mountain; and I have never since heard anything about him.

This is the history of my hermit.

# *thirty-seventh night*

> *A dead woman avenges herself on a living lover. . . .*

THE CEMETERY, crowded with officers, look-ed like a field covered with flowers. The kepis and the red trousers, the stripes and the gold buttons, the shoulder-knots of the staff, the braid of the chasseurs and the hussars, wandered through the midst of the tombs, whose crosses, white or black, opened their mournful arms—their arms of iron, marble, or wood—over the vanished race of the dead.

Colonel Limousin's wife had just been interred. She had been drowned, two days before, while taking a bath. It was over. The clergy had left; but the colonel, supported by two brother-officers, remained standing in front of the pit, at the bottom of which he saw still the oaken coffin, wherein lay, already decomposed, the body of his young wife.

He was almost an old man, tall and thin, with white moustache; and, three years ago, he had married the daughter of a comrade, left an orphan on the death of her father, Colonel Sortis.

The captain and the lieutenant, on whom their commanding officer was leaning, attempted to lead him away. He resisted, his eyes full of tears, which he heroically held back, and murmuring, "No, no, a little while longer!" he persisted in remaining there, his legs bending under him, at the side of that pit, which seemed to him bottomless, an abyss into which had fallen his heart and his life, all that he held dear on earth.

Suddenly, General Ormont came up, seized the colonel by the arm, and dragging him from the spot almost by force said: "Come, come, my old comrade! you must not remain here."

The colonel thereupon obeyed, and went back to his quarters. As he opened the door of his study, he saw a letter on the table. When he took it in his hands, he was near falling with surprise and emotion; he recognized his wife's hand-writing. And the letter bore the post-mark and the date of the same day. He tore open the envelope and read:

"Father,

"Permit me to call you still father, as in days gone by. When you receive this letter, I shall be dead and under the clay. Therefore, perhaps, you may forgive me.

"I do not want to excite your pity or to extenuate my sin. I only want to tell the entire and complete truth, with all the sincerity of a woman who, in an hour's time, is going to kill herself.

"When you married me through generosity, I gave myself to you through gratitude, and I loved you with all my girlish heart. I loved you as I loved my own

282

father—almost as much; and one day, while I sat on your knee, and you were kissing me, I called you 'Father' in spite of myself. It was a cry of the heart, instinctive, spontaneous. Indeed, you were to me a father, nothing but a father. You laughed, and you said to me, 'Address me always in that way, my child; it gives me pleasure.'

"We came to the city; and—forgive me, father—I fell in love. Ah! I resisted long, well, nearly two years—and then I yielded, I sinned, I became a fallen woman.

"And as to him? You will never guess who he is. I am easy enough about that matter, since there were a dozen officers always around me and with me, whom you called my twelve constellations.

"Father, do not seek to know him, and do not hate him. He only did what any man, no matter who, would have done in his place, and then I am sure that he loved me, too, with all his heart.

"But listen! One day we had an appointment in the isle of Becasses—you know the little isle, close to the mill. I had to get there by swimming, and he had to wait for me in a thicket, and then to remain there till nightfall, so that nobody should see him going away. I had just met him when the branches opened, and we saw Philippe, your orderly, who had surprised us. I felt that we were lost, and I uttered a great cry. Thereupon he said to me—he, my lover—'Go, swim back quietly, my darling, and leave me here with this man.'

"I went away so excited that I was near drowning myself, and I came back to you expecting that something dreadful was about to happen.

"An hour later, Philippe said to me in a low tone, in the lobby outside the drawing-room where I met him: 'I am at madame's orders, if she has any letters to give me.' Then I knew that he had sold himself, and that my lover had bought him.

"I gave him some letters, in fact—all my letters—he took them away, and brought me back the answers.

"This lasted about two months. We had confidence in him, as you had confidence in him yourself.

"Now, father, here is what happened. One day, in the same isle which I had to reach by swimming, but this time alone, I found your orderly. This man had been waiting for me; and he informed me that he was going to reveal everything about us to you, and deliver to you the letters which he had kept, stolen, if I did not yield to his desires.

"Oh! father, father, I was filled with fear—a cowardly fear, an unworthy fear, a fear above all of you, who had been so good to me, and whom I had deceived —fear on his account too—you would have killed him —for myself also perhaps! I cannot tell; I was mad, desperate; I thought of once more buying this wretch, who loved me, too—how shameful!

"We are so weak, we women, we lose our heads more easily than you do. And then, when a woman once falls, she always falls lower and lower. Did I know what I was doing? I understood only that one of you two and I were going to die—and I gave myself to this brute.

"You see, father, that I do not seek to excuse myself.

"Then, then—then what I should have foreseen happened—he had the better of me again and again, when he wished, by terrifying me. He, too, has been my lover, like the other, every day. Is not this abominable? And what punishment, father?

"So then it is all over with me. I must die. While I lived, I could not confess such a crime to you. Dead, I dare everything. I could not do otherwise than die— nothing could have washed me clean—I was too polluted. I could no longer love or be loved. It seemed to me that I stained everyone by merely allowing my hand to be touched.

"Presently I am going to take my bath, and I will never come back.

"This letter for you will go to my lover. It will reach him when I am dead, and without anyone knowing anything about it, he will forward it to you, accomplishing my last wishes. And you shall read it on your return from the cemetery.

"Adieu, father! I have no more to tell you. Do whatever you wish, and forgive me."

The colonel wiped his forehead, which was covered with perspiration. His coolness; the coolness of days when he had stood on the field of battle, suddenly came back to him. He rang.

A man-servant made his appearance. "Send in Philippe to me," said he. Then, he opened the drawer of his table.

The man entered almost immediately—a big soldier with red moustache, a malignant look, and a cunning eye.

The colonel looked him straight in the face.

"You are going to tell me the name of my wife's lover."

"But, my colonel—"

The officer snatched his revolver out of the half-open drawer.

"Come! quick! You know I do not jest!"

"Well—my colonel—it is Captain Saint-Albert."

Scarcely had he pronounced his name when a flame flashed between his eyes, and he fell on his face, his forehead pierced by a ball.

# *thirty-eighth night*

*A Baron and his bastard, this story might be called, though, there were also three other little 'children of accidents,' to account for, making four in all. . . .*

As HE DESCENDED the wide staircase of the club, heated like a conservatory, the Baron de Mordiane had left his fur-coat open; therefore, when the huge street-door closed behind him he felt a shiver of intense cold run through him, one of those sudden and painful shivers which make us feel sad, as if we were stricken with grief. Moreover, he had lost some money, and his stomach for some time past had troubled him, no longer permitting him to eat as he liked.

He returned to his own residence; and, all of a sudden, the thought of his great, empty apartment, of his footman asleep in the ante-chamber, of the dressing-room in which the water kept tepid for the evening toilet simmered pleasantly under the chafing-dish heated by gas, and the bed, spacious, antique, and solemn-looking, like a mortuary couch, caused another chill, more mournful still than that of the icy atmosphere, to penetrate to the bottom of his heart, the inmost core of his flesh.

For some years past he had felt weighing down on him that load of solitude which sometimes crushes old bachelors. Formerly, he had been strong, lively, and gay, giving all his days to sport and all his nights to festive gatherings. Now, he had grown dull, and no longer took pleasure in anything. Exercise fatigued him; suppers and even dinners made him ill; women annoyed him as much as they had formerly amused him.

The monotony of evenings all like each other, of the same friends met again in the same place, at the club, of the same game with a good hand and a run of luck, of the same talk on the same topics, of the same witty remarks by the same lips, of the same jokes on the same themes, of the same scandals about the same women, disgusted him so much as to make him feel at times a veritable inclination to commit suicide. He could no longer lead this life regular and inane, so commonplace, so frivolous and so dull at the same time, and he felt a longing for something tranquil, restful, comfortable, without knowing what.

He certainly did not think of getting married, for he did not feel in himself sufficient fortitude to submit to the melancholy, the conjugal servitude, to that hateful existence of two beings, who, always together, knew one another so well that one could not utter a word which the other would not anticipate, could not make a single movement which would not be foreseen, could not have any thought or desire or opinion which would not be divined. He considered that a woman could only be agreeable to see again when you know her but slightly, when there is something mysterious and unexplored attached to her, when she remains disquieting, hidden behind a veil. Therefore, what he would require was a family without family-life, wherein he might spend only a portion of his existence; and, again, he was haunted by the recollection of his son.

For the past year he had been constantly thinking of this, feeling an irritating desire springing up within him to see him, to renew acquaintance with him. He had become the father of this child, while still a young man, in the midst of dramatic and touching incidents. The boy dispatched to the South, had been brought up near Marseilles without ever hearing his father's name.

The latter had at first paid from month to month for the nurture, then for the education and the expense of holidays for the lad, and finally had provided an allowance for him on making a sensible match. A discreet notary had acted as an intermediary without ever disclosing anything.

The Baron de Mordiane accordingly knew merely that a child of his was living somewhere in the neighborhood of Marseilles, that he was looked upon as intelligent and well-educated, that he had married the daughter of an architect and contractor, to whose business he had succeeded. He was also believed to be worth a lot of money.

Why should he not go and see this unknown son without telling his name, in order to form a judgment about him at first and to assure himself that he would be

289

able, in case of necessity, to find an agreeable refuge in this family?

He had acted handsomely towards the young man, had settled a good fortune on him, which had been thankfully accepted. He was, therefore, certain that he would not find himself clashing against any inordinate sense of self-importance; and this thought, this desire, which every day returned to him afresh, of setting out for the South, tantalized him like a kind of itching sensation. A strange self-regarding feeling of affection also attracted him, bringing before his mental vision this pleasant, warm abode by the seaside, where he would meet his young and pretty daughter-in-law, his grandchildren, with outstretched arms, and his son, who would recall to his memory the charming and short-lived adventure of bygone years. He regretted only having given so much money, and that this money had prospered in the young man's hands, thus preventing him from any longer presenting himself in the character of a benefactor.

He hurried along, with all these thoughts running through his brain, and the collar of his fur coat wrapped round his head. Suddenly he made up his mind. A cab was passing; he hailed it, drove home, and there his valet, just roused from a nap, had opened the door.

"Louis," said he, "we start tomorrow evening for Marseilles. We'll remain there perhaps a fortnight. You will make all the necessary preparations."

The train rushed on past the Rhone with its sandbanks, then through yellow plains, bright villages, and a wide expanse of country, shut in by bare mountains, which rose, like bleak ghosts, on the distant horizon.

The Baron de Mordiane, waking up after a night spent in a sleeping compartment of the train, looked at himself, in a melancholy fashion, in the little mirror of his dressing-case. The glaring sun of the South showed him some wrinkles which he had not observed before—a condition of decrepitude unnoticed in the imperfect light of Parisian rooms. He thought, as he examined the corners of his eyes, and saw the rumpled lids, the temples, the skinny forehead:

"Damn it, I've not merely got the gloss taken off— I've become quite an old fogy."

And his desire for rest suddenly increased, with a vague yearning, born in him for the first time, to take his grandchildren on his knees.

About one o'clock in the afternoon, he arrived in a landau which he had hired at Marseilles, in front of one of those houses of Southern France so white, at the end of their avenues of plane-trees that they dazzle us and make our eyes droop. He smiled as he pursued his way along the walk before the house, and reflected:

"Deuce take it! this is a nice place."

Suddenly, a young rogue of five or six made his appearance, starting out of a shrubbery, and remained standing at the side of the path, staring at him with eyes wide open.

Mordiane came over to him:

"Good morrow, my boy."

The brat made no reply.

The baron, then, stooping down, took him up in his arms to kiss him, but, the next moment, suffocated by

the smell of garlic with which the child seemed impregnated all over, he put him back again on the ground,
muttering:

"Oh! it is the gardener's son."

And he proceeded towards the house.

The linen was hanging out to dry on a cord before
the door—shirts and chemises, napkins, dish-cloths,
aprons, and sheets, while a row of socks, hanging from
strings one above the other, filled up an entire window,
like sausages exposed for sale in front of a pork-
butcher's shop.

The baron announced his arrival. A servant-girl appeared, a true servant of the South, dirty and untidy,
with her hair hanging in wisps and falling over her face,
while her petticoat under the accumulation of stains
which had soiled it had retained only a certain uncouth
remnant of its old color, a hue suitable for a country
fair or a mountebank's tights.

He asked:

"Is M. Duchoux at home?"

He had many years ago, in the mocking spirit of a
skeptical man of pleasure, given this name to the found-
ling, in order that it might not be forgotten that he had
been picked up under a cabbage.

The servant-girl asked:

"Do you want M. Duchoux?"

"Yes."

"Well, he is in the big room drawing up his plans."

"Tell him that M. Merlin wishes to speak to him."

She replied, in amazement:

"Hey! go inside then, if you want to see him."

And she bawled out:

"Monsieur Duchoux—a call."

The baron entered, and in a spacious apartment, rendered dark by the windows being half-closed, he indistinctly traced out persons and things, which appeared to him very slovenly looking.

Standing in front of a table laden with articles of every sort, a little bald man was tracing lines on a large sheet of paper.

He interrupted his work, and advanced two steps. His waistcoat left open, his unbuttoned breeches, and his turned-up shirt-sleeves, indicated that he felt hot, and his muddy shoes showed that it had rained hard some days before.

He asked with a very pronounced southern accent:

"Whom have I the honor of—?"

"Monsieur Merlin—I came to consult you about a purchase of building-ground."

"Ha! ha! very well!"

And Duchoux, turning towards his wife, who was knitting in the shade:

"Clear off a chair, Josephine."

Mordaine then saw a young woman, who appeared already old, as women look old at twenty-five in the provinces, for want of attention to their persons, regular washing, and all the little cares bestowed on feminine toilet which make them fresh, and preserve, till the age of fifty, the charm and beauty of the sex. With a neckerchief over her shoulders, her hair clumsily braided —though it was lovely hair, thick and black, you could see that it was badly brushed—she stretched out towards a chair hands like those of a servant, and removed an infant's robe, a knife, a fag-end of packed-bread, an empty flower-pot, and a greasy plate left on the seat, which she then moved over towards the visitor.

He sat down, and presently noticed that Duchoux's work-table had on it, in addition to the books and papers, two salads recently gathered, a wash-hand basin, a hair-brush, a napkin, a revlover, and a number of cups which had not been cleaned.

The architect perceived this look, and said with a smile:

"Excuse us! there is a little disorder in the room—it is owing to the children."

And he drew across his chair, in order to chat with his client.

"So then you are looking out for a piece of ground in the neighborhood of Marseilles?"

His breath, though not close to the baron, carried towards the latter that odor of garlic which the people of the South exhale as flowers do their perfume.

Mordiane asked:

"Is it your son that I met under the plane-trees?"

"Yes. Yes, the second."

"You have two of them?"

"Three, monsieur; one a year."

And Duchoux looked full of pride.

The baron was thinking:

"If they all have the same perfume, their nursery must be a real conservatory."

He continued:

"Yes, I would like a nice piece of ground near the

sea, on a little solitary strip of beach—"

Thereupon Duchoux proceeded to explain. He had ten, twenty, fifty, a hundred, or more pieces of ground of the kind required, at different prices and suited to different tastes. He talked just as a fountain flows, smiling, self-satisfied, wagging his bald round head.

And Mordiane was reminded of a little woman, fair-haired, slight, with a somewhat melancholy look, and a tender fashion of murmuring, "My darling," of which the mere remembrance made the blood stir in his veins. She had loved him passionately, madly, for three months; then, becoming pregnant in the absence of her husband, who was a governor of a colony, she had run away and concealed herself, distracted with despair and terror, till the birth of the child, which Mordaine carried off one summer's evening, and which they had not laid eyes on afterwards.

She died of consumption three years later, over there, in the colony of which her husband was governor, and to which she had gone across to join him. And here, in front of him, was their son, who was saying, in the metallic tones with which he rang out his closing words:

"This piece of ground, monsieur, is a rare chance—"

And Mordiane recalled the other voice, light as the touch of a gentle breeze, as it used to murmur:

"My darling, we shall never part—"

And he remembered that soft, deep, devoted glance in those eyes of blue, as he watched the round eye, also blue, but vacant, of this ridiculous little man, who, for all that, bore a resemblance to his mother.

Yes, he looked more and more like her every moment—like her in accent, in movement, in his entire deportment—he was like her in the way an ape is like a man; but still he was hers; he displayed a thousand external characteristics peculiar to her, though in an unspeakably distorted, irritating, and revolting form.

The baron was galled, haunted as he was all of a sudden by this resemblance, horrible, each instant growing stronger, exasperating, maddening, torturing him like a nightmare, like a weight of remorse.

He stammered out:

"When can we look at this piece of ground together?"

"Why, tomorrow, if you like."

"Yes, tomorrow. At what hour?"

"One o'clock."

"All right."

The child he had met in the avenue appeared before the open door, exclaiming:

"Dada!"

There was no answer.

Mordiane had risen up with a longing to escape, to run off, which made his legs tremble. This "dada" had hit him like a bullet. It was to *him* that it was addressed, it was intended for him, this "dada," smelling of garlic—this "dada" of the South.

Oh! how sweet had been the perfume exhaled by her, his sweetheart of bygone days!

Duchoux saw him to the door.

"This house is your own?" said the baron.

"Yes, monsieur; I bought it recently. And I am proud of it. I am a child of accident, monsieur, and I don't want to hide it; I am proud of it. I owe noth-

ing to anyone; I am the son of my own efforts; I owe
everything to myself."

The little boy, who remained on the threshold, kept
still exclaiming, though at some distance away from
them:

"Dada!"

Mordiane, shaking with a shivering fit, seized with
panic, fled as one flies away from a great danger.

"He is going to guess who I am, to recognize me,"
he thought. "He is going to take me in his arms, and
then call out to me, 'Dada,' and give me a kiss perfumed with garlic."

"Tomorrow, monsieur."

"Tomorow, at one o'clock."

The landau rolled over the white road.

"Coachman! to the railway-station!"

And he heard two voices, one far away and sweet, the
faint, sad voice of the dead, saying: "My darling," and
the other sonorous, sing-song, frightful, bawling out,
"Dada," just as people bawl out, "Stop him!" when
a thief is flying through the street.

Next evening, as he entered the club, the Count
d'Etreillis said to him:

"We have not seen you for the last three days. Have
you been ill?"

"Yes, a little unwell. I get headaches from time to
time."

# *thirty-ninth night*

*One way to get a woman is to dream about her. The trick, however, is to dream about the right woman. . . .*

IT WAS AT THE END of a dinner-party of men, that hour of interminable cigars and incessant sips of brandy, the smoke and the torpid warmth of digestion and the slight confusion of heads generated by the consumption of too much food and by the absorption of too many different liquors.

They were talking about magnetism, about Donato's tricks, and about Doctor Charcot's experiences. All of a sudden, those men, so skeptical, so happy-go-lucky, so indifferent to religion of every sort, began telling stories about strange occurrences, incredible things which nevertheless had really happened, they contended, falling back into superstitions, beliefs, cling to these last remnants of the marvelous, becoming devotees of this mystery of magnetism, defending it in the name of science. There was only one person who smiled, a vigorous young fellow, a great pursuer of girls in the town, and a hunter also of frisky matrons, in whose mind there was so much incredulity about everything that he would not even enter upon a discussion of such matters.

He repeated with a sneer:

"Humbug! humbug! humbug! We need not discuss Donato, who is merely a very smart juggler. As for M. Charcot, who is said to be a remarkable man of science, he produces on me the effect of those story-tellers of the school of Edgar Poe, who end by going mad through constantly reflecting on queer cases of insanity. He has set forth some nervous phenomena, which are unexplained and inexplicable; he makes his way into that unknown region which men explore every day, and not being able to comprehend what he sees, he remembers perhaps too well the explanations of certain mysteries given by speaking on these subjects, that would be quite a different thing from your repetition of what he says."

The words of the unbeliever were listened to with a kind of pity, as if he had blasphemed in the midst of an assembly of monks.

One of these gentlemen exclaimed:

"And yet miracles were performed in former days."

But the other replied: "I deny it. Why cannot they be performed any longer?"

Thereupon, each man referred to some fact, or some fantastic presentiment, or some instance of souls communicating with each other across space, or some case of secret influences produced by one being or another. And they asserted, they maintained that these things had actually occurred, while the skeptic went on repeating energetically:

"Humbug! humbug! humbug!"

At last he rose up, threw away his cigar, and with his hands in his pockets, said: "Well, I, too, am going to relate to you two stories, and then I will explain them to you. Here they are:

"In the little village of Etretat, the men, who are all seafaring folk, go every year to Newfoundland to fish for cod. Now, one night the little son of one of these fishermen woke up with a start, crying out that his father was dead. The child was quieted, and again he woke up exclaiming that his father was drowned. A month later the news came that his father had, in fact, been swept off the deck of his smack by a billow. The widow then remembered how her son had wakened up and spoken of his father's death. Everyone said it was a miracle, and the affair caused a great sensation. The dates were compared, and it was found that the accident and the dream had very nearly coincided, whence they drew the conclusion that they had happened on the same night and at the same hour. And there is the mystery of magnetism."

The story-teller stopped suddenly.

Thereupon, one of those who had heard him, much affected by the narrative, asked:

"And can you explain this?"

"Perfectly monsieur. I have discovered the secret. The circumstance surprised me and even embarrassed me very much; but, I, you see, do not believe on principle. Just as others begin by believing, I begin by doubting; and when I don't at all understand, I continue to deny that there can be any telegraphic communication between souls, certain that my own sagacity will be enough to explain it. Well, I have gone on inquiring into the matter, and I have ended, by dint of questioning all the wives of the absent seamen, in convincing myself that not a week passed without one of themselves or their children dreaming and declaring when they woke up that the father was drowned. The horrible and continual fear of this accident makes them always talk about it. Now, if one of these frequent predictions coincides, by a very simple chance, with the death of the person referred to, people at once declare it to be a miracle; for they suddenly lose sight of all the other predictions of misfortune that have remained unconfirmed. I have myself known fifty cases where the persons who made the prediction forgot all about it in a week afterwards. But, if in fact the man was dead, then the recollection of the thing is immediately revived, and people will be ready to believe in the intervention of God, according to some, and magnetism, according to others."

One of the smokers remarked:

"What you say is right enough; but what about your second story?"

"Oh! my second story is a very delicate matter to relate. It is to myself it happened, and so I don't place any great value on my own view of the matter. One is never a good judge in a case where he is one of the parties concerned. At any rate, here it is:

"Among my acquaintances in society there was a young woman on whom I had never bestowed a thought, whom I had never even looked at attentively, never taken any notice of, as the saying is.

"I classed her among the women of no importance, though she was not quite bad-looking; in fact, she appeared to me to possess eyes, a nose, a mouth, some sort of hair—just a colorless type of countenance. She was one of those beings on whom one only thinks by accident, without taking any particular interest in the individual, and who never excites desire.

"Well, one night, as I was writing some letters by my own fireside before going to bed, I was conscious, in the midst of that train of sensual images that sometimes float before one's brain in moments of idle reverie, while I held the pen in my hand, of a kind of light breath passing into my soul, a little shudder of the heart, and immediately, without reason, without any logical connection of thought, I saw distinctly, saw as if I touched her, saw from head to foot, uncovered, this young woman for whom I had never cared save in the most superficial manner when her name happened to recur to my mind. And all of a sudden I discovered in her a heap of qualities which I had never before observed, a sweet charm, a fascination that made me languish; she awakened in me that sort of amorous uneasiness which sends me in pursuit of a woman. But I did not remain thinking of her long. I went to bed and was soon asleep. And I dreamed.

"You have all had these strange dreams which render you masters of the impossible, which open to you doors that cannot be passed through, unexpected joys, impenetrable arms?

"Which of us in these agitated, exciting, palpitating slumbers, has not held, clasped, embraced, possessed with

302

an extraordinary acuteness of sensation, the woman with whom our minds were occupied? And have you ever noticed what superhuman delight these good fortunes of dreams bestow upon us? Into what mad intoxication they cast you! with what passionate spasms they shake you; and with what infinite, caressing, penetrating tenderness they fill your heart for her whom you hold fainting and hot in that adorable and bestial illusion which seems so like reality!

"All this I felt with unforgettable violence. This woman was mine, so much mine that the pleasant warmth of her skin remained between my fingers, the odor of her skin remained in my brain, the taste of her kisses remained on my lips, the sound of her voice lingered in my ears, the touch of her clasp still clung to my side, and the burning charm of her tenderness still gratified my senses long after my exquisite but disappointing awakening.

"And three times the same night I had a renewal of my dream.

"When the day dawned she beset me, possessed me, haunted my brain and my flesh to such an extent that I no longer remained one second without thinking of her.

"At last, not knowing what to do, I dressed myself and went to see her. As I went up the stairs to her apartment, I was so much overcome by emotion that I trembled, and my heart panted; I was seized with vehement desire from head to foot.

"I entered the apartment. She rose up the moment she heard my name pronounced; and suddenly our eyes

303

met in a fixed look of revealing astonishment.

"I sat down.

"I uttered in a faltering tone some commonplaces which she seemed not to hear. I did not know what to say or to do. Then, abruptly, I flung myself upon her; seizing her with both arms; and my entire dream was accomplished so quickly, so easily, so madly, that I suddenly began to doubt whether I was really awake. She was, after this, my mistress for two years."

"What conclusion do you draw from it?" said a voice. The story-teller seemed to hesitate.

"The conclusion I draw from it—well, by Jove, the conclusion is that it was just a coincidence! And, in the next place, who can tell? Perhaps it was some glance of hers which I had not noticed and which came back that night to me—one of those mysterious and unconscious evocations of memory which often bring before us things ignored by our own consciousness, unperceived by our minds!"

"Let that be just as you wish it," said one of his table companions, when the story was finished, "but if you don't believe in magnetism after that, you are an ungrateful fellow, my dear boy!"

# fortieth night

> *Harlots share many of the traits of their more respectable sisters. They sometimes even bear children. How they rear them is another matter. . . .*

WE MOVED OVER into the garden for our after dinner coffee, and the conversation drifted to light women. What else is there for a lot of men to talk about?

"Ah, those diminutive darlings on their towering red heels!" exclaimed Pierre. "But one of them reminds me of a rather choice incident." And he began his story.

"One evening last winter I sank into one of those awful spells of depression that sometimes take hold of one, body and soul. I was home all alone and I knew that if I surrendered myself to the feeling I would undergo one of those crises of sadness that, if they are repeated too often, end up in suicide.

"I therefore slipped into my overcoat and went out, without in the least knowing what I was going to do. I walked to the boulevards and strolled past the half-empty cafes, for it was raining, or rather misting, and the drizzle dampened one's spirit as well as one's clothes. It wasn't strong enough to cause passersby to seek shelter in doorways; it was one of those rains that are so fine that one does not feel the drops, one of those humid rains that deposit tiny beads of moisture on you and soon cover everything with a froth of icy water.

"What could I possibly do to kill time? I walked and walked, all the time trying to think of some place where I could spend an hour or two, and discovering, to my astonishment, that there is not a place of amusement to go to of an evening, in all of Paris. Finally I made up my mind to drift into the Folies-Bergères, that amusing market-place of light women.

"There were not many people in the big music-hall. In the long horseshoe promenade were only a few stragglers of small means, whose common extraction was flagrantly depicted by their walk, their clothes, the cut of their hair and beards, their hats, their complexions. Once in a while the eye rested on some well-groomed fellow whose clothes looked as if they belonged to him.

"As for the women, they were the same one always meets there. Awful women, homely, fagged out and flabby, walking about with the look of the hunter in their eyes and a ridiculous expression of haughty contempt on their faces. I wonder why they always wear that silly expression? I was thinking that not one of those flabby creatures, puffy in some places and emaciated in others, with big stomachs and thin legs, was worth the louis she has a hard time getting, after she has asked five.

"But suddenly I saw a little woman who looked really

nice and attractive. She wasn't exactly youthful, but she seemed fresh and piquant. I stopped her and, in a foolish way, without a thought, made my price for the night. I did not want to go back to my lonely abode and preferred the company and embrace of this jade.

"So I followed her. She lived in a great big house in the rue des Martyrs. The gas was out in the hall when we arrived. I walked up the stairs slowly, guided by the swish of her skirts and lighting matches as I went. I stumbled many times on the rickety steps and inwardly cursed my foolishness.

"She stopped on the fourth floor and after she had closed the front door behind us, she turned to me and asked:

" 'So you're going to stay with me all night?'

" 'Why, yes,' I replied, 'that was the agreement, wasn't it?'

"It's all right, dear. I only wanted to know. Just wait here, I'll be back in a minute.'

"And she left me standing in the dark.

"I heard her shut two doors and thought I distinguished the sound of voices. This surprised and worried me. The idea of a bully crossed my mind. But, as I have a strong right arm, I thought to myself: 'Well, let come what may.'

"I listened with the greatest attention.

"Somebody was moving about on tiptoe and with infinite precautions. Another door opened and I thought again that I heard a whispered conversation. Presently she re-entered the room with a candle in her hand.

" 'Come in,' she said.

"This speech meant taking possession of the premises for the time being. I went in, and passing through a dining-room that only existed for show, I entered into a bedroom that differed in no way from the usual room of that sort, a bedroom with repp curtains and a silk counterpane that bore several suspicious stains.

"She continued:

" 'Make yourself comfortable, dear.'

"I eyed the room doubtfully, but discovered nothing unusual about it. She disrobed so quickly that she was in bed before I had time to remove my overcoat. She laughed:

" 'Why, what's the matter with you? Have you been changed into a pillar of salt? Hurry up.'

"I imitated her alacrity and soon joined her.

"Five minutes later I was crazy to get out of that bed and go home. But the overpowering sensation of depression and lassitude that had overtaken me earlier in the evening, robbed me of all energy to get up, in spite of the keen disgust I felt for this public bed. The sensual spell which this woman had cast over me, beneath the glare of the music-hall lights, vanished in my arms and nothing remained save the vulgar courtesan, similar to all her sisters and whose kisses smelled of garlic.

"I began to talk to her.

" 'Have you been here long?' I asked.

" 'Six months last January,' she replied.

" 'Where did you live before?'

" 'In the rue Clauzel. But I left there because the janitress was mean to me.'

"And she started to tell me a long story about how

308

the janitress had gossiped about her and maligned her.

"But, all of a sudden, I heard a noise near the head of the bed. First it was a sigh and then a distinct sound, like someone moving on a chair.

"I sat bolt upright in bed and asked:

" 'What's that noise?'

"With perfect calm she replied:

" 'Don't worry, dear, it's the woman in the next flat. The walls are so thin you can hear everything. What rotten houses these are. They're made of paper.'

"My inertia was so strong that I slid back under the bed-clothes; and we resumed our conversation.

"Worried by the foolish curiosity that impels us men to question these women about their first false step, to lift the veil on their first mistake, as if we wished to find a distant trace of innocence, whereby we might love them in the recollection of their past modesty and candor, I pressed her with questions regarding her first lovers.

"I knew that she would lie to me. But what did it matter? Among all her lies I might discover something touching and true.

" 'Now, tell me who he was,' I demanded.

" 'He was a boating man, dear.'

" 'Ah! Tell me about it. Where were you?'

" 'I was at Argenteuil.'

" 'What were you doing there?'

" 'I was a waitress in a restaurant.'

" 'What restaurant?'

" 'At the "Sweet Water Sailor." Do you know it?'

" 'Why yes, Bonafan's the proprietor.'

" 'Yes, that's it.'

" 'And how did the boating-man court you?'

" 'While I was making his bed. He got the best of me.'

"But I suddenly recalled to mind the theory of a friend of mine, a physician, who was at the same time a philosopher and an observer, and whose work in a large hospital brought him in daily contact with ill-famed women and ruined girls, with all the misery and shame to which womankind is subjected by men who have money to spend.

" 'Always,' he had said to me, 'always a girl is ruined by a man of her own class in life. I've volumes of observations on the subject. People accuse the rich of gathering the flower of innocence of poor young girls. It is not true. The rich play second-fiddle to the others and if they gather any flower at all, it's only the second efflorescence.'

"So, turning to my companion, I began to laugh.

" 'Oh, yes, I swear he was, dear.'

" 'You are lying. Tell me everything.'

"She seemed astonished and hesitated.

"I continued:

" 'I'm something of a sorcerer, fair one; I'm a somnambulist. If you do not tell me the truth, I'll put you to sleep and make you give up your secret.'

"She was scared, for she was stupid, as all women of that kind are.

" 'How did you guess?' she stammered.

" 'Go ahead now,' I retorted.

" 'Oh, the first time was hardly anything. It was at

the county fair. The restaurant-keeper had engaged an extra "chef," M. Alexandre. As soon as he arrived he turned the place upside down. He ordered every one around from the boss to the kitchen-maid, as if he were a king— He was a big, fine-looking man, who couldn't keep quiet a minute and who kept yelling all the time: "Bring me some eggs, some butter, some madeira!" And we had to bring the things on the run, too, or he'd say things that made us blush under our very skirts.

" 'After the day's work was done, he sat down and smoked his pipe in front of the door. And as I was passing with a whole lot of dishes he called to me and said: "Come on, kid, walk down to the river with me and show me the place, will you?" '

" 'I, like a fool, went with him, and hardly had we reached the river before he got the best of me. It all happened so quickly that I didn't know what he was doing. He left by the nine o'clock train that night and I never saw him again.'

" 'Was that all?' I asked.

" 'Oh!' she stammered, 'I really think he's the father of Florentin!'

" 'Who's Florentin?' said I.

" 'He's my boy,' she replied.

" 'Ah! I see. And you made the boating-man believe that he was his father, I suppose?'

" 'Why, certainly!'

" 'Did the boating-man have money?'

" 'Yes, he settled an income of three hundred francs on Florentin.'

"I was beginning to enjoy myself. I continued:

" 'That's all very nice, my dear; you girls aren't as stupid as we think you are. And how old is Florentin now, pray?'

" 'He'll soon be twelve,' she replied, 'and is going to be confirmed next spring.'

" 'That's fine. And ever since that time, I dare say, you've practiced your profession conscientiously?'

"She sighed and muttered:

" 'One does what one can—'

"But suddenly a loud noise in the room made me leap out of bed. It was as if somebody had fallen and was trying to scramble to his feet again by holding to the wall.

"I had clutched the candle and was looking around the room in anger and bewilderment. I listened breathlessly, but all was still again.

"She had gotten out of bed, too, and she tried to persuade me to return, by whispering:

" 'It's nothing, dear, nothing at all!'

"But I had at last discovered from whence came the noise.

"I walked straight to a door at the head of the bed, opened it—and caught sight of a wretched little boy sitting beside a big chair, from which he had just fallen. The little fellow stared at me with big, frightened eyes, and opening his arms to his mother, began to whimper:

" 'It wasn't my fault, mama; it wasn't my fault. I went to sleep and fell off. Don't scold me, mama, it wasn't my fault!'

"I turned to the woman and said:

" 'What does this mean, pray?'

"She was distressed and embarrassed. In a strangled voice she replied:

" 'Well, what can you expect? I don't make enough to board him away from home! I'm forced to keep him with me and I guess I don't make enough to pay for a separate room for him. He sleeps with me when I'm alone. When a visitor comes for an hour or two, I put him in the closet and he keeps quiet; he knows. But when a man stays all night, like you, it hurts his back, poor child, to sit on a straight chair 'till morning. —I'd just like to see you. How'd you like to sleep on a chair all night? I guess you wouldn't like it much, either!'

"Her voice was raised to an angry pitch.

"The little fellow continued to sob. He was a poor, miserable, little waif, the very child of the closet, of the cold, dark closet, the child that, from time to time, crept into the maternal bed when it was empty of visitors, to warm his little body.

"I felt like crying myself, and I spent the rest of the night in my own bed."

# *forty-first night*

*A woman wooed is a citadel stormed.*
*This one states her case against car-*
*nal caresses. Her lover refutes her in*
*terms quite unmistakable. . . .*

No, MY FRIEND, the answer must be and remains, no. What you ask of me is both revolting and
disgusting. It is said that God (you must know that I
believe in Him) has spoiled all the good he has created
by giving it some horrible aspect. He has given us the
power of loving, the sweetest joy we have in this world.
But as if he thought love too pure and too beautiful
for us, he has made it subject to the senses—those ignoble
senses of ours which are so coarse and revolting.

He seems to have created the senses as if in derision, as
if intending to contaminate with them all that is truly
delightful in the human body. So deeply has he en-
meshed love in the senses that we can not think of it
without a blush of shame, neither can we speak of it
except in a lowered voice. It hides itself from us, it revolts the soul, it wounds the sight, shames our moral
sense, and even outrages the law. Never again let me

hear you speak seriously of it to me, never!

I do not know whether I still love you. I do know that I am happy whenever I am near you, and when I catch the tenderness in your eyes, and hear the beloved tones in your voice. But I know this. If, through weakness on my part, you obtained what you desire of me, you would from that day on become odious to me. The delicate chain of friendship which now holds us together would be broken. Between us there would be an abyss, an abyss of crime. Let us remain as we are. And . . . love me if you will, I will permit it.

Your friend,<br>GENEVIEVE

MADAME:

Will you allow me in turn to speak to you as frankly as you have to me, without polite phrasing. I will speak just as plainly and unreservedly as I would to a friend who takes his eternal vows.

I also do not know if I love you. I could not really know until after that which revolts you so much has happened.

Have you forgotten the lines by Musset:

Je me souviens encor de ces spasmes terribles,
De ces baisers muets, de ces muscles ardents,
De cet être absorbé, blême et serrant les dents.
S'ils ne sont pas divins, ces moments sont horribles.

This sensation of horror and insuperable disgust, we also experience when we are carried away by the heat of passion, and we let ourselves be mated at hazard.

But when a woman is for us the being of our choice, a creature of continued charm, of infinite seduction as you are for me, the caress then becomes the most fervent, the most perfect, the most infinite happiness.

The caress, madame, is the test of love. When our passion diminishes after the embrace, we have deceived ourselves, but when it increases, *then* we know that we love.

A philosopher, who does not practice these doctrines, has put us on our guard against the snare of nature.

"Nature craves beings," he says, "and to impel us to create them, she has mingled the double enticement of love and voluptuousness in the snare." "And," he adds, "from the moment we give ourselves up to our passions, as soon as the sweet madness of the embrace has passed, a profound sadness falls upon us, we see, we feel and we know the veiled and secret reason which has impelled us in spite of ourselves.

"This is often true,—very often indeed, and it is then that we experience the feeling of disgust. Nature has vanquished our passions, she has thrown us at her will into the arms that opened to receive us, because she decreed that arms should open.

"Yes! I know the cold and violent kisses on strange lips, the fixed and ardent look in eyes that one has never seen before, and will never see again, and all that which I cannot here say, all which leaves in the soul a bitter, bitter melancholy. But when this cloud of affection that we call love has enveloped two beings, when they have thought of each other constantly, for a long time, when during an absence they are forever in the mind, by day

316

and by night, and the sweet souvenir brings to the soul
the features of the beloved face, the smile, and the sound
of the voice, when in thought they have possessed the
absent one, is it not natural then that at least we open
our arms to each other, that our lips meet and that our
bodies blend?

"Have you never had the desire to be kissed? Tell
me, if lips do not call to other lips, and if a look cannot
excite furious and unrestrained passions. Assuredly,
*there* is the snare, the impure snare, you will say. What
does that matter? I know it, I love it, and I will fall
into the snare. Nature teaches us to caress, but hides
her ruse, which is to force us in spite of ourselves to
perpetuate the generations. Well then, let us steal caresses from her, make them our own, refine them,
change them, idealize them, if you wish; nature de-
ceives us, so let us deceive the treacherous one in our
turn. Let us do more than she would have us do, more
than she would dare to teach us. Let the caress be like
a precious metal, brought out roughly from the earth,
we will take it, and work at it, until it is wrought to
perfection, without giving thought to the original de-
sign, or of the concealed caprices of him whom you
call God. And if our thoughts can poetize all things, let
us poetize the caress, madame, even to its most terrible
brutalities, its most ingenious contrivances, and its most
prodigious devices. Madame, let us love the delicious
caress like the strong wine which intoxicates, like the
ripe fruit which sweetens the mouth, like all happiness
which penetrates the body. Let us love flesh, because
flesh is beautiful, because it is white, and firm, and

317

smooth, and soft, and exquisite to the lips and hands. When our artists sought for the rarest, and the purest form for the quaffing bowl—wherein Art could drink to inebreity, what did they choose? They chose a woman's rounded bosom of which the flower resembles that of the rose. I once read in an erudite book, entitled the Dictionary of Medical Science, this definition of the bosoms, which, they say, was orginated by Joseph Prudhomme, who is now a doctor of medicine: "A woman's breasts can be considered as an object that is created for a twofold purpose, that of utility and that of pleasure." If you wish we will pass by that of utility, and speak only of the charm. Would it have its exquisite form, whose call for a caress is irresistible, if it were only destined to give nourishment to the little ones?

"Madame, let us leave it to the moralists to preach modesty to us, and let the doctors give us prudent advice, let the poets—the deceivers who deceive themselves —sing of the chaste union of souls and of incorporeal happiness; let us leave the homely women to their duties, and the rational men to their useless work, the lay breathren to their doctrines, the priests to their commandments, but *we* will love above all else the caress which intoxicates, maddens, enervates, exhausts and revives, which is sweeter than perfume, lighter than the breeze, more acute than wounds, quick and devouring, which forces a prayer, a cry, a tear, a sigh, and which can impel us to commit any crime, or any act of courage. Let us adore it, not in a tranquil, normal, or legal manner, but violently, furiously, immoderately. Let us search for it as we search for gold and diamonds,

318

for it is of greater value, being inestimable and transient. Pursue it without ceasing, die for it and by it. And if you wish, madame, I will tell you a truth which you will not find, I believe, in any book,—the only happy women on earth are those who are loved with this intensity, who do not *want* for caresses. They live without care, without torturing thoughts, with only one desire,—the desire for the next kiss which will be as sweet and as satisfying as the last. The others—those to whom the caress is circumspect, incomplete or rare—their lives are tormented by a thousand restless, disquieting thoughts, by the love of gold, the love of self-conceit, by all the events which in time become griefs. But women who are caressed to satiety have need of nothing, desire nothing, regret nothing. They live in a tranquil and happy dream, scarcely aware of what would be to others, irreparable disasters, for the caress replaces all, cures all, consoles all.

"I have still so much more to tell you."

HENRI.

These two letters written on Japanese paper of rice straw, were found in a little Russian leather pocketbook, under a praying-desk in the Madeleine Church on Sunday morning after the one o'clock mass, by

MAUFRIGNEUSE.